THE
STRONGEST
HEART

ALSO BY SAADIA FARUQI
The Partition Project
A Place at the Table (with Laura Shovan)
A Thousand Questions
Yusuf Azeem Is Not a Hero
*The Wonders We Seek: Thirty Incredible Muslims Who Helped
Shape the World*

THE STRONGEST HEART

SAADIA FARUQI

Quill Tree Books
An Imprint of HarperCollinsPublishers

Library of Congress Control Number: 2024947435
ISBN 978-0-06-311585-9

Typography by Joel Tippie
24 25 26 27 28 LBC 5 4 3 2 1
First Edition

For Abbu

THE
STRONGEST
HEART

PROLOGUE

Once there was a boy who lived with a monster. Not the kind under the bed or in the closet. This monster was real, and it was scary.

Big and loud and furious.

But sometimes this monster was also kind. Sometimes it laughed and told the funniest jokes. Sometimes the monster was weak, and the boy had to help it. At other times, the monster helped the boy.

Often the boy hated the monster and wished it was dead.

And the monster? It didn't hate the boy at all. It wished the boy understood him better. It wished it wasn't a monster.

But if wishes were horses, beggars would ride.

This is the story of the boy and the monster.

Well, mostly. There are other stories in this book too, about animals and fairies and giants. About kings and queens and evil villains. Talking animals and shape-shifting creatures. Demons and gods. Legends and myths.

It's up to you, dear reader, to decide what's real, and what isn't.

1

My new house has a yellow door. That's the first thing I notice about it, because let's face it, yellow doors aren't very common.

I mean, I'm from Queens, New York, which has some of the funkiest people in the world, but I've never seen a yellow door there.

Maybe Houston will be chill. Maybe the yellow door is a sign from God that my life is about to get better. Not that I'm holding my breath or anything. God has never really cared about me. He's got more important things to do.

"Be on your best behavior," Abbu says from the driver's seat.

I drag my eyes from the yellow door and take in the rest of the house. It's gray, with white shutters on the windows and a dark gray roof and no other color. Except for that yellow door, which is completely, I dunno, different.

I stare at it, wondering who painted it and why, and were they a little bit off their rocker when they made that decision?

"Are you listening to me, Mohammad?" Abbu's voice is louder now, the kind that sits squarely between "irritated" and "ready to rumble."

"Yes," I reply quickly. I'm not ready to rumble with him. Not now, not ever.

Which is why I don't remind him that my name is Mo.

I mean, okay, technically, it's Mohammad, which is the most popular name in the world or something. But I'm called Mo by everyone except my dear father (can you hear the sarcasm?). Mumtaz Mirza doesn't do anything he's asked to do. He's—what do they call it in westerns—a law unto himself.

We stare at each other in the rear-view mirror. I can see the top half of his polo shirt, ironed like he's trying to make a good impression, but crinkled at the collar. His face has a sneer built in, like it's a part of his features. Part of him.

That's the worst part. The part that scares me.

Our eyes are the same, medium brown with flecks of black. I want to have exactly zero things in common with this person, so the eye business always gets to me. I come from a long line of South Asian people, aka desi, and almost all of us have monochromatic eyes. Black. Dark brown. Light brown. Charcoal. Caramel. Mocha.

You get the idea.

But Abbu and I have these strange medium-brown eyes with black flecks, like nature decided to play a trick at the last minute.

Abbu runs a steady hand over his hair, then opens the car door and gets out. "Come on, let's go meet everyone."

By everyone, he means his sister, Naila, and her son. This is their house, in the middle of Houston, that we're now going to be living in. We drove two days from New York with all our belongings in the trunk of Abbu's old Corolla, so we could be with family or some stupid thing.

Family is nothing to me. Sad but true.

It's also nothing to Abbu. He doesn't like to meet people. He thinks the human race is a disgrace and that being alone is the best feeling in the world. Who cares about things like parents and spouses and siblings and blah blah?

But apparently we're pretending to be in love with family right now, since we don't have anywhere else to live. Also sad but true. wwSo I'm going to behave like a good boy—yeah, right—and act all thankful that we have a place to stay.

Here's a secret, though.

Secretly, I *am* grateful. I want to know what it feels like to be in a family with other people. Normal people, not Abbu.

So even though I act all tough and roll my eyes, my heart thumps in my chest as I follow Abbu to the yellow door.

* * *

Speaking of secrets, I have many.

You could say I'm a secretive kid. At my fifth-grade

parent-teacher conference, Mrs. Jenner said, "Mo keeps to himself and doesn't share much. He's like the poster child of still waters run deep."

Was I supposed to be flattered or offended? I couldn't tell.

Mama—she was around then—just chuckled like it was funny to be a still water or whatever.

Like I was a deep lake, not a human being with feelings and needs and mountains of fears.

I guess it helped her, thinking of me as a lake. You can leave a lake and drive away, knowing it will be around next year or the year after, if you want to visit again. You can say goodbye to a lake without worrying what it's going to think of you leaving, or how it's going to cope in a house all by itself with a father who's always angry.

Needless to say, there are no more parent-teacher conferences with my mother.

Also not with my father, because he couldn't care less about things like that.

* * *

"Salaam akaikum, salaam alaikum!" A heavyset woman with black hair in a bun and a cheery smile hugs me so tightly I gasp a little. We're standing in the living room now, me and Abbu. The happy woman is Naila Phupo, who of course I've met online lots of times. Abbu loves video calls, because he doesn't have to go anywhere or do anything, but he can still say he's met all his . . . what-do-you-call-it? Social obligations.

Naila Phupo doesn't come across as a hugger on video calls,

obviously. This is something new I'm learning about her. She lets me go, but then smiles and starts hugging me again. "Yakeen nahi aaraha! Tum itne barey hogaey!" I can't believe it, you've grown so big.

"He's thirteen now," Abbu says proudly. "See how tall he is already."

"Just like you!" Naila Phupo finally releases me and grabs Abbu instead.

Okay. This is weird. We're so not a hugging family.

Abbu chuckles awkwardly and pats his sister on the head like she's a puppy.

Naila Phupo lets Abbu go with a little sigh and points behind me. "Apne cousin se milo." Meet your cousin.

I turn. A dude stands near the wall, looking nervous. What has he got to be nervous about? This is his house, and I'm the one who's just barged in with the intention of living here. No offense, but they don't seem rich. The furniture in the living room looks older than the state of Texas. And the house is small.

Being from New York, I can't really complain. The apartments are like shoeboxes there, and I'm not talking the big sneaker boxes. I'm talking those tiny shoes people put on babies, even though they can't walk yet.

I exaggerate, but you get my meaning.

"Hey." I nod to the dude. My cousin. I can't remember his name, but I'm sure someone will tell me.

All three of them look at me in disappointment. Great. I

haven't been here five minutes and I'm already disappointing people left and right.

Of course that makes me want to be obnoxious, because why not? "Whazzup?" I say.

"Mohammad!" Abbu says loudly. "Sahih se salaam karo!" Say salaam properly.

He must be kidding. Since when did he get so religious?

I look at him and realize that he is not, in fact, kidding. He's got that look on his face, the one especially for outsiders. Big, toothy smile. Gleaming eyes. The sneer is still there, but masked until it's almost gone.

Almost, but not quite. It's hiding in plain sight, warning me to be on my best behavior.

Problem is, me and good behavior aren't really on speaking terms. I grit my teeth and hold out my right hand. "Salaam alaikum. I'm Mo."

My cousin smiles nervously and shakes my hand like it's covered in germs. "Walaikum assalam. I'm Rayyan."

Naila Phupo laughs. "He knows that, silly."

The way Rayyan looks at me, one eyebrow raised, it's obvious that he knows the truth. I'd totally forgotten his name. In my defense, he hardly ever came on the video calls, lucky guy. I wouldn't have either, if Abbu hadn't dragged me out of my room and in front of the screen every time.

Anyway.

The silence is awkward, so I sit down on an ancient-looking sofa. The threadbare fabric is covered in faded flowers, and the whole thing creaks like it's gonna break any second. I sit up straight, trying to put my weight on my legs instead of my butt.

Rayyan's mouth twitches. Wait, is this dude laughing at me?

He's tall, but not taller than me. He's also very thin, with his bones sticking out every which way. Doesn't he eat?

Abbu sinks down next to me, putting all his weight on his butt. "Ahhh, shukar."

"How was your trip?" Phupo asks. "We have so much to catch up on!"

I ignore her, because this is officially grown-up talk. You know, the weather, politics, who's married to whom, and other stupid stuff. I don't need to answer, because I'm a kid.

Abbu closes his eyes and mumbles something, so apparently he's not into grown-up talk either. His grin is almost gone now, like it was too exhausting to keep up the pretense.

Naila Phupo chatters on. It takes her twenty minutes to hit on all the highlights: the blistering heat even though it's October, a dirty political campaign for mayor, and the wedding of a relative I've never heard of.

Then she circles back like a pro to the weather in New York and how she's glad she doesn't live in snow, but seeing the fall colors for once in her life would be incredible.

Wow, this lady. She can talk.

All this time, I've been staring at Rayyan's jeans, which are too short for his legs. They're faded, but not in a fashionable way. More like an it's-past-time-to-buy-new-jeans way. His socks peek out of his slippers, which are also faded. Threads hang out of the ends of the laces, and there are scuff marks on both toes.

"What are you looking at?" Rayyan whispers.

I blink. "Nothing."

He narrows his eyes like he knows I'm lying.

His mom's convo shifts to Abbu's new job. Apparently there's a nearby garage that's hired him for a trial run. "We'll see how it goes," Abbu says. "I may not like it."

"It's just for the time being," Naila Phupo says soothingly. "You'll find something else, inshallah."

Abbu nods casually. "I've already got feelers out; don't worry."

He's got an accounting degree, but he's never really held a job for too long. His last stint was keeping the books at a mechanic shop in Queens, so I'm guessing that's where he got this referral from, even though he'd be fixing things instead of doing calculations.

Finally, finally, Naila Phupo stops chattering and stands up. "Dinner will be in an hour," she says with another cheek-splitting smile.

Abbu stands up too, and yawns. "So soon?" he grumbles. "I want to rest for a while."

Nobody mentions how he's being a baby right now. Inconveniencing his sister even though she's made him dinner. Like I said, a law unto himself.

"Koi baat nahi, bhai," Phupo says quickly. No worries, brother. "I'll show you your room."

They walk toward the door, then she turns back like she's just thought of something. "Rayyan, beta, why don't you take Mohammad . . . sorry, Mo . . . to your room?"

Rayyan nods slowly, like the movement is painful. "You mean *our* room."

What they really mean is I'm going to share a room. With another person. Someone I don't know and am not interested in knowing. Like, ever.

This is awful. I didn't share a room even in my baby-shoebox-size apartment in Queens, New York.

Rayyan gets up and goes toward the staircase. He's assuming I'll follow him. I debate what to do. Maybe I can just sleep here on this sofa that's falling to pieces. It's not too bad, once you get used to it.

Abbu turns to me. "Go, fool!" And yup, his sneer is back where it belongs.

I scramble up and hurry after Rayyan before things get any worse.

2

This is what I learn about my cousin Rayyan in the sixty minutes we spend in his room.

Sorry, our room.

One, he's thirteen, same as me. Okay, I knew that already in some corner of my brain, but I hadn't really thought about it. Mama used to tell me she and her sister-in-law were pregnant at the same time. "We attended family events together wearing the same maternity clothes," she'd say, looking annoyed, like it was all my fault.

What can I say? Mama likes to stand out from the crowd.

Two, Rayyan's dad is dead. Again, it's another thing I knew, but not all the details. What I find out today is that he was, get this, murdered.

I think I make a choking sound when Rayyan drops it into casual conversation.

"Shot in broad daylight," Rayyan insists. I think *he* thinks I don't believe him.

Oh, I believe him. It's too bizarre not to be true. "Who was it?" I ask. "Who shot him?"

My cousin's shoulders slump. "That's the real question, isn't it?"

Okay, that means nobody knows. Not even the police. Cool, cool. I have a dozen other questions, but I don't want to look eager, so I decide to take it slow. I'm going to be living here. I'll have plenty of time to get to the bottom of this murder business.

Three, Rayyan's a smart kid, as evidenced by a shelf crammed full of trophies, medals, and plaques. He's got Honor Roll and Winner of Texas Public Schools STEM Award and Regional Spelling Bee Finalist blah blah blah. There's also a bookshelf full of very thick books, mostly nonfiction. Half of them have "introduction" in the title.

Introduction to mathematics. Introduction to the human body. Introduction to engineering. Introduction to machine systems.

Geez, this kid has no life.

Rayyan notices me noticing. "You like reading?" he asks.

I shrug. "I prefer stories. Folktales, to be exact."

He gapes like I've said something blasphemous. "Like what? Davy Crockett?"

I roll my eyes. How Texan of him. "No, desi folktales. Stories from India, Pakistan, Bengal, Sri Lanka . . . ya know."

"How did you get into folktales?" he asks, frowning like I'm a puzzle he wants to solve. "They're not exactly popular with kids."

I pause. The story of how I got into folktales is really personal and a little painful. It all began with a very special dude called Patel Uncle. He was my neighbor, but also basically my friend, even though he was old enough to be my grandfather.

"Maybe I'll tell you someday," I finally reply.

Rayyan nods like that's enough for him. Like he understands personal and painful things.

So now one more thing I know about my cousin is that he thinks Davy Crockett is a folktale worth reading. He needs to be educated about life outside Texas, is what I'm thinking.

The only question I still have about this kid is why he's so thin. I mean, sure, this family isn't rich, but still. He's got his skin hanging off his bones in a way that looks very uncomfortable. I open my mouth to ask, when he points to a pillbox on his desk. "Don't touch that. It's got all my medicines."

Ah, a perfect segue.

"What meds?" I ask casually, like I couldn't be less interested.

Which, you know, I'm not. It's just that I like to have information at my fingertips. I like knowing things, being prepared.

It's the only way to survive in the Mirza family.

Rayyan inspects his scuffed slippers. "Um, I had liver disease when I was younger."

"O-kayyy . . ."

He looks up suddenly. "Don't worry," he assures me. "I'm fine now. But I still have to take pills. They're mostly herbal supplements Mama pushes on me, but still."

"Herbal supplements!" I put my hand on my chest. "Phew. You scared me for a second."

He narrows his eyes. "Are you trying to be funny?"

"Me? No, I never joke." This is one hundred percent correct. It's my line in the sand. I'll do a lot of things for a reaction. Joking isn't one of them.

"Ever?" Rayyan looks surprised.

"Ever."

"Not even a knock-knock joke? But why?"

What is this, therapy? I shrug and move to what I've just learned is my side of the room. It's not too bad. The room is big, and it's got two single beds on opposite ends with a window in the middle. The beds are covered with these stupid plaid quilts, like we're in old-timey Scotland or something. I sit down very carefully on mine, hoping it doesn't creak or tremble like the living room sofa.

When nothing happens, I relax.

Rayyan is still giving me the curious side-eye, so I get up again and unpack my stuff. It's basically a gym bag with some clothes, shoes, a few books. I'm sharing a closet with Rayyan, and it takes me less than five minutes to put everything in.

Then there's my boxing gloves. When I take them out, Rayyan's eyes grow big as plates. "You box?" he squeaks.

This guy's questions never end. "Sometimes," I mutter.

I place the gloves under my bed. They don't go in the closet. I need them close to me, just to feel . . . something. I dunno. It's hard to explain.

Rayyan says, "You should take a nap too, like your abbu."

My neck snaps up. "What . . . he's just tired from all the driving."

"I know." Rayyan's face is blank, like he hasn't just opened up the grossest can of worms in the history of the world.

Does he know about Abbu? Even though they just met, he's my cousin, so I'm guessing nothing is really hidden from him.

I bet they talk about my family when they're alone. Look at that poor loser Mohammad, his dad is totally bonkers.

Ha, if they only knew.

* * *

The first time someone learned the truth about Abbu, I was eight years old.

I was super excited because a friend from school, Jonah Wiley, was coming to our apartment for a playdate.

Okay, a few things to remember here. One, this was a long time ago, before I became all hard and jaded. I used to get excited about things. I used to look forward to stuff.

I also used to call friend visits playdates (ugh), but we'll pretend that never happened.

Two, this was before my life turned into a trash fire. Mama

still lived with us. Abbu was still okay, most days.

Like I said, I was young, and kinda ignorant. "Carefree" is the word I'm looking for here.

Anyway, Jonah came over this one afternoon. Mama smiled. Abbu clapped his back and said, "Welcome, son, it's so great to see you."

I couldn't stop grinning, I remember that clearly.

We played video games in my room. Mama brought out snacks with more smiles, and said, "Let me know if you boys need anything."

We played some more video games.

That's when Abbu started shouting from the next room.

I couldn't tell you what it was about. Not because it was so long ago, but because he was always mad about something and if you tried to think too hard about what his issue was at any particular time, you'd go nuts.

So Abbu started shouting, and then Mama, who could never just ignore the problem, started talking back to him, which made it way worse, as usual.

Abbu doesn't like anyone talking back to him.

What I didn't understand was, if I knew this fact about my father at the age of eight, why didn't my mother? Why didn't she realize that engaging with a bully made things ten times worse?

So here I was sitting with Jonah Wiley in my room, playing video games, and there were my parents arguing away in the other room. I picked up the TV remote and maxed out the volume. The sounds of guns and rockets and people saying "Got 'em!" echoed in the air.

Big mistake.

Abbu strode into the room, eyes bulging. "What is this racket?" he thundered.

Jonah was so startled he dropped his controller and squeaked.

I remained quiet. No engaging with the bully, remember?

Abbu totally ignored my friend. He focused on me and let loose a torrent of words. Something about me being a useless kid, only making noise and playing stupid video games instead of studying and being respectful, et cetera.

He kept going on and on.

My heart pounded, and I felt this wave of heat in my body. I guess it was emotions or whatever? Embarrassment. Fear. Worry.

I didn't make eye contact. I put my controller down and stared at his feet. Well, stared at his dirty socks with a hole in the left big toe, actually.

This was the way to deal with Abbu. Not by arguing, not by showing fear or anger or anything else.

Abbu eventually got tired and left. I shuddered to take in a deep breath. The silence felt almost violent after all the noise.

"Dude, what's wrong with your dad?"

That's when I realized that Jonah was still there. I turned to look at him. He was staring at me with pink cheeks and wide, scared eyes.

"Uh, he . . ." I stopped because I really had no excuse. What was I going to say? My father is sick? Crazy? A weirdo?

At the age of eight, I wasn't even sure why he was like this. He just was.

Like the way our Queens apartment was always cold, or the way I had a tiny mole inside my right elbow.

Abbu was the way he was. Always. Forever.

Later I found out he's got a mental condition. I'll explain all that some other time. It takes me a while to find the words for it.

But back when I was eight, I'd always hoped that all dads were like mine. Maybe it was—what's the word?—testosterone that made men all angry, you know? The guys in the video games definitely acted all macho, full of scowls and snarls. Maybe that was just . . . men.

But Jonah's reaction made me realize I'd been digging my head in the sand.

It wasn't all dads. Not even some dads.

It was just my dad. Abbu.

Jonah insisted on calling his mom and getting picked up early. Abbu grumbled, "Good riddance," and went to take a nap. "If someone wants me to babysit their kid, they better pay me."

Never mind that if anyone was babysitting, it was Mama.

The next morning, Jonah told Alex all about his horrible visit to my house. Alex was supposed to keep it quiet, but he told Juan and Tamika, who then told the entire class at recess.

By the end of the day, all of third grade knew what had happened.

And in classic third-grade style, they'd added to the story.

First, Abbu was ugly and loud.

Then he was a criminal. Oh, some people said he was in the mafia. Honestly, I wouldn't have minded that. It sounded way cooler than the real thing. That he was a dude who couldn't control his anger. That he was unstable. Scary.

So scary.

That afternoon, Sarah Tomlinson sat next to me in the bus. She flipped her shiny blond braid over her shoulder and whispered, "I'm sorry your dad's such a monster, Mo."

* * *

We eat dinner in a little dining area off the kitchen. Naila Phupo flutters around the table, passing dishes of chicken curry, maash daal, and raita. She's also made roti by hand, all fluffy and warm from the stove.

"You've outdone yourself, Naila," Abbu says, pleased. His sneer is in hiding again, and his hair looks combed and styled. The rest has done him good, I guess. He almost looks happy.

Naila Phupo smiles. "It's nothing."

I eat quickly. I can't remember the last time I had such delicious Pakistani food. It's not even fancy, just plain, wholesome stuff that makes me feel happy.

Who knew food could do that?

The chicken is just the right amount of spicy, and the daal

melts in my mouth with creamy goodness. And the roti. Oh my god, it's like heaven.

Naila Phupo is my new favorite person.

Come to think of it, my only favorite person. I grab another roti from the covered plate in the center of the table. It's so good I could eat it plain.

"Slow down, Mohammad!" Abbu growls. "You're so uncouth."

"Let him be," Phupo says, still smiling. "It's a compliment, how he's eating my food." She pats Rayyan on the head. "This one hardly eats."

Abbu calms down a bit. He glances at Rayyan. "Keeping your figure for the ladies, eh?"

Rayyan looks startled. "Er."

His mom shakes her head. She finally sits down on a chair and takes some food. "Bhai," she says in a soft, chiding tone. "We're Muslim."

Abbu scoffs. "So? He can't look at the ladies? Where does it say that?"

I stare at my plate. Who's going to tell my father that yes, in fact, it says in the Quran not to look at the opposite gender, and also that his nephew is in middle school, so chances are he's not looking at any ladies anyway.

He seems the decent type. The good boy.

My opposite.

Naila Phupo clears her throat. "So, tomorrow is school, Mo," she says to me. "Are you ready?"

Wait, what?

My head whips up. "Tomorrow?" I croak. I'd thought it would take a few days to get me registered in school here. Like, wouldn't Abbu have to talk to the admin, show them we live here now? Don't you need documents and stuff?

"Yes, tomorrow," she replies. "I already filled out the forms, and your father signed them on the computer from New York. It's all taken care of."

"But . . ."

She goes on. "Plus, it's mid-October, so you don't want to miss too many days. School starts in August here, you know."

I swallow. The roti seems suddenly dry in my mouth.

Listen, it's not like I hate school or anything. I'm pretty good at studying, you know. And I'm fine being the new kid. I just, I dunno, want to stay still for a minute. There are too many new things, new people, in my life suddenly.

I just need a minute.

"You won't be alone," Rayyan says quietly from beside me. "I'm in the same grade as you. I'm sure we'll share most of our classes."

Naila Phupo beams. "Won't that be nice? Kitna maza aaega!" How much fun you'll have.

I highly doubt that, but I nod. Whatever.

"Good. End of discussion." Abbu slaps a hand on the table. "Pass me the chicken."

3

Alice Walker Middle School is two streets away from my aunt's house, which is great for a lot of reasons.

For example, I don't have to wake up too early in the morning. Like, ten minutes before we need to leave should give me plenty of time to get ready. Only I've forgotten that I have a roommate now, and apparently he takes longer to get ready than a girl dressing up for a beauty pageant.

Choosing clothes.

Taking a shower.

Inspecting his face for, I'm guessing, pimples.

Fixing the laces on those beat-up sneakers that need to be thrown away, like, yesterday.

There are other things too, but I groan and hide my head

under my pillow. I had my usual nightmares all night long, so my head is all fuzzy. "Why are you being so . . . meticulous?"

"Meticulous?" Rayyan looks at me from his desk chair. "That's a big word. Did you learn it from one of your folktales?"

I did, but I'm not admitting it. He looks way too amused for my liking. And not anywhere near as meek as the day before. Maybe he's one of those people who take a while to warm up and show their true colors.

I don't trust that kind of people. Just FYI.

I yawn. "Remind me to wow you with a story later."

"Sure." He goes back to his sneakers. "You better get ready. Mama won't let you leave without eating breakfast."

He sounds grumpy when he says this, but here's what he doesn't know: I'd kill for a mother who insists on breakfast.

Or lunch or dinner.

Or anything, really. Even those herbal supplements on my cousin's desk would be the highlight of my day.

I have this hazy memory of Mama that I sometimes take out from my mind like a shiny treasure.

She sits on my bed, holding a picture book. I'm four years old, maybe five. I'm snuggled up to her, and she's got her arm around me. I don't think I can read yet, but the pictures in the book are bright and colorful. There's a bear in a forest. And a little white boy with blond hair just like hers.

She's reading me the story, and she's rubbing my head, and then she's laughing at something funny the bear said. Or maybe the boy said it, since bears can't talk.

On the other hand, it's a children's picture book, so maybe the bear *is* the one talking.

Who am I to judge?

So, basically, I had a mother once too.

Oh, she's still around, don't get me wrong. Still my mother. Still alive and well, but far, far away from me on some work thing. She hasn't read with me or smiled at me in a long time, not that I need her to. I'm a big boy.

I climb out of bed, grab some clothes, and head for the bathroom. "You didn't answer me," I call out. "Why're you being so meticulous? Is this going to happen every morning, because let me tell you, I'm rethinking this whole room-sharing arrangement."

There's silence, which is okay. I don't need someone talking to me while I pee. It takes me ten minutes to get dressed, brush my teeth, and straighten out my hair. It's long, almost to my chin. Perfect, really, because it hides the fake earring I wear in one ear.

Not completely hides, mind you. What would be the point of the earring if people couldn't see it?

Abbu hates my entire look. Oh yeah. Mission accomplished.

When we get to the kitchen, Naila Phupo's already there. She's made us parathas and omelets, which kinda shocks me. I was expecting cereal or a protein bar at the most. "You did all this?"

"Only because it's your first day," she replies merrily. "Don't get used to it."

I breathe a little easier. I don't want to hate on my cousin for having such a perfect mom. Especially since he's looking at his plate with a scowl.

I forgot Rayyan's allergic to eating. I slap him on the back. "Dig in, dude!"

*　*　*

Another benefit of your school being close is that you can walk instead of taking the bus.

I don't like school buses, because they're smelly and make me nauseous. Also, you never know when somebody you don't like will sit next to you and say something horrible.

An example: Sarah Tomlinson's comment about my father in third grade. I've hated school buses since then. Go figure.

I pull my backpack higher on my shoulder and follow him. "What's your school like?" I ask Rayyan.

"It's school," he replies with a grunt.

I give him a thumbs-up. "Genius response, dude. So helpful."

He gives a sad little laugh. "Eh, you just have to keep your head down and not make waves."

"But I'm a master wave maker," I protest. "Tsunami-size waves."

Rayyan groans. "That's all I need."

I raise my eyebrows. "What? You thought this earring was for show?"

"It's not . . . your ear isn't really . . . ," he stutters.

I scoff. "No, it's not pierced, but this is still an earring. Gives a certain message, ya know? And I'm just waiting till I'm old enough to get tattoos."

His eyes bulge. "Seriously? Isn't it, like, against Islam or something?"

I grin. I'm not really serious.

Okay, maybe fifty percent. "I'll see how I feel when I'm eighteen," I tell him.

He sighs. "I have a whole list of things to do before then."

"Like what?"

He swallows like he's getting ready to tell his biggest secrets. "Van Meter High School. Valedictorian. Early college. Pre-med."

I don't know what this Van Meter thing is, but it sounds ultra boring. "Whoa," I say. "Slow down, Sheikh Chilli."

"Huh?"

I stop and give him my best are-you-for-real look. "You don't know Sheikh Chilli? Never heard his stories?"

"I told you that I prefer . . ."

I shake my head and start walking again. "Sheikh Chilli's stories are funny, but they have deep messages. Well, all folktales do. But his most famous one is the khayali pulao."

Rayyan frowns. "Pulao is the rice dish Mama makes on Saturdays. But why khayali?"

"It means imaginary."

He grits his teeth. It's obvious from the way his lips pinch together and his jaw gets a muscle tic. "Yes, I know that. But why? Was this Sheikh Chilli a cook?"

Ugh, this dude.

* * *

Here's the thing with folktales, or folklore, or whatever. They don't follow a set genre or category. You can have ghost stories, monster stories, love stories, or war stories. You can also have stories with jokes or morals or absolutely nothing. Shocking, I know.

I guess that's why I like folktales. They don't have rules.

If you wanted to introduce folktales to a newbie, you'd begin with a short, funny story. Maybe a moral. Or a joke.

But as I've said before, I don't like jokes.

In stories, Sheikh Chilli is this goofy guy whose whole life is a never-ending series of stupid antics. I'm talking being attacked by a bear and offering him vegetables from his basket kind of stupid. Or sitting on a tree branch while cutting it down stupid.

FYI, the real Sheikh Chilli was the complete opposite. A wise saint who taught a Mughal prince. I don't know where the stories of his being a total loser came from, but they're a part of South Asian folklore now.

Anyway, once upon a time Sheikh Chilli goes to the market for eggs. In some versions, it's a pot of oil, but eggs sound better, maybe because of the omelet I ate for breakfast. It doesn't matter.

So the sheikh buys some eggs and puts them in a basket,

and puts the basket on his head like one of those washer-women we see in pictures of villages.

Basically, carrying things on your head was a legit way of transporting goods back then. You know, if you didn't have a donkey or horse.

Sheikh Chilli starts to walk back to his house, and probably the journey is boring. Without the radio or Bluetooth, you've got lots of time to think, right? Only thinking is this guy's biggest problem. He always gets into jams when he's thinking too hard. So he thinks about the eggs and how much each of them costs. Only now that he's got them, what if they all hatch, and he ends up with a lot of chickens? And guess what those chickens will do when they turn into hens?

Lay more eggs!

Then he thinks he'll come back to the market with a whole lotta eggs and sell them every week or whatever schedule hens lay eggs on. I don't know, I'm not a farmer. But Sheikh Chilli thinks he'll become rich selling all these eggs. Maybe there's an egg shortage and he can charge a lot. Or maybe the current egg seller dies, and Sheikh Chilli takes over his business. Who knows how this guy's mind works? It's a mystery.

Anyway, he's planning to get rich off eggs, and then he'll build a house instead of living in his little cottage or whatever. (This part I'm guessing, because the stories don't say what sort of house Sheikh Chilli lives in.)

So now he's planning his house as he walks with that basket on his head. It's gonna have lots of rooms, one for eating and

27

one for sitting, and several rooms for sleeping, blah blah. But then he'll be lonely in that big house, obviously, so he'll need a wife. Since he'll be a rich dude at that point, Chilli the Egg Merchant or whatever, all the girls will fall at his feet. He'll get married to the most beautiful one, obviously, since this is his imagination. And then they'll have a nice family with servants and kids, then grandkids, all the while selling eggs.

Or maybe by this time, he's branched into other foods, like milk or butter. Maybe he's bought a bakery or a butcher shop too. He's Sheikh Chilli, after all. Anything's possible.

By now, he's close to his house—sorry, cottage—thinking about his grandkids and how he's going to play with them, when he bumps into somebody passing by and drops . . . guess what? His egg basket.

Yup. All the eggs are smashed on the ground.

That's basically his dream going up in flames. Or yolks or whatever.

Sheikh Chilli starts yelling at the person, saying he won't have his big house or his lovely wife or his grandkids now that his eggs are smashed.

That makes the other guy laugh, like duh. "Stop making khayali pulao, Sheikh sahib," he says. "You need to stop thinking and start doing."

* * *

Rayyan is the best type of listener. He doesn't interrupt me until we reach the school. Then he nods slowly and says, "That's a good story, even if it's made up."

28

I shrug. "It's a folktale. There's some truth and some lies. But it's all good."

Rayyan opens the big wooden door for me like a total gentleman. "I'm not cooking khayali pulao, though," he says quietly. "I'm actually doing something to achieve my dreams."

Seeing as we're roommates, I know I'll probably learn all about his *doing something* very soon.

It's gonna make for great storytelling.

4

Texas schools are weird.

There's the pledge of allegiance in first period, which is fine. My family may be from Pakistan, but I'm an American through and through. I can recite the pledge. Well, kinda.

Here's where it gets tricky, though. There's another pledge after the first one. Get this: allegiance to the Texas flag.

What the . . . ?

Does anyone else think this is messed up? Why on earth are we pledging our loyalty to a state? It boggles the mind.

I look around homeroom. Rayyan is standing next to me. He's got his right hand on his chest, and his eyes are closed. Ugh, the Goody Two-Shoes.

Some kids are looking around. A few have their eyes closed

like Rayyan, but I suspect they're dozing.

Good news, most students think swearing to the Texas flag is a bit much.

Our homeroom teacher is a dark-haired lady named Mrs. Perez. I know this because there's a big sign in cartoon script on top of the whiteboard. *Welcome to Mrs. Perez's Class.* I'm guessing she's the English teacher because she's got *The Chronicles of Narnia* and *A Wrinkle in Time* quotes all over the walls. There's even one from *Ghost,* by my favorite author, Jason Reynolds: "You can't run away from who you are, but what you can do is run toward who you want to be."

That's me in a nutshell, ladies and gentlemen. Or at least, trying.

Anyway, the pledges end, then there's a moment of silence—don't ask—and then morning announcements. I tune out.

We're reminded to put away our phones, otherwise there will be consequences. Neither Rayyan nor I owns a phone (unbelievable, I know!), so we're fine. The rest of the class scrambles to put their devices away. I roll my eyes and tune out again.

The teacher gets started with, you guessed it, *A Wrinkle in Time.* She reads some pages, then passes around a handout with questions.

Mrs. Whatsit tells Meg that her faults will be useful in her adventure. Usually, our faults are things that we want to change. Why do you think she says this? Write out a list of your faults and think about how they might be useful in your own adventures.

Er, no thanks.

I look over at Rayyan, who's busy writing his response. What's he gonna say? My faults are not eating enough? Studying too hard? Someone should tell him overproductivity isn't a good look.

I've seen kids like him before. There were a few high achievers in my old school. Only I stayed very, very far away from them. I preferred to maintain a certain, ahem, reputation.

Aka, my faults. Yes, Mrs. Whatsit, I have a bunch of 'em. Let's see. Mo Mirza's list of faults.

Bad boy, obviously. Doesn't care about anything. Steals from the bodega near his apartment. Stay away from him, he might just beat you up.

(In my defense, the only thing I ever stole was an apple or a banana, when my parents couldn't be bothered to feed me. Nothing major.)

Yeah. Everyone in my old school knew my rep. And the kids who stayed away from me the most? Kids like Rayyan.

Only now, Rayyan is my cousin and my roommate, so he can't really stay away, can he?

English ends, and we go to the next class. And then the next, and the next. It's all a blur, partly because I'm half asleep after a night of bad dreams, a strange bed, and Rayyan's snoring.

And partly because every single class is boring, which, to be honest, I was expecting. They're mostly honors classes, which means more studying. More textbooking, more teacher lecturing, more ugh.

I mean, I'm a good student, but please. Let's not go over-board with the academics.

I zone out for most of the day. A walking, talking zombie, that's me. Rayyan chatters as he points out things around the school. The library, the chess club hangout (shudder!), the water fountain that never works. The one that does.

The cafeteria, and how it's Wacky Wednesday, which means cheese nachos or whatever.

Spoiler alert: I don't care.

Also, the cafeteria is wild. The entire back wall is a gigantic mural of cowboys and horses. I'm not kidding. I spend most of my lunch staring at it, trying to figure out if it's a scene from the artist's imagination or some real-life history lesson.

Finally we get to last period, which is—drumroll, please—biology. In case you're wondering: we don't have to study all of science this year. Honors students have ninth-grade biology even though we're in eighth grade. We actually get to sit in a science lab instead of a regular classroom.

Look, I'm not a science nerd or brainiac. I'm definitely not planning to go to med school like Rayyan or anything. But this class, this subject, seems cool so far. There's a full-size plastic skeleton standing in the corner near the windows, and that alone makes me smile. He's wearing a backward cap on his head—sorry, skull. Red clown shoes are on his feet.

Pretty funny, even for someone like me.

The biology teacher is called Mr. Pigao. He's thin, with floppy black hair, and get this: he's wearing a lab coat. It should make him look dorky, but it doesn't. He's grinning, but who wouldn't be if they stared at a clown skeleton all day? Or maybe because it's the last class of the day and he gets to go home soon. Who knows?

"Mr. Pigao is my favorite teacher," Rayyan tells me as he sits down on the lab chair next to me.

I eye him sideways. "You mean all the others *weren't* your favorites?"

He acts like this is a real question, and not sarcasm. "You'll see. Mr. Pigao's amazing."

Okay. Just because the dude wears a lab coat and smiles at everyone doesn't make him amazing.

When the bell rings and everyone settles down, Pigao waves to me. "Seems like we have a new student in the class! Please introduce yourself, my friend."

I groan, because this is exactly what every new student needs: to be called out on the first day.

Again, sarcasm. It's my go-to.

I keep sitting. None of the other teachers had me stand up and introduce myself like this was first grade. Most of them just ignored me, or called out my name and said welcome. "Uh, hey," I begin. "I'm Mo. From New York City."

"Well, Mo, from New York City," Pigao says with an easy smile, "welcome to my class. We're starting a new unit called body systems. Hope you like it."

"You mean anatomy," Rayyan says.

Pigao tilts his head. "Sure, if you want to call it that."

"I do."

Well, this is interesting. Rayyan has been quiet in every class. He's taken notes and kept his head down, even when a dude called Frankie threw rolled-up balls of paper at his head in algebra. So either Pigao is really his favorite, or cousin dear is trying for a personality change.

My guess is the first one.

"Shut up, loser," comes a voice from the back.

I turn my head. It's Frankie.

"Now, buddy, you know the rules of my class," Pigao says. "Be kind and thoughtful. Never use hurtful remarks."

Is this guy for real?

Frankie apparently thinks the same thing, because he scoffs. But he doesn't say anything, so I guess Pigao's rules are good for something.

"Let's begin." Pigao claps his hands once and leans against his desk. "The human body is a combination of systems that work together to perform . . . what?"

"The functions of life." Obviously, this is Rayyan. He says it so confidently.

"Good, Rayyan!"

"Lucky guess." It's another kid, but he's sitting right next to Frankie and they're dressed exactly alike—hoodies and jeans with ripped knees, even though I'm a hundred percent sure both are against the dress code.

Although my earring isn't school appropriate either, so let's just leave it.

Pigao ignores the Frankie clone. "Functions of life are the

processes we need to survive and be healthy," he tells the class. "Can someone give me an example?"

A few kids raise their hands, Rayyan included. Here's another thing different from my old school. Nobody raised their hands there. We just said what we wanted to say.

People in Texas are really polite, I guess.

Pigao chooses a girl at the back of the class. "Yes, Monique?"

"Well, we need to eat to survive," Monique says slowly. "That means we need a way to digest our food, right?"

"Right." Pigao points to a boy. "What else, Eli?"

"Thinking," says this Eli character. "We need a brain to think."

Pigao grins. "Absolutely. You kids are on fire!"

All this time, Rayyan is standing straight up, waving his arm in the air like he's got the best news to tell. I want to laugh, but I'm pretty sure that's against one of Pigao's class rules or whatever. No laughing at geeks, even if they're your relatives.

Especially if they're your relatives.

"What about you, new kid?" Pigao says. "Mo, right?"

I've gone from wanting to laugh to wanting to scowl in the space of two seconds. I thought I was giving off a pretty clear message with all my slouching and not making eye contact. Also, I'm not raising my hand like Rayyan here, so why is he even calling on me? "Er, yeah," I say. "I'm Mo."

It must be obvious at this point that I'm stalling. I have no idea how to answer.

What? I said I liked the class, not that I'm any good at it.

"Give me another example of life functions," Pigao says. "What do we need to survive? To live?"

I wanna say love, or affection, but I know that's not the reply Pigao is looking for. Honestly, that's a me problem. I'm the only one who knows that without those things, the body is just a husk.

A bad boy with a fake earring and a fake nasty attitude to hide the fact that there's no life inside his skeleton.

Speaking of skeletons, the plastic dude in the corner gives me an idea. I say, "Walking. Running." A few kids snicker, which makes me scowl more. "I meant, movement in general. Using our bones and things."

Pigao gives me a kindly smile. "Yes, you're right. We need our bones to move properly, to get away from predators, et cetera."

I lean back against my chair. I hardly ever participate in class, so it was nice to get an answer right. Then I remember the snickers behind me, and turn my head. I'm guessing it was Frankie and his clone.

They're both smirking at me, so I stare at them to show them I'm not scared.

On the contrary, I can beat them into a pulp and drink them for breakfast with my eyes closed.

* * *

"Biology is so much fun," Rayyan says as we walk out of class.

We've got homework, so I wouldn't exactly call it fun. It's

reading two whole chapters of the textbook, but now I'm thinking I could ask Rayyan to read it aloud for me, since he likes the class so much. "If you say so," I grumble.

"I do," he insists. "We're having a science fair at the end of the semester. I can't wait!"

Ugh. Seriously? A science fair? I'm so gonna fail this class.

Frankie and his goon come out of the classroom behind us. Frankie pushes Rayyan out of the way, while his goon shoves me with his shoulder. Hard.

"Hey!" I am so ready to pound these jokers into the ground.

"Move!" Frankie growls.

Rayyan takes my arm and moves us both away from the dynamic duo. "Forget them. They're not worth it."

I send them dirty looks as they walk away, looking smug. Do they think I'm letting this go? Uh, nope.

To be continued.

Rayyan starts walking down the hallway. I hurry to catch up with him. This school is huge, and I don't wanna get lost. "Where are we going? Isn't the exit that way?"

I know this because the hallway is full of kids, all rushing in one direction.

Just to be clear, we're going in the opposite direction.

"I need to see someone." Rayyan leads me down a hallway and stops outside a set of double doors. A sign on the door says LIBRARY.

"Why are we here?" I ask. My old school didn't have much

of a library. It was a small room cramped with shelves and musty books that smelled like they were a hundred years old.

"It'll just be a minute."

I follow him, because I'm super curious. What kind of library does Alice Walker Middle School have? Rayyan walks to the librarian's desk, but I don't notice. I'm gazing around with my mouth open.

Imagine this: high ceilings. Brightly painted walls. Shelves, shelves, and more shelves. Armchairs in the middle that look like you could sink right into them and never leave.

Me. I'd sink in and never leave.

There's a youngish African American man at the desk. Glasses, button-down shirt, khaki slacks. He's got the whole librarian vibe. He holds out a folder. "Rayyan, so glad you dropped by."

"Sorry I'm late, Mr. Trent." He takes the folder carefully, like it's precious.

The man looks at me. "New student?"

I nod.

"You like reading?"

Another nod. I'm going for cool here, ya know?

Trent smiles. "You can come by anytime to borrow books. I keep the library open for an hour after school."

I say, "Thanks, I will." And guess what? I totally mean it.

When we're back in the hallway, Rayyan opens the folder again and shows me the papers inside. The top one looks like an application form. "For NJHS," he says.

Am I supposed to know what that is? I'm still dreaming about the library.

I peek at his face, and yes indeed, I'm supposed to know. Still, I'm a stubborn kid. "What's NJ whatever?" I ask.

Rayyan sighs. "NJHS. National Junior Honor Society."

I don't let up. "Uh-huh?"

"It's a very prestigious student society," he explains. "Helps you get into college."

I narrow my eyes because maybe he's teasing me or something. "Dude, that's NHS, in high school."

How do I know this? Jonah Wiley's big brother, Matt, was president of the National Honor Society last year, and he gave a presentation about the dangers of social media to the entire middle school.

A mandatory presentation. That lasted forty-five minutes. Followed by Q and A.

Yup, just another reason to detest the Wiley family.

Rayyan puts away his folder and starts walking toward the school exit. "NHS is even more prestigious. But everyone knows it's hard to get into. NJHS members get into NHS much easier."

"So you're preparing for high school by joining some club in eighth grade?"

"I'm not joining, per se. This is just the application form. It's got a list of requirements, and if they think you're good enough, they invite you to join."

I can't help it. A laugh bursts out of me. "You're kidding? It sounds like a secret society or something. Will you be wearing a cloak and having meetings in the night under a full moon? Maybe chant something in Greek?"

Rayyan stops and turns. His jaw is clenched, and he's holding his backpack with white knuckles. "Don't make fun of me."

I stop too. "Hey, dude, I didn't mean to—"

"Yes, you did. Everybody does. Why would you be any different?"

"I . . ." Honestly, I have nothing to say here. He's not wrong.

He turns back and starts walking again. We're almost to the exit, and we still have two long streets to go before we get home.

His home. Where I'm staying, thanks to the kindness of his mother.

Ugh, why am I so bad?

"Sorry, man," I try again, making my voice all sincere and stuff. "Really, you want to join this junior society, be my guest. In fact, I'll even help you."

We're outside the school by now. Rayyan doesn't stop walking, but he turns his head to stare at me. "You will?"

"Yeah, anything you need. We're cousins, aren't we?" I'm being completely truthful too. I'll help this dude. How hard can it be, right?

He rewards me with one of his shy smiles. It's like the sun coming out from behind clouds or something. "Thanks, cousin."

5

Abbu's in a mood when we get home.

Look, that's nothing new. He's often in a mood. Outraged, or delusional. Or both. Sometimes, when he's really bad, he gets hallucinations too. The last time that happened was three years ago.

We call them episodes, like his life is a sitcom that goes on for about thirty minutes at a time, and then ends with a cheerful "See you next week!"

Nope. That's not how it goes at all.

When I get home, we hear Abbu talking loudly about his favorite subject: aliens. "They're definitely watching us, Naila, mark my words. Everybody knows this. Everybody!"

"Oh really?" Naila Phupo repeats. It's obvious she's smiling, and I can just picture her round face full of joy, her eyes sparkling like she's happy to be alive. "I didn't know this, bhai, so it's not everybody."

Abbu scoffs. "You're the oblivious kind, sister." But his voice isn't harsh. It's almost . . . happy too. Loud and brash, but happy at the same time.

Well, as happy as he can possibly be, which isn't much most days.

"I'd rather be oblivious than worry about aliens watching me as if I'm on some reality show!" Naila Phupo retorts. "Hai Allah! Can you even imagine?"

For context, Rayyan and I have entered from the front door and are standing in the hall taking our shoes off. Abbu and Naila Phupo are in the kitchen, off the left side of the hall. I can't see them, but I can hear the clinking of teacups against saucers, so they're probably having their afternoon chai.

"Haven't you read about Area 51?" Abbu says impatiently. "It's in . . . which state is it? Arizona? New Mexico?"

"Nevada."

"Yeah, that one. They've got all sorts of test subjects down there, alien aircraft and whatnot. You know this, Naila! I used to tell you all about it when we were kids."

"But those are just stories, bhai."

Abbu scoffs. "That's what they want you to think!" This is accompanied by thumps, then tinkling of china. I don't need to peek into the kitchen to know he's thumping his fist on the table. He loves doing that, to show how serious he is. "What's

43

next? You'll tell me you don't believe in the Bermuda Triangle either? How gullible can you be, sister?"

Rayyan turns to me with a strange look. "What's going on?" he whispers. "Is all that true? Area 51? The Bermuda Triangle?"

He's got a glint in his eye, like he likes the idea. Ugh, how is my father so convincing? So . . . in control? In New York, everyone in the apartment building used to call him King, and me Little Prince.

Just so you know, every time someone used that name, I reacted. If they were an adult, or female, I usually sent them a glare. If it was a dude my age, I punched him.

Yeah, don't call me Little Prince. Like, ever.

"Nah," I reply. "My dad's got a big imagination."

Did I just cop out? Did I just gloss over the fact that my father has delusions?

Yup. I'm not telling anyone the truth. It's embarrassing, and pathetic and ugh, whatever.

"He seems cool," Rayyan says. "Your abbu, I mean."

I make a strangled sort of laughing plus crying sound in the back of my throat. I don't do it on purpose, it just comes out, all demented and emotional-like. Rayyan isn't wrong, in some twisted way. Abbu has this—what's the word?—aura around him. He can hide his scowl and his sneer, and make his eyes all innocent until everybody thinks he's cool.

They don't see the monster hiding right under the skin. Lurking.

And just when you get lulled into the fairy tale, he blinks and whoa! The cool guy is gone and the monster is out, prowling for victims.

Aka me.

Abbu and Naila Phupo start talking about something else. "Remember that park behind our house growing up?" she says. "They shut it down a couple of years ago. Such a waste!"

"The one where I used to push you on the swings? Unbelievable!"

"You were the best swing pusher, bhai, I swear to God!"

I whirl away from Rayyan and run to our bedroom. It's all the way upstairs, which is good. I need some distance from the insanity in my life.

The horrible sitcom that never ends, where the hero is actually the villain, and nobody can tell because he keeps his true nature hidden.

*　*　*

These are some of the ways my abbu is not cool.

One, he left me in the car for two hours when I was five. He went to play cards at some casino in Atlantic City, or something. It was fine, though. It wasn't summer, so the car didn't get too hot.

I was fine.

Two, he didn't feed me for the week Mama went to San Diego for a conference. I was seven. He told me I was a big boy and could take care of myself. It was okay, though. There were lots of snacks in the pantry.

I now hate Oreo cookies, but that's okay.

Three, he drank too much one time and almost crashed the car. This was last year. I was in the back seat. I got two lacerations on my face, but it doesn't really matter. They didn't need stitches. The car didn't even hit anyone, technically. It just went through a barrier and for about forty seconds we drove on the wrong side of the highway.

I know, because I counted.

* * *

Once upon a time, there was a jackal.

What's a jackal, you may ask. Well, I've never seen one in real life, but I've looked it up. A jackal is a canine. You know, like a dog, but it looks more like a fox. It's got a bushy tail and delicate ears, and a little snout and whatnot.

People have pretty negative views of the jackal, let me tell you. When you call someone a jackal, it means you don't respect them, and you think they're a thief or a freeloader or someone who takes advantage of others.

A bad person.

The animal, though. That's something else. I've seen pictures, and the jackal is beautiful. This goes especially for the golden jackal, which lives in South Asia. It's sleek and wiry, very much like a fox.

Anyway, so the jackal in this story is hungry, once upon a time. He searches for food in the forest, and can't find any, and then he gets chased by a group of dogs, so he runs straight into a town. He runs, runs, runs, trying to find a place to hide and maybe even steal some food. Wouldn't that be amazing?

The jackal obviously has no clue about towns and humans. He goes into a dye shop and falls into a big drum of blue dye. The right word is *indigo* or something, I think. He comes out of the drum completely covered in this indigo.

To those who don't know the difference between paint and dye, look that stuff up. He's not covered in paint. His fur is dyed blue.

Sorry, indigo.

Mr. Jackal runs back to the forest, relieved that nothing happened (or so he thinks). He meets other animals, and nobody can recognize what he is because he looks all wrong. They don't really like jackals, on account of their being predators and eating their babies, and other gross stuff.

But Mr. Jackal is clever. He realizes that this is a chance he'll never get again. He can change his identity and pretend to be someone else. Someone good. Someone important.

Really, the sky's the limit. And nobody will know, because jackals aren't blue. As long as he doesn't make that howling slash barking sound that's the hallmark of his species, he'll be golden.

Get it? Golden jackal? But the punchline is that he's now blue.

Or indigo. Whatever.

There's more to this story, don't worry. I'll come back to it later.

* * *

The next day at school, one good thing and one bad thing happen.

The good thing first.

Pigao hands out worksheets of the human skeleton. I think it's kiddish stuff at first, but then I get a closer look. You've got to label a bunch of bones, and you can't just write things like *leg* or *jaw*. You have to use the actual terminology, like *femur* and *mandible*.

"Don't ask Indiana Bones to help you with these," Pigao jokes, pointing to the skeleton in the corner. The cap and clown shoes have been replaced by a black T-shirt and chunky rings on every finger. "He doesn't have any brains, as you can see."

Rayyan giggles. He giggles, I tell you.

We get started on the worksheets, but there's a problem. Only two kids in the class have read the textbook like we were supposed to. Most of us don't know how to label this worksheet.

I'm not worried, though. I like challenges.

Oh, and guess who the kids are who've done their homework? Rayyan: no surprise.

The big surprise: Frankie.

Yup, the same Frankie who made fun of Rayyan and shoved him the day before. That guy.

In my experience, bullies are kids who don't do well in school. They suck at life, so they take it out on other, weaker kids.

Frankie, though, isn't one of those kids. Come to think of it, he answered a lot of teachers' questions correctly my first day. And today, apparently, he's read the chapters of our textbook explaining the parts of a skeleton.

Go figure. I'm officially shocked.

Pigao, though, doesn't seem surprised by any of this. The lack of knowledge in ninety-nine percent of the class. The know-it-all smirk of Rayyan and Frankie (weird how their smirks are pretty much identical).

"Don't worry," Pigao says cheerfully. "We'll make it a group project."

Everyone groans, because you can't be a middle schooler and not despise group projects.

"This will be good practice for the science fair," Pigao says. "You'll need to work in groups for that."

Yeah, I'd totally forgotten about the stupid science fair.

"Worksheets, Mr. Pigao?" Eli whines. "We're not in elementary school."

Pigao snaps his fingers. "Ooh, how about we make it a competition? The group with the most correct answers wins . . . something."

Wow, so motivational.

"Like what?" Eli asks, sitting up.

Pigao wags his eyebrows. "We'll see." He divides the class into two. One has Rayyan as the group leader, and the other has Frankie.

Guess which group I'm in.

Yup, it's Frankie's group.

I'm not ashamed to report that I glower at him the whole time. I haven't forgotten how he slammed into me after school the day before, and how he called Rayyan a loser.

My cousin may be a loser, but I'm the only one allowed to call him that.

Anyway, both groups go through the worksheet with the group leaders helping out with the answers. Personally, I feel like this isn't the best way to learn. We could easily have looked up the answers online if that's all we had to do. We got our fancy Chromebooks, ya know.

I look over at Rayyan's group, and he's actually letting the kids guess and talk it out, instead of just handing them the answers like candy on Halloween.

Frankie, though, is the opposite. He just points to a blank and grunts out the answer like he's doing us all a huge favor.

We get through the skull and vertebrae while I glower, as I said before. By the time we get to the humerus, I've had enough. "Stop feeding us the answers, dude," I whisper. "Let us figure it out ourselves."

"Ooh, look who's all concerned about education," Frankie whispers back with a laugh. "Dude."

Okay, so he doesn't like the word *dude*. I make a note to always use that when talking to him.

"Dude, what's your problem?" I ask, leaning back.

"My problems?" he cackles. "Let me count the ways."

My mouth hangs open. I know this is a reference to some

poem. I just can't figure out which one, or even where I heard it. It's not like I'm into poetry or anything, but I've read some, thanks to Patel Uncle.

Anyway, in this moment in biology class, I'm more focused on how this beefy guy with beady, hateful eyes is quoting poetry.

You know those dreams where everything is normal, but one thing sticks out because it's got no connection to the others? Like, you're in your room in your old apartment and everything is the same, even your mom who doesn't live with you anymore (doesn't love you anymore, maybe, possibly), except for this one weird plant in the window that grows and grows until it wraps its vines all around you and your room and suffocates you to death?

Okay, maybe not exactly like that. But you get the picture. Frankie quoting poetry to emphasize his bullying chops just seems out of whack.

Kinda like the jackal with the blue skin. Totally whack.

"Leave me and my cousin alone, okay?" I whisper shout.

He taps the worksheet. "Pelvic girdle," he says to our group calmly. Then to me, "Or what? Whatchu gonna do, loser?"

I narrow my eyes. Is this guy serious? "I'll do whatever I want," I reply in a hard voice. I also crack my knuckles, just so he knows who he's dealing with.

Frankie laughs out loud. As in, loudly.

I *so* want him to get into trouble, but he knows exactly

what he's doing. Pigao lets us talk and laugh and even snack in class.

It's true. For example, at least five people are eating a variety of things as they work on the human skeleton right this minute. Mini pretzels, chips, raisins. A girl is actually eating a bowl of strawberries like she's in a rom-com.

Well, not a bowl per se, more like a plastic container like the kind you put leftovers in. But you get my drift. It's still cheesy.

Pigao barely even looks up at Frankie's braying jackal laugh. He's got his nose in his computer screen like he's reading some super important document.

I want to do something violent. Something bad.

Nobody laughs at Mo Mirza.

Frankie goes back to the worksheet. "That one's called the fibula," he tells strawberry girl.

She smiles brightly at him. "You're so smart, Frankie."

Ugh. Excuse me while I puke.

And that, my friends, was the one bad thing I said happened at school. Otherwise, everything was peachy. Rayyan's group got the most worksheet answers correct, and Pigao gave them each a bag of mini M&M'S.

And guess who Rayyan shared his M&M'S with? Me, of course.

We left the class smiling, and I ignored Frankie even though I had a pit in my stomach.

Frankie may have fooled everyone into thinking he's smart

and helpful. Me? I'm never fooled because I know too much about people and how awful they can be.

This dude is the jackal hiding under blue skin, but I can see him clear as day.

Just like Abbu.

6

"It's Saturday," my father says.

Actually, he grunts.

I know why he's grunting. Saturday afternoons are a specific kind of torture.

Well, not for him, because he just ignores things he doesn't like. Sadly, I can't do the same.

But it's not afternoon yet. It's Saturday morning, and Naila Phupo has made a feast. Brunch, she calls it.

"My wife never cooked all this traditional breakfast," Abbu says, waving his hand over the table.

That's right, ladies and gentlemen. My dad always calls my mom "his wife." Never actually uses her name. She's like Voldemort, she who must not be named.

I mean, I don't blame him. Names have power, you know. They make you feel stuff. And why would you want to feel anything for someone who abandoned you?

Because here's a thing I try not to think about too much: She didn't just abandon me. She abandoned Abbu too.

Or, ya know, her husband.

"She was busy," Naila Phupo says defensively.

Abbu shakes his head. "She was always busy," he says angrily. "Busy, busy, busy."

I don't know why he's talking about her. He hardly ever does. But since today's Saturday, she's probably on his mind more than usual. He's dressed to reflect his mood, like always. No ironed polo shirt today. He's in his plaid pajama pants and a short-sleeved T-shirt, but it looks clean and he's tried to comb his hair.

It's like he's fifty percent human, fifty percent monster peeking out from behind the mask.

His words put me on edge. *He* puts me on edge.

But what else is new? I try to relax and eat. The breakfast is so delicious, I want to write poems to it.

How do I love thee, O halwa poori, let me count the ways.

(And then I realize that's the poem Frankie was quoting, one of Elizabeth Barrett Browning's sonnets. And then I realize that Frankie is not an ordinary eighth grader, because most eighth graders aren't reading Victorian poets.)

To distract myself from thoughts of Frankie, I say, "Mmm, Phupo, this is awesome!"

She beams like I gave her a million dollars. "Take some more, beta," she says, pushing another fluffy fried circle of breadlike goodness into my hands.

"Don't give him more, he'll get fat," Abbu says. He's shoveling huge morsels of poori wrapped around aloo choley into his mouth like there's a race he needs to win.

Phupo smacks him on the arm. It's just a tap, really. "Don't say that, bhai."

"I'm right," Abbu insists. "Those things are greasy. God knows how many calories they have."

I grit my teeth. Not gonna say anything. Not gonna say anything. Not gonna . . .

"You've got high blood pressure," I mumble. "You're the one who shouldn't be eating this delicious food."

Three things happen at once.

First, Abbu's face transforms into a thundercloud. His jaw works as he tries to swallow his poori so he can hurl some insults at me.

Second, Rayyan stares at me like I've committed the worst sin. Talking back to a parent, ya Allah, what disrespect!

Third, Naila Phupo, bless her heart, leans over and pulls me into a hug. "So glad you liked the brunch, beta!" she says, beaming. "That one doesn't appreciate my cooking at all!"

That one, aka Rayyan, scoffs. "I like your cooking, Mama," he protests.

"Oh, you do, huh?" She scoops some halwa and puts it on his plate. "Then eat this!"

His shoulders drop. "Ugh, halwa is too sweet!"

"It's supposed to be sweet!" Phupo pushes his hand toward his plate. "Now eat!"

I choke on a piece of poori. Not because I'm upset or mad (when am I not these things?), but because of her. Naila Phupo.

She's so . . . nice.

Cheerful. Happy.

And I don't get it. She's got nothing to be cheerful about. She lives in a crappy old house. Her husband is dead. Murdered, no less! She works some kind of job—I'm not sure what yet—to support a kid who's been seriously sick, from what I can tell.

And now she's taken on a horrible brother and his stubborn son.

Like, what makes her smile? Why isn't she crushed and broken under all the hits she's received?

It's mind-boggling, truly.

And a little sickening, like the halwa she's made. So sweet that you don't trust its sweetness even though it's delicious.

Or maybe she's fine, and I'm just unsettled because it's Saturday.

* * *

In our room, stuffed with greasy food, Rayyan spreads papers on his bed.

"Don't tell me you're doing homework?" I groan, flopping down next to him.

"What's wrong with that?"

57

I stare at him, because it's a genuine question. Like, he really wants to know why I object to homework on Saturday. "Uh, because it's the weekend."

"So?" He shrugs. "More time to study."

I sit up. "No! Absolutely not!"

"What would you rather do?"

"What I always do on weekends." I reach under my bed and take out my boxing gloves. "Fight."

We head out to the backyard. The one positive about Rayyan's family not having much money is that the backyard is a wasteland. No flower beds. No grass. There's a big tree in one corner, which is perfect for our needs.

"Get me a pillow," I say.

Rayyan looks confused. "Um, for what? You taking a nap out here?"

I chuckle. "You'll see."

He rolls his eyes and heads back inside. "And rope!" I shout after him.

He whirls around, his eyes popping. "Rope? Where am I supposed to . . . ?"

I wave him away. It's his house. I'm sure he knows where things are kept.

A few minutes later, Rayyan is back with a big fluffy pillow and a straggly rope. I take the things from him and get to work.

"There you go!" I show him my masterpiece.

Well, I'm being sarcastic here. It's more like a beggars-can't-be-choosers kind of situation. I've placed the pillow smack dab in the middle of the tree trunk, at face level. It's fixed in place by the rope, which I've tied tightly around the tree.

"What is it?" Rayyan asks, looking perplexed.

I pull on my gloves and get into position. Leaning slightly forward. Legs apart. Hands close to chin. "Our very own boxing bag."

"You . . . you can't be serious," he gasps. "You're a kid! And this . . . this is a pillow on a tree, not a boxing bag!"

"It's close enough."

He watches, horrified, as I throw quick jabs at the pillow, one after the other. Then I mix it up with a few upper cuts. "Who taught you?" he asks.

"YouTube."

He lets out an incredulous laugh.

I get it. I'm probably too young to be doing this. But it's how I back up my reputation. Bad Boy Mo, with the too-long hair and the earring and the snarky attitude, knows how to fight. Like, Muhammad Ali style.

Get this. I don't actually fight other people. Abbu would be furious if I ever got suspended from school for fighting. Or for anything, really. But here's a secret: knowing these boxing moves, having this—what's it called, persona? It helps build me up as someone to be scared of.

What can I say? I learned from the best.

Abbu's monster scares me. My monster scares everyone else.

Yeah, it's the trickle-down theory or something. I dunno.

Rayyan watches me as I box. I'm not putting a lot of

weight behind my hands, but it's enough to get the blood pumping.

Enough to tell myself I'm the real monster. Someone who can't be beat.

"Why do you do this?" he finally asks. "Because of your nightmares?"

I freeze. How does he know?

Rayyan shrugs. "You talk in your sleep."

Am I supposed to apologize? I'm not sure. It's not like I ask the dreams to come and drive me nuts.

I decide to ignore the topic. "I box so that nobody messes with me," I reply. "You should learn too. I don't like Frankie and his goons messing with you."

"There's just one goon," Rayyan protests. "And I'm not into violence. I'm a pacifist."

I raise one eyebrow. "You mean, you like being bullied?"

"They're not that bad." His voice is very low, like a lie trying to hide itself.

I go back into my boxer's stance. "Whatever you want to tell yourself."

Rayyan sits on a little brick near the tree. I think it's left over from a flower bed or something. Maybe once upon a time, this place was a beautifully tended garden. Who knows?

"Frankie's been saying mean stuff to me since elementary school," Rayyan continues in his low voice. "But it's nothing I haven't heard before. Too thin. Too smart. Orphan. Goody Two-Shoes."

I bite my lip, because wasn't I thinking the same thing about him a few days ago? "That was before," I tell him. "I'm here now. That crap will stop."

"How? You going to beat him up? Then you'll be no better than him."

I pause to look over my shoulder. "Here's a tip for you, my dear cousin. I'm worse than any bully you can imagine."

Exhibit A: Jonah Wiley in third grade, a week after the monster incident. I got tired of him saying stuff to me in the hallways and after school, so I kicked him hard and made him fall down. There was lots of blood from his nose, and possibly a bruise on his ankle too.

This was before I taught myself how to box.

Exhibit B: the kids in my Queens apartment building, talking about Mama never being home and saying bad words about her. Hey, I was ten and I knew what those words meant. You shouldn't ever say that about girls, FYI.

By then I knew how to box. So I taught all those kids a lesson.

Yeah, I never pretended to be a good person, you know?

It's obvious Rayyan doesn't believe me, though. He shakes his head and looks away, a sad look on his face. Maybe he's imagining the garden when his dad was alive. Maybe he's thinking of the days he was sick.

Or maybe he's pitying me.

I've got no idea.

* * *

Saturday afternoon.

I've showered and changed into jeans and a nice navy blue T-shirt. I've taken the earring out.

Yeah, it's that kind of afternoon.

"Mohammad, you ready?" Abbu growls from his room. It's Naila Phupo's guest room, basically.

I go in. My father's sitting at a desk, his laptop in front of him. There aren't any lights on, so the room is on the dark side.

We wait for the video link to connect. It's through a secure government site, so it takes forever.

"We should switch on the light," I say, looking around. "It's too dark."

"It's fine," Abbu replies shortly.

I focus on him. He's still wearing his pajamas and T-shirt combo. The T-shirt with the old stain on the front. "You should change," I say.

Okay, I whisper. I'm not exactly sure I want to give him a direct command, because who knows how he'll react?

Abbu scowls at the laptop. "I don't need to get dressed up for that woman."

Okay then.

We wait. And wait. The regular time is two p.m. Eastern but we're in Texas now, so it's one p.m. Central. "Are you sure you got the time right?" I ask.

Abbu growls warningly. He sounds like a monster sometimes too, which messes with my head. A lot.

After five more minutes, the screen lights up. It's an incoming video call.

It takes another half a minute for Mama to come on the screen.

The first thing she says is this: "Why is it so dark?"

"Uh . . . ," I begin.

"Turn your laptop toward the light, Mo. I can hardly see you."

I don't want to move. I'm too busy looking at her. Her small face with a perfect little frown between her perfect eyebrows. Blond hair tied in a ponytail. Blue eyes framed by glasses.

She looks the same as always. I want to reach out through the screen and hug her.

Nope, not happening. Not even if she was in this room with me.

"Mo! Can you hear me?"

"Sorry." I jump to do what she says. There's a lamp on the desk. I push the laptop closer to it. "How about this? Is it better?"

"I suppose it'll have to do."

"Okay, good." I smile nervously, hating myself for it.

Here's what you need to know about my mother. She's brilliant.

I don't mean she's smart and sassy (although that's also true). She's literally a genius, like her IQ is a hundred and seventy-five, and she's got a photographic memory that recalls things perfectly, even what she had for breakfast three years ago.

Anyway, Dr. Rebecca Eckert has a PhD in engineering. Currently, she's a fellow for UNESCO, studying water systems in poor countries. A fellowship is a special job for a short period of time, like one or two years, I dunno. Right now, she's in Greece working with refugees in a camp there, making sure they have clean water and everything.

A regular Mother Teresa, my mom is.

"So, how are you?" she asks me briskly. It's her style, I guess. She calls it no-nonsense.

I call it no emotion. Same difference.

Before I can reply, Abbu leans forward. "What do you care how he is? You left him. You don't care about him."

I sigh. Usually he lets me speak for a few minutes before getting started on his grievances.

Mama gasps. "How can you say that, Mumtaz? I love him! I'm his mother! But the families here *need* me. They have no safe drinking water! Can't you understand that?"

"Oh, yeah! And your own son doesn't need you, does he?"

Mama's eyes flash. "He's got his father, doesn't he? Why don't you step up, stop drinking and gambling, and actually be a parent for once?"

"I'm the only parent he has, wife!" Abbu roars.

Deep breaths. Deep, deep breaths.

I stand up and say, very loudly, "I'm fine, Mama. The new school is great. I'm in honors classes, which means ninth-grade biology and algebra."

The adults stop their fighting and turn to me. "That's to be expected, Mo," Mama says. "You're my son, after all. Smart."

Abbu grunts, but he doesn't say anything. For now.

I sit back down. I think if I keep talking about school, she'll listen. "We're learning about the human body in biology class. It's really interesting."

"Biology?" Mama's face breaks into a rare smile. "That's amazing, Mo. How are you liking it so far?"

"I'm liking it a lot." I want her to smile more, so I add, totally lying, of course, "I think we're going to do research too, dig in deep about some topics."

Actually, this could be true. I bet I'll have to do this for the science fair.

"Humph, research!" Abbu barks. "We don't need more researchers in this family."

Mama's smile fades. "What does that mean, Mumtaz?"

"I'll tell you what it means. . . ."

This time I don't even bother with the deep breaths. I turn around and leave the room. The pillow on the tree is waiting for me in the backyard. I left my boxing gloves on the patio steps, because I knew I'd be coming down here again after the call.

I always practice my jabs after one of Mama's calls.

It's the way I spend Saturday afternoons.

7

In Naila Phupo's family, Sundays are for the Almighty.

Let me explain.

I've learned that my aunt works at the Islamic center as an administrative assistant. "There's a mosque, and a community hall, and a youth program, and so much more!" she says happily as she drives Rayyan and me to this magical place. "I don't work on Sundays, but I still like to go, because that's when they have all the best programs."

The best programs? What does that even mean? My family never went to any sort of Islamic center even when we were an actual family. Abbu thinks religion is for the weak. Mama isn't Muslim, and she turns her nose up at every Muslim event. I can't even remember celebrating Eid much, except for video calls with Rayyan's family.

Listen, don't judge me. I have bigger problems than whether I get presents for Eid.

"The programs are *not* fun," Rayyan tells me from the passenger seat.

"Don't say that." Phupo smacks his arm lovingly. I'm learning this is her go-to move. It's a soft smack, full of affection, but still. I'm not a fan.

Rayyan taps the folder in his lap. "I'm going to complete my work," he warns her. "Just telling you in advance."

Her shoulders slump. "Beta . . ."

"It's important stuff, Mama!" Rayyan gives her that stubborn look of his. It's the same when she's pushing him to eat something and he doesn't want it.

Phupo sighs. "Okay. Just . . . at least show Mo around and introduce him to everyone."

Yay, lucky me.

We drive about twenty minutes, which would seem far in New York terms, but in Houston, apparently it's right around the corner. We're also moving very, very slow. Phupo has an old Nissan that looks like it saw better days in the eighties.

Now it's just trying not to die.

"Too bad bhai didn't want to come," she says out of the blue. "He would've enjoyed himself."

Does she know her brother even a little bit?

"He . . . er . . . wasn't feeling like it, I guess."

That's an understatement. Abbu was grumpy because everyone had plans for the day except for him. He'd shouted at me for eating breakfast too slow, then at Naila Phupo for making noise in the kitchen, then at the birds for tweeting too loudly outside his window.

Also, his blood pressure was too high.

Third, in his words, "The FBI surveils all the mosques in America. Why would I want to show my face at such a dangerous place?"

Rayyan had watched quietly and said nothing. As usual.

My face had flushed with embarrassment and annoyance.

So yeah, Abbu is not with us this fine Sunday afternoon. There is zero complaint on my end.

We reach the mosque and I literally jump out. I'm happy to see some of Houston, even if it's just the local Muslim hangout.

The place is humungous. There's a big mosque with a golden dome and a white minaret. A sign on the side says WELCOME TO KHADIJAH MASJID. Next to it is a gray building with tall glass windows. Lots of people are entering and leaving. Lots more people are standing or sitting on the grass outside.

Naila Phupo joins a group of ladies who look her age. "I'm going to attend a lecture about women's empowerment," she informs us.

"Go, women!" I say.

Am I being sarcastic? Yes.

Am I kind of jealous because the lecture sounds cool? Also yes.

Rayyan sits on a bench in the grass and opens up his folder.

"You really brought your homework?" I ask, sinking down next to him. "You don't want to attend a lecture or something?"

"The kids don't have lectures," he complains. "They have Sunday school."

Okay, it doesn't sound too bad. I had a couple of Christian friends who attended Sunday school at their church, and I always wondered what that was all about. It sounds babyish, but also sort of interesting.

"So you don't attend Sunday school?" I ask. "I thought you were all about education?"

Rayyan shrugs. "Sometimes. But last week they were talking about how God has a plan for everything, and that made me sort of mad."

"Why?"

He frowns. "God's plan is to make my dad die? To make me so sick I can't eat anything without my stomach hurting?"

"Er . . ."

Too late, he's on a roll now. "Maybe it's God's plan to send me a bully who makes fun of me every day, and an uncle who's scary but also kind of pitiful—"

I hold up a hand, because . . . what?

"Are . . . are you talking about Abbu?" I stammer.

Rayyan stops. "Sorry, you know what I mean."

"Pitiful?" I'd never use that word to describe my father. Not even if all the other words in the dictionary were taken and that was the only one left. Plus, the other day, Rayyan was calling Abbu cool. "How is he pitiful?"

Rayyan stares at me. "Well, he's sick, isn't he? He gets all angry and upset and thinks aliens are after him, because of his sickness. Right?"

"No," I say, a little louder than I need to, probably. "He's just a horrible person. A monster."

Rayyan's forehead wrinkles like he can't figure something out. "You . . . you don't mean that. You know he's sick, right?"

* * *

Here's the thing. I hate calling my father sick. I don't say it, don't feel it, don't tell other people about it.

It's like an excuse. It's like asking people to feel sorry for me. Poor Mo, sad bad boy, Dad's sick in the head and Mom's left, boo-hoo.

No. I'm stronger than all that noise. My struggles are my own. I don't need to tell anyone about Abbu's condition.

But let me lay it all down today.

Abbu has paranoid schizophrenia. It's a mental illness that messes up your brain and doesn't let you think or act like a normal person.

You may have uncontrolled anger. Check.

You may get addictions. Check.

You may get delusions of grandeur. Check. Paranoia. Check. Hallucinations. Ah, yes, those too sometimes. Check.

The symptoms of schizophrenia aren't the same for all patients. Some don't get Hulk-level angry. Some don't have hallucinations. But all of them have one thing in common:

they can't take care of themselves or their responsibilities.

It means their exterior is hard and tough, like Indiana Bones in Pigao's classroom. No softness, no humanity.

Just a monster.

* * *

It starts to rain a little, so Rayyan puts away his folder and leads me into the gray building. There are a bunch of meeting rooms on the first floor, some empty and some full of people. I see Naila Phupo and her friends in one of the rooms, listening to a woman wearing a hijab.

Normally Naila Phupo doesn't wear hijab. But today she's wearing shalwar kameez, and her hair is covered with a dupatta. I'm guessing it's her mosque outfit.

Who am I to judge? Sometimes we all want to fit in. I mean, I took out my earring before we left home. Didn't need the raised eyebrows or the disgusted faces.

Upstairs there are classrooms filled with kids of all ages. In one room, teenagers watch something on a flat screen. I see a flash of Arabic letters. In another, little kids are sitting on a mat. A woman is reading them a story. I look at the title. *Yasmin the Explorer.* I smile, because I read all the Yasmin books in first grade.

She's awesome.

In another classroom, a few kids our age are writing in notebooks. The teacher is a man who looks kinda like Abbu, holding a Quran.

"I'm supposed to be in there," Rayyan whispers.

"You're being bad, eh?" I smirk. "I love it."

"Shut up. I'll go later."

We pass a small library (which makes me think of Walker Middle's incredible one) and an art room. They're both empty. Then we get to the last door, which says Office. Rayyan opens the door and steps inside.

"What's this, your secret hideout?" I ask, following him.

There are two desks facing each other, both with computers and other office stuff. You know, things like staplers and mugs full of pens and those big old-fashioned phones with cords. There are bookshelves on the walls and a printer-scanner combo in the corner. Under the window is a worn-out leather couch.

"This is where Mama works," Rayyan tells me.

"What does she do, exactly?" I ask.

He shrugs in a classic don't-know-don't-care gesture. "She's kind of like an office manager. Answers phones, files paperwork. Deals with the community."

My eyes bug out. "What, like if there are people protesting the mosque outside?"

He scoffs. "No, like if the toilet breaks, she's the one to call the plumber."

This guy's a real joker. I grab a pen from one of the desks and throw it at his head. "What are we doing here?"

Rayyan sits on the couch and opens his folder again. "I need to review the NJHS application."

"Boring."

He doesn't answer. He picks up the pen I threw at him and starts reading the form. It's, like, five pages long.

While he reads, I check out Naila Phupo's desk. I know which one is hers by the scarf dangling on the desk chair. I've seen it in the house too. It's silky black with white teardrops.

There's a picture of her and Rayyan at the beach. They look happy.

I try to remember if there are any pictures of me and Mama anywhere on this planet. I'd even take one of us at her office desk.

There aren't. Not a single one.

You know who she's taken tons of pictures with? The refugee kids, that's who. I know this because she mailed us a magazine a few weeks ago. It was a UNESCO publication, and on the cover was Dr. Rebecca Eckert surrounded by happy, adorable refugee kids. She sat in the middle of them, holding a little boy in her lap, looking like a cat that ate a whole forest full of canaries.

Or wherever canaries live. I dunno.

Rayyan makes a loud, aggravated sound. It distracts me big-time, which is perfect, because I don't want to think about my mother anymore. She takes up way too much headspace, anyway. "What's up?" I ask.

"Aargh, it's just this application! It's stupid!"

I wait for more.

Nothing. No explanation. He looks like how I imagine the disgruntled bear would look in this one folktale called "The

Bear's Bad Bargain." An old woman promises to feed a bear some kichri in exchange for chopped wood, but in the end, she hoodwinks him. He's not happy, obviously.

"When's the application due?" I ask.

Rayyan waves his hand. "It's not due until February. I'm trying to get a head start on some of the items."

It's like he's speaking gibberish. "Why?" I insist. Whoever heard of starting on work *early*? Like, months early. This is madness.

"Because . . ." He sighs, like talking to me is too hard. "Look, the service section. I need to be volunteering somewhere already. I need to have a lot of hours, so I need to start now. Get it?"

"Like, *now* now?"

He nods sadly. "Yup, it's already too late, probably."

Okay, let's not get melodramatic. "Well, then, find something to volunteer for."

"Okay." He looks at me with big eyes, like I'm going to solve all his problems. "You said you'll help me."

"When did I . . . ?" Then I remember. It was on the way home from school after my first day. "Yup, sure, I can help. What kind of things are you interested in?"

"Anything. I don't even care at this point."

I snap my fingers. "Hey, maybe this place has some work for you."

He frowns. "The Islamic center? Like what?"

"I don't know." I pick up his papers and walk toward the

door. "Maybe fixing those broken toilets you were telling me about."

"Be serious. Please."

I pull him to the art room we saw earlier. On the door is a flyer. *Volunteers Needed for Sunday Art Class. No Experience Necessary.* "How about helping kids paint?"

"I know nothing about painting," Rayyan protests. "I'm all about STEM."

I shrug. "Come on, how hard can it be? You're already coming here on Sundays, it's like killing two birds with one stone."

"Must you be so violent?" Rayyan takes out his pen and writes both our names on the sign-up sheet. "There. Happy?"

I mean, I wasn't expecting to be dragged into this volunteer business. But whatever. Cousins, right?

I slap him on the back. "See, problem solved! Aren't I a genius?"

* * *

After her lecture, Naila Phupo takes us inside the mosque, where we offer Zuhr prayers.

That's a first for me, offering prayers in congregation. I gave up praying around the time my parents decided to become horrible people.

But this space is gorgeous, and the light filtering in through the stained-glass windows makes me feel a weird sort of peace. Like, puts me in a trance or whatever.

I like it.

We're in a huge room carpeted in red and yellow lines. The

men stand up front, and the women behind a thin partition. We're led by a middle-aged uncle with a salt-and-pepper beard and crinkles around his eyes. "That's Imam Shamsi," Rayyan whispers.

I don't care. I just want to be in this space with my thoughts.

Imam Shamsi starts the prayer. To my surprise, his voice is seriously melodious. Like, he could get a gig on Broadway if this imam work doesn't pan out.

I follow along with all the other guys. Rayyan is on my right, and the person on my left looks like he's in high school. There are a lot of uncles around me. Also, a lot of kids. Naila Phupo is somewhere behind us, with the rest of the ladies.

Like a slow wave on the ocean, we all stand and bow and prostrate on the ground together. Then we stand again and repeat the cycle, over and over.

I try to open my mind to God.

I try to ask for something. Beg for something.

But my soul is quiet. For now, being in this space is enough.

Maybe, one day, I'll be able to ask for what I need.

8

My second week at Alice Walker starts with a bang. Literally.

I'm walking down the hallway to the first class when I bump into an angel. I'm not even kidding.

Let me count the ways (and yes, I'm channeling my inner Frankie, which is gross, but whatever).

Tall. Light blue jeans and a purple blouse. Curly black hair down to her shoulders. Dimples.

Ah, the dimples do the trick. Ladies and gentlemen, it's official: I've got a crush.

"Excuse you!" the angel cries when I bump into her. "Look where you're going, new kid."

I'm speechless. And breathless.

She's rude. Like, a lot.

Doesn't make my crush any less, but now I'm adding—what's that word?—*masochist* to my personality traits. You know, Mo Mirza's list of faults.

Other items on the list: cowardly. Unlovable. Unfunny. Eats too much candy. Can't make a good left hook. Can't sing.

"Sorry," I say, trying out my bad-boy smirk just in case it works on her.

It doesn't. She gives me a dirty look and flounces away.

Yes, she actually flounces. I wouldn't have thought that was possible in tight jeans, but there it is.

I sigh. "Who is she?"

Nobody's around to answer me. Rayyan left me at the front entrance to go to the restroom before class. Something about his stomach rumbling.

No worries. I'll find the black-haired beauty myself.

* * *

Once upon a time, there was a prince of Egypt named Saif-ul-Malook.

Egypt, you say? Isn't that far from Pakistan, or South Asia, whose folktales Mo Mirza specializes in?

Yes to both. Basically, the prince was from Egypt, but this is indeed a desi folktale, because it centers around a stunningly beautiful lake in northwest Pakistan with the same name. Lake Saif-ul-Malook. You just have to wait to see the connection.

So, Saif is a prince of Egypt. One night, he sees a fairy named Badri Jamala in his dreams, dancing in a lake and generally having a good time. He's immediately smitten. Another version of the story says he sees her image on some old coins, but I don't like that version. Let's face it, you can't see enough on a coin to fall for a person. It's basically an outline, not the real face.

A dream, though. That can be real enough to make you feel stuff.

Saif wakes up in the morning and tells his family he's leaving to find this Badri fairy. He's got no clue where she lives, or who she is, but he's determined. She could be a serial killer, for all we know. But she's pretty, so it's all good.

Saif searches everywhere. He travels for six years, asking everyone he meets.

Yup, you heard that right. Six whole years. No worry about his kingdom or his family. Begging on the streets, yada yada. This guy has what we call a goal-oriented mindset.

One day, though, his mindset is rewarded. Finally. He meets a wise old man who gives the prince a magical cap. It's a mythical thing that can take you anywhere your heart desires.

(We interrupt this broadcast to announce that if Mo Mirza had this cap, he'd be traveling to a certain refugee camp in Greece, pronto.)

Anyway, as soon as Saif puts on the cap, he's whooshed away to this beautiful place, a lake in the Naran Valley (that's near the Himalayas, FYI). He's shocked, A. because of the instant travel thing, and B. because this is the place he saw in his dream six years ago!

But there are no fairies dancing in the lake. No Badri.

Then Saif gets another jolt. The cap isn't an ordinary magical cap. It comes with a jinn. Long story short, the cap belonged to Solomon, who ruled the jinn, et cetera. The jinn dude has some bad news. The fairies aren't easy to see, since they're not human. There's one way to make that happen, though. Maybe, no promises. Saif should set up camp and pray for forty days or something. The prayer thing is called chilla, in which you don't eat anything, only sit and pray for forty days.

Brutal, I know.

Saif decides he's been begging on the streets for years, living the life of a homeless person, how hard can a chilla be?

Answer: pretty hard. He gets weak and exhausted by day forty, but when the chilla is over, guess what? There's all this light and music and he finally—FINALLY!—sees Badri Jamala. The beautiful fairy queen is at the lake with her entourage or whatever.

Or maybe she's always been there, only now he can see her.

Doesn't matter. They're finally on the same plane of existence. He sees her, she sees him. Saif's heart leaps in his chest (I'm only guessing, since I wasn't there, but it makes sense that he'd be super excited to find her after six years and forty days).

Typical love story, eh?

Nope. If you thought this was the end, that Saif and Badri lived happily ever after, you'd be wrong.

Well, they do, but not immediately. There are villains to defeat first.

But that's a story for another day.

*　*　*

I go to first period, planning ways to search for Badri.

I mean, the rude but pretty girl I crashed into. Same thing.

So what if I imagine myself as Prince Saif-ul-Malook going around like a beggar searching for his fairy queen? There's nothing wrong with it. That's what folktales are for, to inspire and motivate us, right?

Thankfully, it doesn't take me six years to find her. Nor do I have to stay hungry for forty days. No offense to Prince Saif, but I don't think any girl is worth that much.

Good news: she's already sitting in class.

Bad news: it's music class, which . . . ugh. Who thought teaching eighth graders how to read sheet music was a good idea?

Here's the story of why I despise music class.

In fourth grade, my friend Zed threw up in a recorder, I kid you not. I don't know what Zed's deal was. Maybe he was sick. Maybe he was nervous because the music teacher, Miss Romano, wanted him to play "Mary Had a Little Lamb" in front of the whole class.

Zed made a lot of excuses. Like, he didn't remember the tune. Also, that he lost his recorder. Miss Romano brought out an extra recorder, then glared at Zed and told him to "Come up here and get it over with."

Honestly, some people shouldn't be teachers. They're not cut out for it.

Anyway, Zed slowly went up to the front of the class with the spare recorder. He was sweating and his hands were trembling.

I should mention here that Zed isn't a coward. He's a cool dude, always in Marvel villain T-shirts and wearing an earring just like mine. In fact, we'd gone to a shop down the street to buy our earrings together. His name is Zubair, but he hated it even more than I hated Mohammad, so he changed it to the letter *Z* as pronounced in British English. Zed.

So Zed started "Mary Had a Little Lamb," but he didn't even get through the first line before he puked in the recorder.

Gross, I know.

You'd think that's why I hate music class. But it's not. There's more to this disgusting story.

The next week, Miss Romano called me to the front of the class to play "Happy Birthday." Only nobody had bothered to clean the spare recorder the week before, so I put my mouth on the exact same spot where my best friend puked.

Yup. Good times.

*　*　*

At Walker Middle, music is an elective. This should mean there's a choice, but ironically, it's the complete opposite in my case. I'm in this class because all the other electives were already full. Ugh. One of the downsides of starting school in October.

Rayyan is in computer science, which . . . double ugh.

This room is full of a bunch of eighth graders from different sections. Normally, I'd be okay with it, because I'm not in the business of making friends. Today, though, I'm searching for a friendly face, because I need answers.

Unfortunately, I find Frankie sitting four seats away from me. He catches my eye and shakes his head slowly, like a pendulum.

What? Is that supposed to be threatening?

I roll my eyes and look away. Eli, from Pigao's class, is right next to me. "Hey," I whisper. "How's it going?"

The music teacher, Mrs. Nguyen, is talking about . . . something. I have no clue what. Eli turns sideways and shrugs. "Okay."

Hmm, not a great conversationalist. I can respect that.

"Um, do you know that girl?" I ask, nodding to the front of the class.

Eli gives me a puzzled look. "Carmen Rodriguez. Why?"

I shrug. "Haven't seen her before, that's all."

"She's in a different eighth-grade section."

I lean back in my chair and relax. I spend all of class staring at the back of Carmen Rodriguez's head. Her hair is pretty, all . . . curly and stuff.

This is the first time in my entire life I don't despise music class.

* * *

"Sorry you had to tough it out alone in Mrs. Nguyen's class," Rayyan says in biology.

The bell hasn't rung yet, and Pigao is talking to another teacher in the hallway. The plastic skeleton in the corner is wearing a top hat and purple cape. I smile, thinking of Carmen's blouse. "It wasn't too bad."

Rayyan looks unconvinced. "Really? What did you learn?"

"Something called musical note architecture. But who listens to teachers, right?"

"The music students put on a performance at the end of the year," Rayyan tells me. "So I think it's in your best interest to listen."

Yikes. I did not know that. "Fun!" I say with an exaggerated happy face. I'll have to make sure I'm not using a recorder for my performance.

The bell rings, and Pigao strolls inside with his hands in his lab-coat pockets. The kids in the class have already started snacking. The menu is grapes and baby carrots. Yeesh.

"Good afternoon, students," Pigao says. "Today we're starting on muscles. That's another important system in our anatomy."

A few of the guys start showing off their biceps. "I'm a gym rat," Frankie boasts.

"That's not something to be proud of, my man," I say.

He gives me a dirty look, which I totally ignore.

Check it: I'm a master at ignoring things I don't like.

Pigao claps his hands. "Before we begin, turn in your skeleton charts, please."

There's a shuffle as we hand over the charts. "So what did

you learn about the human skeleton last week?" Pigao asks. "Any revelations?"

There's silence. Well, you can hear someone chomping on carrots, but that's it. I lean forward. "It's cool," I say.

A few kids laugh.

"Indiana Bones would definitely agree," Pigao says, also laughing a little.

I gulp and try to explain. "Well, what I meant was, it's amazing how much our bones do for us. We don't even realize."

"That's anatomy in general," Rayyan adds. "All the systems in our body are doing cool things, but we don't even realize until one of them stops working."

"Hmm," Pigao says. "If you had to describe the skeleton in one adjective, what would that be?"

Everyone has answers to that. Hard. Tough. Protective. Pigao hands out a single candy at every response.

The candy is my favorite, Kit Kat. Maybe that's why I decide to break my own rule and speak up in class twice in a row. "How about . . . impenetrable?" I say.

"Nerd!" Frankie whispers behind his hand. His goon snickers.

"Thanks," I reply dryly. Literally nobody has ever called me a nerd before. Also, this guy who spouts poetry is gonna call me names? Whatever. "Takes one to know one."

"Enough." Pigao tosses me a Kit Kat. "Time to talk muscles."

9

One thing about me. I'm not into shopping, like at all.

Sure, I like buying new stuff. Sneakers. T-shirts. Boxing gloves. What can I say, a guy needs things.

But we live in the twenty-twenties, right? We can buy almost anything we need online. So many cool stores have websites to order from. Then why go shopping? Malls are for losers.

Guess what I'm doing this Friday afternoon? Going to the mall.

With Abbu.

Yeah, I already know it's not gonna be fun.

Apparently I need a new jacket. Winter is coming up, and my current one is NYC-weather approved. You know, fit for snowstorms and temperatures in the single digits.

Houston winters need a different kind of jacket, I'm told. "Get fleece or nylon," Naila Phupo told us before we left. "Something lightweight."

Shudder. That sounds awful.

The mall is half an hour away, and Abbu talks the whole time. All his favorite topics make an appearance: I need to study hard, not get into fights like in my old school; I need to eat proper food, not the junk I like so much; I shouldn't worry, things will get better—in fact they'd already be better if only his wife had stayed with us instead of galivanting across the world.

Here's the problem. I hate this man so much that I can't even agree with him when he's saying the right thing. Like, I know things would be better if Mama hadn't gone to Greece, but when he's saying it in his grumpy, entitled voice, I just can't keep quiet.

"Mama's doing something great," I grumble. "You should support her."

Never mind that in my heart, I don't support her even as much as a grain of sand.

Abbu laughs in this ugly way he has. "Yeah, that's what everyone says. What a great woman I married."

This is true. Everyone makes it a point to remind him—us—how incredible Mama is. How self-sacrificing. She'd have to be, to marry a monster like him, right?

* * *

Some ways in which Mama is incredible.

1. She's a doctor. Okay, so not a medical one, but still. Her research keeps people healthy, and even saves lives sometimes. Once she wrote a report on diseases in the water pipes in old inner-city houses. She was on the news talking about it for weeks afterward.

2. She took care of Abbu for fifteen years. And let me tell you, Abbu is a full-time job. He needs someone to do things for him when he can't, because of, you know. Schizophrenia. Like, making sure he takes his meds, and making sure he eats and takes a bath and doesn't burn down the apartment complex in one of his rages.

3. She took care of me when I was little. I mean, sure, she's my mom, so she had to. But she didn't have to remind me about it all the time, did she? Like, "Look Mo, I'm making you dinner again when I could've been working," or "God, Mo, why did you have to get sick the same day as my very important meeting?"

4. She's currently helping a camp full of refugee kids with no regard to her own safety. As I've mentioned many times before. Yay, Greece, you lucky dudes.

*　*　*

You may be wondering why my parents are married. They've got zero in common, not even their ethnicity. Definitely not their intelligence.

That's where you'd be wrong. Abbu is pretty smart, in his own way. One time I saw him add a long line of numbers on a receipt and come up with the right answer in just a few seconds. All he had to do was stare at the receipt intensely, lips moving, and he'd added it all in his head.

Secretly, I was impressed.

On my face, I didn't show anything.

Mama and Abbu met in college. She was in the engineering department, and he was an accounting student. They had a math class together or something, and got to talking. I'm guessing they weren't always angry with each other. "He swept me off my feet," Mama once told me, a long time ago.

Then she shook her head like she was totally regretting this sweeping business.

Whatever. They got married, had a kid, started hating each other, and now I'm stuck in the middle.

* * *

"I'm not going to spend the whole evening in this dump," Abbu warns me when we reach the mall. "Buy the first jacket that fits, and let's leave."

Sure, whatever.

Here's how the shopping spree goes.

Shop number one: no jackets. They're all out. How is that even possible?

Shop number two: all they have are those huge, puffy jackets that make you walk like a penguin. Abbu insists I buy one of those, but I beg and plead and he says okay.

Shop number three: all the jackets are either too expensive or too ugly. A few are both. Yikes.

By this time, Abbu is sick of me and my jacket needs. He thinks the guy at the counter is after him or something, and we need to hustle out of there.

What he means is anyone's guess. Abbu gets like that sometimes, imagining all kinds of over-the-top things. People are after him. His soda might be poisoned. He's being followed by the secret service.

He could write thrillers and become a millionaire, if he got out of his own head.

"Which one do you want, Mohammad?" Abbu growls at me. He's keeping one eye on the counter, where the guy is listening to music on his earbuds.

"Er," I riffle quickly through a bunch of clothes. "I don't know."

I mean, I know what I don't want. They're mostly hideous.

Abbu grabs a black one. "Is this fleece?" he asks the counter guy.

"Check the label."

Abbu's mouth tightens. "He's supposed to help customers, the ass. I should call his manager."

But he won't. He doesn't actually do anything. He only threatens.

Abbu shoves the jacket at me. "Try it on."

I do as he says. Thankfully, it fits. I don't even care what it looks like at this point. I can tell this shopping trip is a bust. I'm getting this jacket or none at all.

We stand at the mirror, and I get a flash of a memory. Abbu

and me, getting ready for my fifth-grade graduation. Mama was going to meet us in the school auditorium, so us two guys got ready by ourselves.

"Big day, eh, Mohammad?" Abbu said in a happy tone. "Can't believe you'll be in middle school soon."

I couldn't either. I passed the middle school every day and it looked really big and scary, not that I'd ever say that out loud. Another thing I couldn't believe: my father being nice and kind. He helped me put on my jacket and checked my hair in the mirror. Then his own. "We'll get Thai food on the way home, to celebrate," he said.

I nodded eagerly, already planning what I'd order. Most people loved pad thai, but my favorite was beef satay. Yum.

Behind my back, I crossed my fingers. *Please don't get angry. Please don't argue with Mama. Please don't get angry.*

It worked. Everything went well. I got my certificate. Zed and I took lots of pictures on his dad's phone. Mama and Baba didn't argue at all, not even about what food to order.

So, basically a miracle.

Abbu pays for the jacket. I'm expecting him to rush us out of there, but he stops and points to a sign next to the credit card machine. "You're hiring?"

The guy looks up. "Uh, yeah. You want a form?"

"Sure." Abbu takes an application form while I stare at him. He's looking for a job? I thought he was working at the garage.

I don't ask, though. I'd rather not start a conversation with him.

We head out. Abbu orders some fast food at a drive-through. Two cheeseburger combos. "Shouldn't we get something for Phupo and Rayyan too?" I ask.

Abbu looks irritated. "Why do we need to do that? She's probably cooked already."

I grit my teeth. The way he's looking at me, I know he's ready to erupt. But this is important. "She's always cooking for us. We should bring her some food."

Abbu shakes his head. "You're too soft, that's your problem. Even with that earring, you can't be a tough kid like your father."

I think about Pigao's skeleton. Underneath all our soft skin and flesh, we're basically a tough set of bones, right? I decide I can be just as tough as Indiana Bones. We're basically the same inside, me and that plastic skeleton.

Abbu drives up to the window and adds a few more things to his order. Two more cheeseburgers, plus chicken nuggets, fries, and milkshakes. The lady at the window shakes her head, but he gives her his best charming smile. She smiles back and does what he says.

The food comes out in big brown bags lined with grease and smelling ah-mazing. Belatedly, I wonder if Naila Phupo eats halal food only.

But I'm not poking the tiger again. If she doesn't eat this food, Rayyan and I will have a feast.

＊　＊　＊

"Oh my god, I love Whataburger!" Rayyan says with his mouth full.

I'm grinning, because it's nice to see him eat. "What *is* that, anyway? Whataburger?"

"A Texas specialty," he replies. "Like, California has In-N-Out, and New York has Shake Shack."

"Wait, I saw a Shake Shack in the mall here," I protest.

"Yes, but its origin is New York City, right?" He slurps some milkshake loudly. Gross.

"Yup, just like me." I lean forward. "Their shroom burgers are my favorite."

Rayyan makes a face, because ya know, mushrooms.

We're sitting in our room, on our beds, the food on the side table between us. Legs dangling down to the floor. Music on.

"My turn next," I say, pointing to the laptop that's streaming a cringey pop hit.

"Sure."

I lean over and find my favorite song. It's an old Nazia Hassan hit, "Aap Jaisa Koi."

Rayyan, obviously, has never heard it before. "What on earth is this?" he asks, mouth open.

"I dunno, it's from the eighties." I'm lying again. I know exactly who sang it (Nazia Hassan, British Pakistani teen singer), when (1980), where (the Bollywood film *Qurbani*), and so much more.

Judging from Rayyan's face, he knows I know all this. "Why are you like this, Mo?" he asks all serious-like. "How?"

I scoff. "Like what? Into eighties hits?"

"Into Urdu or Hindi songs," he replies. "You're American. Your mom is a white American. Your dad doesn't seem like the type of guy who listens to music at all. What gives?"

I shrug and eat some fries. Actually, Abbu is very much into music. Oh, he can't stand current tunes, sure, but he'll talk your ear off about the ancients, as he calls them. He's got albums of classical Indian music in his boxes somewhere. Slow, soothing, heart-wrenching sounds.

I shake my head. "It's just music, dude. Calm down."

"It's not *just* music," Rayyan insists. "It's also other things, like those folktales you like. And the poem you were reciting the other day, from memory! Who does that?"

My neck is getting hot. Since when does mousy cousin Rayyan make fun of me? "I do that," I say firmly. "Nothing wrong with that."

Rayyan gives a little smile. "I know. I didn't mean . . . I guess I think there's a story behind it."

I relax. "Good thing I love stories."

*   *   *

How I got into old music and even older folktales.

Mama had just finished her PhD and started a new job at UNESCO. It was a junior researcher position, different from the fellowship business, but close enough that she was ecstatic. Went around for days smiling at everyone.

I was nine, I think. By this time, I knew my father was a monster and my mother was a researcher. That was their identity.

My identity was the lost bad boy. I was happy with it too. It meant I could stay up late and get into fights at school, and not care what anyone thought about me.

I mean, I'm still the same, only now I hide it better.

Anyway. The day before Mama's new job started, she had a big argument with Abbu. I could hear them from my room, even though I'd shut the door and climbed under my blanket and put the pillow over my head.

Here's a play-by-play. The constant shouting. The ridiculous accusations—Abbu saying Mama was a spy. Mama calling Abbu a no-good freeloader. And so on and so forth.

Anyway, when it was quiet again, Mama came into my room and said, "Starting tomorrow, you'll be going to the downstairs apartment after school."

I peeked from behind the pillow, alarmed. "I don't need a babysitter!"

Mama sighed. "Yes, you do, Mo. I won't be home in the afternoon anymore. And your father doesn't come home until late. You know that."

"Why can't you be home earlier?" I said foolishly. "Just tell your new job that you have a kid. They'll understand."

Mama stood up, hands on her hips. "One kid isn't as important, Mo, when there are thousands of kids and families I'm helping with my research. They need my work to continue."

"What about me?" I whispered from under the blankets.

But she'd already walked out of my room.

The next day after school, I reported like a good little soldier to apartment 1G. An elderly man with graying hair and thick glasses opened the door. He was wearing a light green kameez over white pajamas—not the kind you slept in, but the kind that came with a certain type of South Asian clothes. Oh, and he was desi. I should have led with that.

"So you're the doctor's little boy, eh?" He pulled me inside and shut the door. "I'm Patel. Your new friend."

"You mean babysitter."

Patel Uncle frowned at me. "You a baby?" he asked.

I glared back at him. "Of course not."

"Then how can I be a babysitter?" He turned away and sat on a big, overstuffed armchair. "At the most I'm a boy sitter. Or a kid sitter."

I looked around. The room was overflowing with books. Books crammed into shelves that went all the way up to the ceiling. Books in stacks on the floor. Books on the coffee table. "Have you read all of these?" I whispered.

Patel Uncle chuckled. "Most of them."

That was it. I was sold. I smiled, and it felt like my smile had come out on my face after a long time.

I spent a lot of afternoons in Patel Uncle's apartment. He was a retired professor of South Asian literature. His family was scattered all over the country, and some were in India. None of his kids lived in New York.

I guess I became like his grandkid, maybe. He's the one who taught me what desi meant, and how we all lived together at one point in history, all the Indians and Pakistanis and Bangladeshis. How our languages were similar, especially Hindi and

Urdu. How our cultures were intermingled even though we were now separate countries.

I read his books, and he told me stories.

I also told stories, sometimes. But mine were of the true variety. Mama, Abbu, Zed, everything else.

Patel Uncle had this old music player called a gramophone, and he played old Indian classics on it. Kishore Kumar. Lata Mangeshkar. Ravi Shankar. I brought my laptop and played him more recent music. We had arguments over which decade had the best music.

Patel Uncle also liked English poetry. That's where I read "How Do I Love Thee? Let Me Count the Ways," among other sappy poems.

Only now I've met Carmen Rodriguez and poetry no longer feels sappy. Dude, I wish I could tell Patel Uncle about my crush.

I can't, though, because he's far, far away in Queens, and our afternoon chats are over. Khatam.

That whole chapter of my life is over.

10

"Did you talk to your mother yesterday?" Naila Phupo asks on the way to Sunday school.

My breath stops for a second. She's never asked me about Mama before. Rayyan turns halfway in the passenger seat, looking at me.

Just looking, nothing else.

What's with that face, anyway? Does he pity me or something? Last I heard, he's got a dad who got murdered. Maybe his dad was a drug dealer. At least my mom's a high-profile water expert dedicated to helping others, blah blah blah.

"Mo?" Naila Phupo says, peering into the rear-view mirror.

Okay, so she's not letting this go.

I clear my throat. "Yeah, we talked. It was fine."

Which, of course, is a lie. They're never fine, our chats. I got in a few words about the latest biology class—we've moved on from muscles and started blood circulation—before Abbu began interrupting. Where did Mama keep all his documents? What doctor should he go see for his blood pressure? Why could she help other people but not her own family?

Et cetera, et cetera.

Then Mama got mad. Said some things like, and I quote, "You're a grown man, why do you need someone to take care of you? What's wrong with your blood pressure, how high is it now? I'm not surprised you're not taking your meds, you never could do anything by yourself. My country needs me, the refugees need me. What are you doing to help the world, eh, Mumtaz?

Ya know, same old, same old.

Naila Phupo extends her arm backward and gives me an awkward pat on my knee. "Mujhe pata hai tumko mama yaad aati hoogi." I know you must be missing your mama.

I shrug, because what am I supposed to say to that? It's not even *missing* at this point. It's more like a fiery hatred at what she's done. Just left me.

Left me alone with a monster.

Whatever. It's a good thing I don't need her anyway. "I have you, don't I?" I say to my aunt with a little wink, bad-boy style.

She beams like I've paid her the best compliment. "Of course, beta. That's right. Come to me whenever you need anything."

Rayyan rolls his eyes.

I kick the back of his seat, then thank his mom. "Shukriya, Phupo."

At the Islamic center, Rayyan and I jump out as soon as the car stops. "Be good, boys!" Naila Phupo calls out.

We wave to her and head to the gray building. This time, the art room isn't empty.

In fact, it's buzzing with energy and chaos.

Oh. My. God. Kids, so many kids. All little ones, probably first and second graders. A few toddlers run around the big wooden table in the middle of the room, laughing it up. Then one bumps into another, and they both fall on the floor.

"No way," Rayyan whispers next to me.

"This is the class we're supposed to teach?" I say, horrified, just as a little girl with pigtails and a cheeky grin pushes past me. "We should quit. It's not like we're getting paid."

Rayyan turns to me with narrowed eyes. "We can't quit! We're here for my NJHS application. I need this!"

I huff. "Okay, fine, whatever."

He looks around. "Who's in charge here?"

"Dude, it's us!" I whisper-yell. How is he not getting this? "*We're* the idiots in charge."

"Actually, it's me." There's a sound from the doorway, and I turn around. It's Imam Shamsi, with his gentle smile and salt-and-pepper beard.

"Er, sorry," I mutter, my heart sinking. Did he hear me say "idiots"? Is that considered a bad word by religious Muslims?

The imam turns to the room and holds up his hands. "Assalamo alaikum, children!" he calls out loudly. "Please settle down!"

And like magic, the hooligans settle down.

Yeah, they're still grinning and nudging each other, and I even see one kid kick his friend. But they all sit on the stools around the table and zip their mouths like good little children.

"Welcome to art class," Imam Shamsi says. "These two young men are your teachers. They'll help you make drawings and paintings, and whatever else you want to do."

A boy with thick glasses raises his hand. "Sculptures too?" he asks. "I saw a show about sculptures on TV yesterday."

The imam sighs. "That's up to them," he says, nodding to us. "Boys, why don't you introduce yourselves?"

I'm pretty sure he knows us already, because he'd called Naila Phupo a few days ago to make sure we'd be volunteering as promised. Abbu had freaked out when he'd heard the news. "Volunteering for the religious nutcases now, eh, Mo?" he'd sneered. "Just wait until your grades start falling and you become a fundamentalist. Don't expect me to bail you out when that happens."

I'd fisted my hands behind my back and ignored him.

What I didn't say: "When have you ever bailed me out of anything, old man?"

"Well?" Imam Shamsi is looking at us expectantly. What does he want us to tell our names for? He already knows them.

I get the feeling that he knows everything about everybody here.

Imam Shamsi nods toward the class. That's when I realize the intros are for the kids' benefit. They're looking at us like we hung the moon. I guess we look pretty amazing to them, since most of them can't even tie their own shoelaces yet.

The girl with pigtails waves at me. She's got chocolate on her cheek.

At least I hope it's chocolate.

Ugh, what have I gotten myself into? This is really not good for my bad rep. I nudge Rayyan, so he knows to go first. It's his thing, after all.

"Um, sure, I'm Rayyan," my cousin says nervously. "I'm in eighth grade."

The kids go "Oooh" like eighth grade is heaven. Ha! If they only knew.

Rayyan nudges me, basically saying it's my turn. I try to smile. "I'm Mo, also in eighth grade."

This time, there's no oohing and aahing. The kids look confused. "Mo's not a Muslim name," Pigtail Girl says sadly. Her grin is gone.

Glasses Boy leans closer. "Are you one of the Three Stooges? My nana likes to watch that show, but my ammi says it's very vi-violent."

Imam Shamsi chuckles. "I'm sure Mo is short for something, isn't it?"

I grind my teeth. "It's short for Mohammad."

Immediately, half the class raises their hands and starts chattering excitedly.

"Oh, my brother's name is Mohammad!"

"My dad's name is Mohammad too!"

"Guess what? I'm Mohammad!"

Whoa. These little ones need to. Calm. Down.

The imam looks satisfied. "Well, I'll leave you to it, then. The class is two hours long, and you can break it up any way you want. Teaching, artwork, playtime. It's all up to you."

"Uh, sure?" Rayyan says weakly.

"Supplies are in the closet back there," the imam continues. "Oh, and snacks too. How could I forget the snacks?"

The kids cheer loudly at this. Two kids start high-fiving each other. Seriously, who are these little devils?

The imam smiles at everyone and, get this, he leaves.

The kids stop cheering, thankfully. "What are we doing first, Rayyan bhai?" someone asks.

Rayyan and I look at each other, petrified. This is not what I was thinking when I made him sign up as a volunteer. I envisioned kids my age. An art teacher. A quiet, artistic atmosphere with everyone doing calligraphy or something.

These kids would rather draw trees and animals, I'm guessing. Maybe Pokémon, if they're into that sort of thing. To tell you the truth, I'm ready to bolt.

"What should we do?" Rayyan asks me, panicked. "Two hours! We have two whole hours!"

I take a deep, deep breath. I've been taking care of myself

since I was old enough to walk. I can figure out a two-hour class. "Imam Shamsi said we could do whatever we wanted, right?"

He chews his lip. "Well, I'm sure there are limits to that."

I head toward the supply closet. "We'll keep within limits. Probably."

* * *

One thing we learn: two hours is way too long for little kids to sit still.

About one and a half hours too long.

But we manage, because we're awesome. I like to think that our first day as volunteers is pretty darn good. We hand out construction paper and tubs of crayons, then shout out ideas of what to draw. All kinds of animals. The sun. The earth. People. Buildings. Spaceships.

Rayyan has the brilliant idea to connect the artwork to Islamic concepts, since we're in a mosque and all. I roll my eyes, because God really doesn't care about kids doing art. But I let him do what he wants, since it's his class, essentially.

He talks to the kids about God being the Creator, making everything in our world beautiful. The kids sit and listen, because he's also handed out packets of mini cookies at the same time. Genius, this guy.

"Some things are ugly," one kid says. He's wearing an ugly yellow sweater, so I guess he knows what he's talking about.

"Yeah," Rayyan says patiently. "But beauty is in the eye of the beholder."

"Is that from a Taylor Swift song?" a girl asks. "My sister's always saying weird stuff and calling it Taylor Swift."

Rayyan laughs. He lost his panicked slash terrified look somewhere in the first thirty minutes of the class. "It means that something *you* may find ugly, someone else may find beautiful."

"Like clothes," Yellow Sweater Dude says. "My mom buys horrible clothes for me, but she says they're the latest fashion."

Both Rayyan and I laugh at that. These kids are funny, I'll give 'em that.

Then all the kids start laughing and throwing cookie crumbs around.

In fact, everything we say is met with giggles and cheers, like the kids are overjoyed at hanging out with us.

I mean, we *are* eighth graders, so basically we're heroes.

It's almost enough to make me forget the dumpster fire that is my life.

After snacks, we do a little wiggle out, but without music, because ya know, mosque.

Then we go back to drawing. More words get thrown around, but somehow they're all fashion related now. Trousers. Shalwar kameez. Dupatta. T-shirt. A dinosaur wearing a T-shirt. Another dinosaur.

Here's a shocker: the drawings aren't bad at all.

At the end of the class, everyone has at least two drawings to take home. I'm imagining they all have devoted moms and dads who'll put their artwork on the fridge and take pictures to send to equally devoted grandmas and grandpas.

Ugh. Whatever, I don't care.

"That was a pretty good class," Rayyan says when everyone's left.

"Yup," I reply. Nobody cried, nobody screamed and threw a tantrum. No furniture was destroyed.

I'm counting all that as a win.

Another win: getting to know the kids a little. Pigtail Girl is named Sana, and her family's from Turkey. Glasses Boy is Yusuf from Bangladesh. There's Farhan, a dude in a helmet who doesn't talk much, but he makes the most incredible abstract art. Just scribbling violently with crayons like he's got beef with the construction paper. There are two boys named Mohammad; one is five years old, the other is seven. That one's the oldest in the class.

Even the two toddlers had drawn quietly for the most part. Halfway through, they fell asleep on the floor, which is weird but also adorable.

Weirdly adorable.

I'm not sure why these kids are in an art class when there's the rest of Sunday school going on around us. They could be learning about the five pillars of Islam or memorizing hadith. When I ask Rayyan, he just shrugs.

"Maybe they're delinquents," I say, picking up crayons from the floor.

Rayyan scoffs. "That would be you, not your students."

"Hey!" I throw a crayon at him and pretend to be offended.

Rayyan gathers extra paper from the table. "They're too young for regular Sunday school," he tells me. "I remember starting classes when I was eight, I think."

"I've never been to Sunday school," I admit.

"Eh, you're not missing much."

Look, I'm not against Sunday school or religious studies, or anything like that. I mean, I'm not an atheist. I still believe in God and the Holy Prophet and the Quran and all that other good stuff.

I guess I've just become disillusioned. I don't think God cares for me, so in return I don't care for Him. Simple.

If someone has a different relationship with the Big Guy, then that's fantastic. They're lucky.

Rayyan puts the crayon tubs back into the closet. "Can I ask you something?" he says quietly.

"What?"

"Was your chat with your mom *really* good?" he asks. "Or were you just saying that to get Mama off your back?"

My shoulders slump. I'm so tired. Like, I want to fall down to the floor like those toddlers and just sleep for a year. "It was the same as always," I admit. "She and Abbu spend most of the time shouting at each other. She hardly talks to me."

His eyes widen. "I'm sorry."

"It is what it is. I gave up caring about them a long time ago."

Rayyan sighs. "I say the same about my abbu, that I don't care that he died. That he was killed. But in my heart, I know it's not true. I do care. That's why it hurts."

I have so many questions in my mind. Who killed his father? Why? But the rest of what he's said catches up to my brain a few seconds later. All my tiredness falls away. My annoyance level goes up to the roof. "That's why it hurts?" I mimic. "What weakness is this? Things only have the power to hurt us if we let them."

Rayyan looks startled. "I guess . . . I guess I'm not that strong."

"Everybody's strong, man," I insist. "We've all got those hard skeletons. Our bones protecting our soft insides. All we gotta do is stay vigilant. Don't let the feelings in."

11

We've almost finished cleaning up the art room when Naila Phupo peeks in. "Rayyan! Mo! Come with me. I want you to meet a friend of mine. She's got a son your age."

"Mama!" Rayyan groans but drags himself out.

He's such a good little boy.

"I'll finish cleaning up here," I say. I need some alone time. Two hours with the Energizer Bunny kids has drained me.

When they've left, I pick up the rest of the papers and stack them neatly in the supply closet. Then I walk around the room for a final check. I don't want Imam Shamsi to think we didn't do a great job.

In the back, there's a big plastic storage container.

I open the container and see a bunch of oil paints and

canvases. I stand and look at them for a long time. Just staring. I'm sure if someone passed by and saw me, they'd wonder what the heck I was doing.

Good question. I don't really know.

All I do know is, my heart is beating wildly.

Like I'm doing something wrong, but also something right.

In Pigao's class on Friday, we studied a bunch of did-you-know facts. Like, did you know that the human heart beats a hundred thousand times a day? Or that your heart muscles work twice as hard as the leg muscles of a sprinter?

Who knew?

All I know is that the oil paints and blank canvases are calling to me. I grab one canvas, a couple of brushes, and some paints.

Not the bright colors like pink or blue.

Nope. I grab the black and dark brown and maroon. Oh, and some dark gray too.

I set everything neatly on the table. Only I'm not sure what to do next. I've never really painted before, outside of art class in elementary school. My inner voice is screeching at me. *Stop! You're not an artist, Mo.*

How hard could it be, though, if the little toddlers and Sana the Pigtail Girl could do it?

I realize I don't have everything I need, so I go back to the storage container and get a paint tray. I think it's called a palette.

By the time I get back to my seat, excitement and nervousness are bubbling inside me like lava. My inner voice has gone from telling me to stop this foolishness to shouting, "Do it, do it, do it!" Like a daredevil at an extreme sports challenge.

With trembling hands, I put some paint on the palette and mix it with the brush. Then I hold the brush over the canvas. I try different positions, hand straight, hand upright, switch hands, et cetera.

Finally, I get comfortable enough—barely. Take a few deep breaths to bring my heart rate down.

And then I paint.

Well, it's more like stabbing the canvas with darkness, but it's also painting in a raw, wild way. Like, pouring all my hurt and anger and hopelessness onto the canvas in front of me.

One brushstroke for all the things I wish I had, like Mama back in my life, and Abbu gone forever, and Patel Uncle still nearby to talk to.

One brushstroke for all the things in my life that are unfair, like how I had to move across the country, and share a room with someone, and share oxygen with stupid bullies like Frankie.

One brushstroke for Abbu. The biggest, darkest, ugliest stroke.

When I finish, I realize I'm sweating. The canvas lies in front of me like a thing that's been torn apart with claws and fury. The paint lines are jagged. Raw.

Look, I know it's not perfect. The art museum's not gonna knock on my door anytime soon. I have no technique and I don't know what I'm doing. I've used up too much paint on half the canvas and too little on the other half.

But it's done, and it's mine, and it's as ugly as my feelings, so that's something. It's like looking into a mirror, but seeing your insides instead of your face.

Everything exposed, finally.

Scary, but also good, you know?

* * *

Lunch is Pizza Hut's cheese pizza, and we eat at tables in the small gym. I'm just shocked this place has a gym in the first place.

And look here, a sign for the Good Bros Soccer Team, whaaat?

Maybe we should've asked around if they needed sports volunteers instead of art teachers.

"You okay?" Rayyan asks. "Why are your fingers black?"

I look down at my hands. "Oh, uh, it's paint."

"Paint?"

I pass him some pizza. "Never mind. Tell you later."

P.S. That's a flat-out lie. I'm not gonna tell anyone about what I did. It's not like I plan to make a habit of it.

A few of our art students wave to us from the kiddie table. "Rayyan bhai! Mohammad bhai!" they yell.

Naila Phupo passes by with a pitcher of water. "Tum dono to mashoor ho." You two are famous.

I try to smile at the kiddos, but I'm really unsettled right now. It's like after that paint sesh, all my frozen feelings have melted and overflowed, and now there's nowhere to hide them.

"You sure you're okay?" Rayyan asks again.

"Just eat your pizza, man," I mumble.

I'm on my third slice—stupid overflowing feelings don't make me any less hungry, apparently—when Imam Shamsi joins us. "I'm sorry for leaving you in the lurch like that earlier," he says. "I was late for a meeting."

"That's okay, Imam sahib," Rayyan replies. "We enjoyed it."

"You're doing a commendable thing, mashallah. My regular volunteer was older, but she got married recently and moved to Chicago. I hope you two can stay for a while until I find someone more permanent."

Rayyan tells him about his NJHS application, and assures him we're here to stay.

"How about you, Mohammad?" the imam asks gently, his eyes crinkling with amusement. "Enjoying the art class?"

I shake my head, still focused on the black paint on my fingers. "Beggars can't be choosers," I say in a rough voice.

Rayyan looks appalled. "He's just kidding, Imam sahib."

I'm really not. Exhibit A: a canvas with oil paint crusted on it like a crime scene at the back of the art room.

* * *

Once upon a time, there was a wise man named Watayo Fakir. He lived in Sindh (that's a province of Pakistan, FYI).

One evening, Watayo attends a wedding feast in the village. The host knows how respected this dude is, so he gives

Watayo a very important job: to distribute the platter of sweets among the guests after the ceremony. In Urdu we call them mithai. They're desi desserts made from a variety of things like flour, sugar, ghee, blah blah. Some are cooked. Some are fried. Some are hard and brittle, while others are soft and gooey.

But. They. Are. All. Delicious.

So Watayo's been tasked with handing mithai over to the guests. For me, this would be simple. Just divide and distribute. Basically, use your math skills. But Watayo doesn't do anything the simple way. He asks the host how he wants the mithai to be distributed. The host's got a hundred other things to do. I'm guessing he's the father of the bride or the groom, which is why he needed Watayo's help in the first place. So he just shrugs. Who cares, just do it.

But he doesn't say this to Watayo, because, you know, respect.

"Would you like me to distribute it in the godly way, the way the Almighty would do? Or would you rather I distribute in the worldly way?" Watayo asks.

Now, if I'd been at this wedding, I'd have realized there was a catch to this question. There's no way Watayo is asking something so simple. But the wedding guests are hangry and they want their sweets, so they reply, "Our Creator is just. Do as He would do."

So what does Watayo do? He gives the first guest a huge portion, and the second one a very tiny piece. The third guest he sends back empty-handed. Then the next few guests get big portions, so nothing is left for anyone else.

Naturally, everyone is shocked and angry. They ask Watayo why he's being so unfair. So unjust.

To which Watayo replies, "This is the way of the Almighty. He gives little to some people and a lot to others. And to some, he gives nothing."

The wedding guests quickly return all the mithai and ask Watayo to distribute it again in the worldly way.

In other words, by straight division, the type you learn in elementary-school math.

* * *

At home, there's more stuff that makes me feel those jagged, lavalike emotions.

Abbu's drunk.

Yes, I know we're Muslim. I think I've already established that my father has no connection with his religion. I don't know if it's a schizo symptom or what, but he's very loudly and proudly anti-religion.

Anyway, Abbu's drunk, and I'm responsible for hiding it, because Naila Phupo will definitely throw us out of her house if she discovers this very haram behavior.

Yay, lucky me.

Let me set the scene: Abbu, sprawled in bed, snoring. Empty beer bottles, all over the floor. Fast-food wrappers, also on the floor. Oh, and a half-eaten burger in the bed, squished under Abbu.

The smell is horrendous, but he also doesn't like to shower much, so.

I get a garbage bag from the kitchen and clean up the room. I check Abbu's pulse like I learned from YouTube. It's one hundred beats per minute, or close enough.

So he's not dying.

Here's an ugly secret. For a minute there, when I first came in, I thought he was dead. The emotions in me rose up like choppy waves. Happiness, then shame for feeling happiness, then worry about what would happen to me if he died, then anger at him and his bad decisions . . .

Like I said, lucky me.

I guess Watayo Fakir was right. The Almighty gives some people absolutely nothing.

12

On Monday morning, Mrs. Nguyen hands out packets called "Understanding the Nature of Sheet Music." I can't even look at it, it's so mind-numbingly boring.

I'm not the only kid in the class having this reaction. There are a lot of shuffling feet and side-eyes. "When will this ever help us in real life?" Frankie asks.

Stupid Frankie. I don't care that I agree with him. He's annoying. "You didn't have to take this class, you know," I remind him. "It's an elective."

"Shut up!" he hisses.

Mrs. Nguyen has really good hearing. She frowns at Frankie, then turns to the class. "I know this seems boring to some of you, but don't worry, we'll get to actual music in the next class."

Actual music? I hope she doesn't mean Beethoven.

Oh, and Rayyan was right, there's an end-of-year performance, so I'm dead, ha.

I spend the rest of music class staring at Carmen's back. She's tied her hair into a single braid, with a red bow at the end. I stare at that too.

Lunch is on the track field, for some weird reason. We're told to grab our trays from the cafeteria and head outside. "The weather is great, enjoy yourselves outside for once!" Coach Andrews calls out. He's the soccer and football coach.

"Don't let life be full of regrets," Coach Emilio adds. He's the track and volleyball coach.

I learned the other day that Coach Andrews and Coach Emilio are married to each other. The reason I found this out was because a group of quote unquote concerned parents protested outside our school last week about their "devil lifestyle corrupting innocent kids."

There were signs and everything.

Sometimes I wish I was back in New York, because I don't get Texas.

Other times, I'm sorta glad I'm experiencing such strange customs, like saying y'all to everyone, and pledging allegiance to the Texas flag, and protesting things that aren't other people's business. It's how those nature photographers must feel, hiding in a strange habitat for days just to take one award-winning picture of an ugly bird or something.

"We don't want a life full of regrets, do we, kids?" Coach Emilio shouts.

"No, sir!" everyone shouts back.

Well, mostly everyone. Not me, because that would be totally uncool.

Only now, I'm sitting on the bleachers, thinking random thoughts about my life. And, ya know, my regrets.

For instance, Mama has this gold necklace that's been handed down from her great-grandmother in Italy to her grandmother and mother in New York, and then to her. It's supposed to go to the next girl in the family, but I'm not a girl. Duh.

That's one regret in my life. If I was a girl, Mama could hand the necklace over to me.

I'd have other problems, like getting periods and trying to walk in heels, but I'd figure it out.

Another example. Patel Uncle gave me this big book with illustrated stories from the Puranas. I didn't know until much later that it was quite expensive.

How did I know? Abbu took it from my room and sold it at a used-book store. He was nice enough to come and say thank you. And then ask if I had any other treasures hiding under my bed.

That's one more regret in my life. I should've hidden my treasures better.

"You've got that look on your face again," Rayyan says, nibbling on his PB&J sandwich.

I pick up an apple from my lunch tray. "What look?"

"Like you want to die, but you also want to kill someone."

I shrug. "Accurate."

I take a bite out of my apple and watch the other kids. Frankie is holding court like a king in the center of the field. A lot of kids are standing around him, smiling up at him like lackeys. Even the coaches are hanging out near him.

Ugh, this dude annoys me just by existing.

"He's the coaches' favorite," Rayyan tells me, since I apparently said that last part aloud.

Coach Andrews pats Frankie on the back. Double ugh. "Why?" I ask in sick fascination. "What's he play?"

"Everything." Rayyan shakes his head. "Football quarterback. Soccer goalie. Chess champion."

"Are you serious?" I scowl. "How is that possible?"

"They say he's a genius."

"Well, they're stupid." Okay, not my best retort, but I can never think of something too clever on the spot. Call it another item on Mo Mirza's list of faults.

*　*　*

Remember the story about the jackal who falls into the vat of indigo dye?

It's time to continue that story.

So Mr. Jackal has been living in the forest disguised as something else, thanks to the indigo dye covering his body. Nobody knows exactly what he is, because let's face it, there aren't any big blue canine-looking animals on planet Earth.

In the beginning of this whole fiasco, the other animals would run away from him, terrified. He doesn't understand what's going on until he catches sight of himself in a puddle of water. That's when he figures out that he's now different. He realizes he can hide his true nature under this indigo dye.

He calls out to all the terrified animals, "Friends, don't be afraid of me. The Creator of the jungle has sent me to be your king."

Of course, the animals aren't highly intelligent, so they believe him. He doesn't look like anything they've ever seen, so he must have been sent by the gods above, or whatever.

So basically, they all start to fawn over him and rush to do his bidding. He makes them chase away all the other normal-looking jackals. He makes them hunt for him and feed him and overall treat him like a celebrity.

Forget the lion, it's the jackal who's the king of the jungle now. Everyone fears him, or adores him, or some weird combination of the two.

But one day, Mr. Jackal hears some other jackals in the distance, howling away. He totally forgets that he's in disguise, and he joins in the howling. What can I say? It's a jackal's nature to howl with the rest of the pack.

It takes a few minutes for the other animals to realize that their king from the other realm, sent directly from the Creator, is actually a jackal. An animal they despise.

They jump on him and tear him to pieces.

Well, some versions say they run him out of the jungle, and he disappears, never to be seen again.

But I prefer the first version. It's more fitting.

* * *

I'm halfway through my apple when Frankie and his goon walk over to us. Really, it's not even walking. More like sauntering. Swaggering. Whatever an ape would do if he felt like showing off in front of other apes.

"Hey, losers," Frankie calls out to me and Rayyan.

I sigh. I guess he's still pouting over our spat in music class. "Don't you have any other insults in your repertoire?" I ask.

Okay, I deliberately use a very. Big. Word. You know, just to see how it's taken.

The other guy frowns, like he doesn't understand what I just said. Frankie, though. He narrows his eyes at me in a calculating way.

I know he understood me just fine.

He scratches his jaw in a mocking way. "Hmm, would you rather I call you a poisonous bunch-backed toad?" he asks. "Or maybe a filthy worsted-stocking knave? Creative enough for you?"

"Huh?" his friend says.

"Huh?" Rayyan says.

Me? I'm too busy being speechless because I'm pretty sure this guy just quoted Shakespeare. A lot of it.

Reminds me how Patel Uncle would shout, "Friends, Romans, countrymen, lend me your ears!" whenever he wanted to tell me something important.

Ah, good times.

Only . . . there's no way Frankie knows Shakespeare. Right?

Omagawd, my head is beginning to hurt.

When I don't say anything, Frankie scoffs and turns to Rayyan with a hand stretched out. Like he's a king or something. "Give me your lunch."

Rayyan immediately holds out his lunch box. Meanwhile, I'm still staring with my mouth wide open. I shake my head to get back in the game. "What? No!" I snap.

"Nobody's talking to you, Yankee."

I laugh . . . what's the word? Sardonically. "You do know the Civil War was, like, a hundred years ago, right? I'm not a Yankee, and this isn't a plantation."

"A hundred and fifty," Frankie says.

My laughter dies. "What?"

"The Civil War was more than one hundred and fifty years ago," he explains patiently. Sorta mockingly.

If you think this statement will irritate the heck out of me, you're right. That headache is now a throb in my forehead. I really need this dude to stay in one lane. Bully or geek. Ignorant or well read. Stupid or genius.

In what twisted reality can you be both?

Jackal and blue wolflike creature?

Abbu or monster?

This last thought is like gasoline to my internal fire. It's way too close to my nightmares, and those seriously creep me out.

I scramble up and lean forward until I'm really close to Frankie's face. I can see his zits and everything. "I don't care about history," I say in a very low, very controlled, hopefully scary voice. "I care about my cousin. He's under my protection. You don't mess with him."

Frankie scoffs. "Under your protection? What are you, the mafia?"

I smirk. Show him my knuckles, which are all raw after this weekend's boxing session. Pillow on a tree. Who'd believe it?

Frankie's friend starts sweating. "Maybe we should go, Frankie," he whispers. "This guy looks cut."

Frankie and I stare at each other for long seconds. One . . . two . . . three . . . four . . .

He swallows and steps back. "I'd beat thee, but I should infect my hands," he says in a casual tone.

Uh, what? Did he just . . . was that . . . ?

Man, I don't even know at this point. I'm just glad to see him walking away. The goon follows.

"Sure!" I yell. "Keep telling yourself that."

I sit back down next to Rayyan. He's looking at me like he's never seen me before. "I'm under your protection?" he squeaks.

I smirk again. "Yup." Inside, though, I'm all fired up. Someone has to protect the downtrodden animals of the forest.

Er, kids. I mean kids of this school, obviously.

Frankie may have fooled the coaches and teachers, but he can't fool me. I'm an expert monster detector.

"Wow, I'm honored," Rayyan says.

I take a bite of my apple. "You just keep your head down and let me take care of the baddies."

He eats the rest of his sandwich in one swoop. "Great plan."

By Tuesday, things have calmed down. In English class, Mrs. Perez makes us write an essay about the themes of good versus evil in *A Wrinkle in Time*. I use Frankie as my inspiration for the evil part. He gives me dirty looks all day, but stays away.

After school, I decide to go to the library. You know, just to make sure it wasn't all a dream.

It's not. It's very real, and very incredible. Reminds me of Patel Uncle's living room, lined up and down with book-shelves. I wonder if this one has any folktales.

I browse through the nonfiction shelf and find a book about art. Styles of painting and stuff like that. "You like art?" Trent the Librarian asks as he scans the barcode.

"Not really," I reply. "But I'm trying."

"What do you *really* like?"

I decide to tell him. He looks cool. "Ancient tales. Stories that shouldn't make sense, but they do if you think about them."

"Hmm." He looks at me thoughtfully. Then he blinks and asks, "Are you hungry?"

"Um, excuse me?"

With a smile, he reaches under his desk and brings out something round, wrapped in plastic. It's a snickerdoodle cookie.

With a rush, I'm back in second grade. Mama and I made a big batch of snickerdoodle cookies for my school bake sale.

Well, Mama made the cookies. I stood on a stool at the

counter and watched. Her hands moved in quick, sharp motions as she sifted the flour and rolled the balls of dough. She let me roll each ball in the cinnamon before flattening them into circles. "My mother used to make these cookies with me," she told me.

My eyes widened. "Grandma?" This was the white-haired lady who'd visited us the year before during summer break.

"Yes, she loves baking."

"Do you love baking too?" I asked. I'm not sure, but I really wanted to know. If the answer was yes, I'd love baking too. It would be my new thing. I'd totally replace video games with cookies.

"Not really, Mo." Mama smiled slightly. "But I love hanging out with you, buddy."

So basically, she lied.

Trent the Librarian watches in shock as I drop the wrapped cookie back on his desk and walk backward. "No thanks, I'm not hungry."

* * *

On Wednesday, Pigao hands out some information about the science fair.

Here are the details of this stupid event.

When: two days before winter break. Aka the least serious time of the year. In my old school, kids dressed up as elves and reindeer that week. Our principal was always Santa Claus.

What: science projects by sixth, seventh, and eighth graders.

Perfect. We'd be compared to a bunch of little kids. No competition, seriously.

Where: the gym. Aka the place where I've received sixteen thousand dodgeballs to the head.

How: groups of two or three, working on a topic we've studied in class. I nudge Rayyan and whisper, "You and me, dude," and he nods so fast he almost falls off his chair.

Why: because teachers hate us and want us to fail spectacularly.

After the info dump, Pigao makes us take a biology quiz on our Chromebooks. "Time to test your knowledge about the circulatory system," he announces with glee.

Ninety percent of the class groans.

Who doesn't groan? My cousin Rayyan, of course. Frankie, ugh.

And also, interestingly, me.

I dunno, this anatomy business is really growing on me.

I glance at Indiana Bones, who's wearing a long blond wig and a bright green scarf wrapped around his—her?—neck. Then I get started on my quiz. The circulatory system is made up of the BLANK and thousands of vessels called BLANK and BLANK.

Heart, arteries, and veins. Bingo!

Blood carries BLANK and BLANK to different parts of the body.

Hmm, that would be oxygen and nutrients. Oh yeah.

Tiny vessels that connect the larger ones are called BLANK.

Okay, I must admit that stumps me. I peek at Rayyan's screen and he's typing something starting with C.

Ooh, got it. Capillaries.

I end up getting one hundred percent, which is pretty great for a kid like me. I can't wait to tell Mama.

Then I remember I hate her, and change my mind. I'll tell Naila Phupo instead. She'll be happy for me. She might even cook me biryani or something. Last week Rayyan got an A in math and she made him gulab jamun. That's probably my favorite of all the mithai in existence.

As Patel Uncle would say, food is her love language (insert massive eye roll here).

Frankie's looking at my Chromebook screen with a scowl. "Did you cheat?" he whispers in my ear, almost.

I glare at him. Hasn't he heard of personal space? "Of course," I reply. Gotta keep that rotten-kid reputation solid.

However.

The true story of how I got a hundred on my biology quiz.

First off, don't worry, I didn't study, per se. In case you think I read the assigned pages over the weekend, you're dead wrong.

What I did do was listen to Rayyan reading them aloud while I punched the pillow in the backyard. It's not my fault. He likes to watch me, the weirdo, while staying a good distance away from the tree. Also while reading whatever homework we've got assigned. This weekend I also learned about the Declaration of Independence, and some random facts about Python.

The computer language, not the animal.

After the quiz, Pigao puts up a slideshow about blood.

Frankie and his goon slow clap like idiots.

"In ancient times, blood was a big mystery to people," Pigao begins.

Listen, I'm surprised. He's never talked about things like history before.

"What did they think?" Eli asks from the back of the class.

"Well, they obviously didn't know what blood consisted of, like red and white cells, and plasma." Pigao leans back against his desk. "A famous second-century physician named Galen taught that blood was made in the liver from food we ate. Then it entered the veins and was transported to the rest of the body."

"Whoa," Rayyan says. "They didn't know much about anatomy."

"Well, you have to understand, that was thousands of years ago," Pigao replies. "They didn't have the tools we do now. That meant they believed lots of things about the human body that weren't true."

"Not if they were Arab or Persian," Rayyan says. "Ibn Sina and Al Razi, anyone? And what about Al Khwarizmi?"

There's crickets in the room. Even Pigao is nonplussed. "I'm sure you're right, Rayyan," he finally says.

"Nerd!" someone who sounds very much like Frankie coughs into their hand.

I snap my fingers. Time to change the subject. "They used

to drain blood from a sick person, right? To help them get well?"

Pigao's face lights up. "Yes! They used leeches, or sometimes just bloodletting. Cutting a vein and letting out what they thought was dirty blood."

Some of the girls squeal. "Ew!" Monique cries. "Why are we talking about this?"

The guys laugh, cuz they want to seem tough.

Except for me. I don't think bloodletting is anything to laugh about.

Wanna know why? It was one of the treatments for schizophrenia before people wised up. Other inhumane treatments:

Shock therapy. Like, electrodes to your body.

Lobotomy. Yup, that's opening up the brain and taking out part of it.

Opium or morphine. Really hard-core drugs with lots of nasty side effects.

Straitjackets. Not to mention manacles, waistcoats, and padded cells.

Oh, and something called hydrotherapy, in which you get pushed into cold water for hours.

13

Abbu is not well.

This is code for drunk and possibly in pain, not that I care.

It's Saturday, and he's been hiding in his room since the night before. Naila Phupo interrogated him on Friday evening, which was kinda funny.

"Have you found a job yet, bhai?" she asked as we ate dinner. She'd cooked shami kabab and mixed moong masoor daal, which is the best combo in the world. Rayyan and I had formed the kabab patties, so excuse us if they looked a little lopsided.

They were still extremely delicious.

Abbu grunted. "You trying to tell me something, Naila?"

She went red at that. "Kya? Bilkul nahi!" What? Of course

not. "I just want to make sure you're not wasting time. Maybe the garage will take you back. Allah ki marzi." It's God's will.

Abbu also looked red now. Ha. It would be funny if I wasn't worried about his anger erupting at the kitchen table like a tidal wave.

Here's the thing about Abbu's job history: it's seriously messed up. He can't work anywhere for too long, because of his anger issues, plus the delusions and paranoia. One time, when he worked for the transportation department of NYC—this was when I was in fourth grade—he started telling everyone that aliens were using the trains to infiltrate the city. He insisted he was being watched by men with green faces and black eyes.

Needless to say, he was fired. Too many people complained he was harassing them.

Abbu and harassment? I dunno. It's more like he keeps saying stuff he believes out loud until people get rid of him.

Or, you know, they leave.

Which brings me to Saturday afternoon, when Abbu is hiding in his room from his sister's questions, and I have Mama all to myself on the video call.

I'm equal parts excited and nervous.

"So how are you, Mo?" she asks briskly, like always.

I clear my throat. I've put the laptop on a little stool in the backyard, where there's plenty of light. "I'm fine, Mama. I miss you."

Wow, look at me, being so honest and all. What can I say,

I'm a risk-taker. She's either going to tell me she misses me too, or say I'm too old to be acting like a baby.

Mama purses her lips. She's wearing a plain white T-shirt, and her gold necklace hangs from her neck, taunting me. "I miss you too, munchkin," she finally says with a sigh.

Okay, I hate the nickname, but she hasn't called me that in, like, five years, so I'll take it.

"How's the refugee camp?" I ask. "Any new kids?"

Secretly I'm hoping she'll say the following: all the kids are great, and they're getting resettled into proper homes, and the world is perfect because there aren't any more wars, and so the camp is closing down, and therefore she's coming back.

Phew. Seems like I *am* a baby who believes in unicorns and fairies.

Now you understand my obsession with folktales, huh?

Mama, of course, launches into descriptions of the camp. How overcrowded it is, and how it leads to more illnesses, and how the families have very little food and some are basically starving, and how despite her hard work, the water system still isn't providing clean water to everyone.

Horrific stuff, really. After a minute, I tune out because I don't have the bandwidth to feel sorry for poor refugee kids.

I guess I'd feel bad for them, if I was normal. But mostly I hate them because they're the reason my mother isn't here with me.

So . . . yeah. What does that make me?

Ladies and gentlemen, meet Mo Selfish Mirza.

"How's school?" Mama asks when she finally stops talking about the camp. "Are you getting good grades?"

A flash of my biology test passes through my mind. I shrug. "I'm doing okay. We have to perform a musical in front of the class at the end of the year, which is freaking me out."

Mama's eyes light up. "Oh, that sounds magical. I performed in a musical in elementary school with Nathan. We had so much fun!"

I frown. "Uncle Nathan?" He's Mama's younger brother, but she hardly ever talks about him. Or you know, to him. I don't even know where he lives. I know basically nothing about him.

"Yes, he lives in Houston. I, uh . . ." There's movement behind Mama, and she looks off-screen. Someone says something, and a kid cries out sharply.

Wait, what? I have an uncle in my city? Right here?

Why didn't she tell me before?

I'm staring at her with my mouth open and my eyes blinking like a tool, when Mama says, "They've just brought in some new refugee families. Everyone has to help. Bye, munchkin."

And now I really, really detest that nickname all over again.

* * *

Rayyan finds me in the backyard, hunched over the laptop.

"Are you done with your video call?" he asks. "We need to decide on our science fair project."

I shake my head. "I am *so* done."

"Okayyyy." Rayyan peers down at me. "What's wrong?"

I look up at him. His eyes are so close that I notice the black flecks in them, just like mine. It distracts me for a second, because I never knew we had that in common.

It makes sense. Rayyan is literally the only sane person in my life right now. I can't count Naila Phupo because she's too cheerful. Even when she's scolding Abbu, she's got that gleam in her eye that tells everyone she's only mad for the right reasons.

Because she cares or whatever.

Plus, her anger is like a spring shower, comes and then goes away without leaving any destruction.

Abbu's anger is the tidal wave I already mentioned. Or like a hurricane that can leave you wounded and distraught.

Rayyan, though. He's like me, only way thinner.

And now I discover his eyes are like mine too. Maybe that's why I share what I'm feeling right now.

"I found something out today," I tell him slowly. Carefully, testing the words out. "My mama's brother, Nathan, lives right here, in Houston."

Rayyan frowns. "You didn't know?"

"Nope." I scoff. "Maybe Mama just forgot to tell me?"

Rayyan looks shocked, like the idea of forgetting a relative is incomprehensible. "Where exactly in Houston?"

I'm still stunned, so I just mumble, "No idea."

"Maybe my mama will know," he says. "Or Mumtaz Mamoo."

The last person I'm asking about anything Mama related

is Abbu. He'll just start complaining about how she left him blah blah. "It's okay," I say. "I doubt this guy's interested in being my uncle. He couldn't be bothered to ever meet me, right?"

Rayyan sighs. "You don't have all the information, dude. You should ask some questions, try to get to the bottom of this."

"I don't care," I insist.

"Really?" He frowns again. "You look like you care a lot. You look . . ."

"What?" I ask when he stops.

"Like, devastated?"

I think about this. Am I devastated, really? "I guess it would've been nice to have a normal person in my life, you know? Especially after I moved here and everything changed for me. He could've helped me settle in, showed me around or something."

"That's what we're here for, cousin!" Rayyan looks indignant, like I've insulted him.

I mean, he's not wrong. Naila Phupo and Rayyan have been my lifesavers. I don't know what I'd have done in Houston without them. "Forget it." I shake off my thoughts. "Wanna box with me?"

Rayyan looks at me closely, like he wants to say more but can't think of how to say it. Finally he turns and heads toward the door in the backyard fence. I realize he's holding a soccer ball under his arm. "Not today," he replies. "We're going to the park."

"What about the science fair project?" He's always so focused on his studies. I can't believe he wants to play soccer, of all things.

Maybe he's doing it to distract me.

Like I said, lifesaver.

* * *

Turns out, there's a park on the street next to ours. It's got a swing set and a rusty slide, plus there's a decent-size field. It's overgrown with weeds, but it's still good enough to kick a ball around.

I'm too antsy, though. Soccer is the furthest thing from my mind.

Rayyan doesn't enter the park like I expect. He passes it and turns into the next street, where there's a bigger intersection. I follow, because where am I going to go? On the far left are a few shops, plus an old rundown gas station.

He stops at the stop sign. Just freezes.

Ten seconds. Twenty. Thirty.

There aren't any cars, or even people around us. "What are we waiting for?" I finally ask.

Rayyan nods toward the gas station. "That's where my abbu was killed," he says.

Listen, the hair on the back of my neck stands up straight. This topic is extremely unexpected. "Where?" I croak.

"In that gas station, on San Jacinto Street."

"What happened?" I'm half sure he won't actually tell me. The other half is wondering if this tale of murder and misery is even true. I've never heard anyone else mention it.

But then, turns out I have an uncle nobody talks much about either.

Just goes to show how much I know. Or, ya know, secrets people keep for no reason.

Rayyan leads me back to the park. We sit on the swings, and he starts talking. "Abbu was paying for gas inside the store when a masked man came in. With a gun, obviously."

"Obviously."

"He asked for cash and things, the way any robber would," Rayyan continues. "And then the guy at the counter started talking back to him or something, and . . ."

I gape. "What? Who does that when there's a guy with a gun in front of you?"

"He was new. Filling in for the regular guy." Rayyan waves away my concerns. "Anyway, they got into an argument, and the robber started shooting."

"Whoa."

"Yup," Rayyan nods sadly. "Abbu got shot just because he was standing there, holding his hands up and everything."

I try to imagine the scenario. Guys with guns. Shooting. Killing.

Dying.

My heart is thumping extra hard. "Did the guy working there get shot too?" I ask.

"No," Rayyan replies. "They've got those bulletproof screens in front of the counters, remember?"

Maybe? I didn't know that was a thing. "How old were you?"

"Eight," he replies.

So the year I discover that my dad's a monster, my cousin finds out his dad is dead? Yikes.

"We had reporters hanging around the house for a few weeks afterward," Rayyan says. "They used to call out the details of the case to us, to see our reactions."

A wave of anger crashes over me. "What were the police doing all this time?"

"They didn't have any leads, no witnesses, nothing."

"What about the guy working there? He was a witness."

"He didn't have anything to tell that the videos don't show. The killer was masked. He ran away after shooting Abbu, so he didn't even take the money."

"Wow," I whisper.

"Yup."

We sit in silence for a while. This is a lot to take in, and I wonder how Rayyan took it when he was eight years old. And how Naila Phupo took it when she's always so cheerful. Did she smile and say "Allah ki marzi"?

"You wanna watch the police press conference?" Rayyan asks out of the blue.

"What, now?"

He laughs a little. "No, it's on my computer at home. Right now, we play soccer."

* * *

Once upon a time, a group of girls are gathered around a well, gossiping.

Cause, ya know, girls.

They're talking about weddings and marriage gifts and jewels. Again, cause, girls.

One of the girls, though, isn't like the others. Her name's Bopoluchi. She's poor and has no money or jewels. But she can't be admitting all that, so she lies and says she's got a whole trunkload of those things.

Too bad for her, there's a robber hiding in the bushes listening to her. The next day he goes to her house dressed all nicely and holding a bunch of gifts. Says he wants her to marry his son in the next village.

Bopoluchi's parents agree, because why not? They used to get married without seeing the other person in those days. It was cool.

So the robber and the girl start their journey. They walk and walk, until they finally get to the robber's cottage. That's when he reveals himself as the big baddie, and tells her there's no son. Bopoluchi will be marrying him.

Mwah ha ha ha.

He leaves her with his old mother, and goes to get food or something for the wedding.

But Bopoluchi is quite a smart girl. She starts to plan her way out of this predicament. The old woman, who's basically her guard right now, helps her put on a wedding dress. Then she asks about Bopoluchi's beautiful hair. She wants to know how it got so long, because ya know, the old lady's almost bald at this point.

Bopoluchi tells her she used to pound her head with a mortar and pestle. You should look it up. A mortar is one of those cup thingies made of stone or marble, and it's got a clublike thing to grind whatever's in the mortar. That's how they used to grind grains and spices in the olden days. Some of the mortars are big, like buckets, or even troughs. Just depends on how much you've got to grind.

Anyway, the old woman is ready to try this unique way to grow long, beautiful hair. She brings out the mortar, which is the big kind, and sits down with her head leaning into it. Bopoluchi happily takes the pestle and starts pounding on her head.

Obviously, the old woman dies.

Bopoluchi exchanges clothes with the dead body (gross) and runs away in disguise (smart). I'm guessing she's smirking as she runs, knowing she got the best of the villain or something.

Meanwhile the robber dude comes back and sees his bride on the floor, blood all around her head. Then he realizes that's not his wife but his mother, and he's furious. He runs out, trying to find Bopoluchi, who, of course, is back at her village by then.

The robber waits a few days, planning his revenge. One night he comes to her house with three other robber friends. They pick up the bed Bopoluchi's sleeping on and carry it away. What they don't know is that Bopoluchi is hiding her billhook in her sheets, because she knows the robber's gonna come back for her sooner or later.

Oh, FYI, a billhook is a knife that was used to cut through small trees and shrubs and rope and things.

Bopoluchi wakes up while she's being carried away. Quick as a fox, she leans down and chops off the heads of three of the robbers, one after the other. Now only the original robber, who wanted to marry her, is left. He's scared out of his wits, and he climbs up a tree to escape the wrath of Bopoluchi.

But remember she's smart? She lights a fire under the tree, probably still smirking, and the smoke is so heavy, it suffocates the robber. He falls to the ground and dies.

Bopoluchi goes back to his cottage and steals all his money and jewels. Only is it called stealing if he stole it first from someone else? Who knows?

Anyway, she's rich now, and doesn't need a husband. I'm guessing she lives happily ever after.

14

"Are you like Muhammad Ali?" Pigtail Girl asks me.

Rayyan and I have just entered the art room at Sunday school. All the kids aren't even here yet, because we made it a point to come early.

Ya know, professional-like.

Sana is one of the early birds. Her pigtails are a mess, and she's wearing her T-shirt backward. I'm guessing she's a real artistic type, even though she's probably six or seven.

"How do you know I box?" I ask.

Sana's mouth drops open. "You box? Like a real . . . boxer?"

I curl my hands into fists in front of my face. "Yeah, you better stay on my good side!"

She giggles. "Okay. I will." Then she frowns. "So that's two ways you're like Muhammad Ali."

I put my hands down. "What do you mean?"

Sana's face is classic are-you-kidding. "Your name is Mohammad," she says patiently.

"I know that," I reply, also patiently. "But usually I go by Mo."

"Well, this is masjid, so you go by Mohammad here."

Okay then. Good logic.

The door opens and more kids come in. Soon we have a full house.

The quiet kids. The average, sunny-disposition kids like Sana. The hyper little ones who can't stop moving and jumping around.

"What's the snack for today, Mohammad bhai?" somebody asks.

"Yeah," another one says. "I'm starving."

The two hug their stomachs and groan, and basically act like they're dying or whatever.

Rayyan and I share a look. We'd both forgotten what hooligans we're teaching here. I wanna climb up on the art table and let out a roar, maybe threaten them a little, so they'll calm down.

But I don't think that will go over well with the Sunday school admin. So here's what I do.

"Listen up, kids. If you settle down, I'll tell you a story."

Rayyan raises an eyebrow. He knows by now that my folktales can be pretty gory.

The kids quiet down quickly. They sit at the table with their hands on their laps, faces turned to me with expectation.

Ha! I wanna smack my chest and howl with satisfaction. But that won't go over well with admin either. Also, the kids will probably see it as a signal to completely let loose.

I grab a stool. "Okay, let's see. Have you heard the one about the Brahmin's daughter who marries a tiger?"

The kids' eyes grow round. "No!" they say.

The guy in the ugly sweater—this time it's black-and-white checks—asks, "What's a Brahmin?"

"A priest, I guess," I reply. "Someone of high class in India."

"This is America," Sana tells me helpfully.

"My stories are all from India," I reply. "Well, what used to be India. Now it's Pakistan, India, Bangladesh, Nepal. . . ."

There's silence. Most of the kids have no idea what I'm talking about. Rayyan covers his smile with his hand.

I kick his foot with mine. He better not make fun of me.

The oldest kid, a dude named Tahir, frowns at me. "Brahmins are Hindu. We're Muslim."

"Yeah . . ."

"And human beings can't marry animals," he continues. "It's against the laws of nature."

Ladies and gentlemen, we have a genius in our class. I scowl, because I don't need anyone smarter than me in my student body.

Before I can put this little punk in his place, Sana speaks up. "It's just a story, Tahir. Don't freak out for no reason."

Tahir flushes.

I wanna give Pigtail Girl a high five, but I keep my hands locked down. No need to fan the flames.

I get started on the story. It's got enough twists and turns to keep the kids—what's the word? Enthralled. They're listening with round eyes and their entire bodies are leaning forward.

I get it, I really do.

Stories are powerful. They transport you to fantasyland. They let you imagine things that could never happen in real life. Like the Brahmin's daughter, who's fooled by a tiger disguised as a handsome man, and gets imprisoned by him. And her brothers who come to rescue her, and use all sorts of things on the way to help her. An ant, a palm shrub, a donkey.

For the first time, I realize why Patel Uncle's folktales make me so . . . enthralled, I guess.

They help me imagine a different life. A life where I'm the one in control, because I'm the storyteller.

"Wow," Sana says with a sigh when I finish the story. "That was amazing!"

"Another one!" cries one of the hyper toddlers.

Rayyan stands up and claps his hands once. "Next time," he says. "Now let's get drawing."

They draw for an hour. It's the same as last week, when Rayyan and I call out things to draw, and they compete with each other. Like, whose coloring is the best, and which cat looks the most realistic. I get the idea to have them draw all the animals in a zoo, so they want to look up pictures of zebras and lemurs and chimpanzees.

Rayyan's brought his laptop, so he pulls up some photos, and there's complete silence as the kids try their best to copy the animals.

It's cute.

I try, you know. I really try to get out of my head and enjoy these kids and their laughter and silly drawings that look nothing like the real thing. For instance, there's a cow with legs longer than a skyscraper and a curly tail like a pig.

And there's an octopus with a face like a human being, I kid you not. It's a female with a hijab and big eyelashes, and the kid who made it says it's his mom.

Who wouldn't think that's adorable?

Me, that's who. I can't focus on anything. I'm stewing over so many things, I'm like a pressure cooker with the lid close to blowing off. Telling the story earlier helped distract me, but as soon as that was over, things went back to being gray thunderclouds for me.

I want to know more about my uncle Nathan. I want to know where he lives, and I want to meet him.

I also don't want to meet him, because he obviously hates me and doesn't want anything to do with me, ha.

My mind is a jumbled mess, kinda like Abbu's probably is all the time.

And that's the worst part, you know? My fear that I'm just like him. That one day I'll lose my mind too, and then I'll have a kid who I'll hate and continue the cycle.

Oh my God, someone save me from my own thoughts.

"We should go to the zoo," Rayyan whispers to me.

I jerk my head up. "There's a zoo here?"

"Yeah. And lots of other things too." He taps his chin. "You haven't done any sightseeing yet."

"That's because I'm not a tourist."

We stare at each other, a little startled. It's the first time this thing has been officially acknowledged. Mo Mirza is here to stay.

Maybe one day Houston will feel like home.

I mean, my folktales have talking mice and tigers that change into men, so who knows? Anything is possible.

Even if right now just breathing seems difficult.

* * *

With tortured feelings, I take out another canvas from the back of the class.

The one from last week is behind the storage container. Its jagged, uneven paint mocks me big-time.

You can't even paint right, boxer boy.

I tell that stupid voice in my head to look up Van Gogh, whose paintings are weird but sell for millions. Sometimes art is ugly and doesn't make sense. Sometimes art is just a way to vomit all your pain out of you.

Sometimes art is medicine.

And sometimes it's fantasy.

Listen, here's the truth. I've been dreaming about coming back here and painting again since last Sunday. And when

I flipped through the book I got from the library, I became even more motivated.

Rayyan was stunned to see me dressed up early in the morning, ready to go to the mosque. "Didn't know you enjoyed teaching a bunch of wild children so much," he teased.

I shrugged. "It's not bad."

What he doesn't know is that I'm enjoying something else much more: the secret painting class.

Where I'm the teacher and also the student.

Where I can spill all my insides onto the canvas without anyone judging me or asking questions. Or telling me that art is supposed to be pretty and why don't I use more than one color, and maybe shape a few things out instead of these blobs of . . . nothingness.

Nobody knows about the nothingness that lives inside me.

I gather the canvas and paints and sit at the art table. I can't wait for that first jab of the paintbrush, dripping with thick oil paint, all over that canvas.

So I don't wait. I begin.

First brushstroke, full of bloodred paint.

They say blood is thicker than water. But my blood is weak. Mothers, fathers, now even uncles, apparently. All weak blood. Fake.

Another stroke, this one blue. So many layers that it seems almost black.

A third stroke, dripping all the way from the top to the bottom like the circulatory system.

Then red, ragged and rough.

It's wet right now, of course, so it looks soft and uncertain. Wait until it dries. Then the uneven paint will look serrated and crude. Long lines and sharp curves, all rough and edgy.

Just like the arteries and veins of a monster.

*   *   *

At home, Rayyan makes a list of science fair projects. "We could do the one with taste and smell," he says.

"What's that?" I ask.

He looks at me like I'm stupid. "You put a clothespin on your nose, then taste different juices with a blindfold on."

I mock-shudder. "I'm not putting a clothespin on my nose. Or a blindfold."

He sighs. "How about demonstrating the blind spot?"

"No. Sounds weird."

"Best ways to cool body temperature?"

"Um, no. Sounds stupid." I'm sick of this topic, so I decide to change the subject. "How about showing me the press-conference video now?"

Rayyan brightens. He drops his notebook and gets his laptop from the desk.

That's when I start to think it's not a great idea. What if he collapses? He's not exactly the poster child of health and happiness. "Are you sure?" I ask.

"Are *you*?" he retorts.

"Why wouldn't I be?"

He shrugs. "You're looking stressed out these days. Yesterday after art class, you didn't come for lunch. Where were you?"

I'd like to tell him, but I've decided that my painting is a secret for now. I don't know what I'm doing, and my artwork is so very, very private.

And bad. It's really bad.

But.

If he's showing me his family's worst moments, maybe I can show him my dreadful paintings.

They're not winning any awards, but at least they're mine.

Rayyan's still looking at me. Waiting for a response, I guess.

"Uh, just hanging out by myself," I mutter.

Yes, I'm aware it's the world's weakest excuse. Who hangs out by themselves in a Sunday school building? I should have said reading or something like that.

Rayyan doesn't say anything else. He settles on his bed with his laptop, and I climb in after him. "Want some popcorn?" I joke.

Then I stop, because no jokes for Mo Mirza.

Thankfully, Rayyan thinks I'm serious. "I don't like popcorn," he replies, and presses start on a video.

Immediately, I'm pulled in. A police officer stands at a lectern. On his left are a few other officers. On the right is a woman and child.

Wait, that's Naila Phupo, or at least a version of her from another dimension or something. No smile. Puffy, red eyes. The child, of course, is Rayyan. He's totally different, mostly because he's shorter, and has meat on his bones. I guess this is before his illness.

He looks like a baby. A big, sad baby.

Behind them, there's a blown-up picture of Rayyan's dad on an easel—the same picture I've seen in the living room.

"That's Abbu," Rayyan whispers.

"What was his name?" I ask.

"Zafar."

The police officer starts talking, and let me tell you, I'm riveted. The video is of bad quality, but everyone's feelings are jumping off the screen like they're physical things.

Phupo's despair and grief. Rayyan's confusion. The police officer's anger.

"Last night, there was a crime at the Shell gas station on San Jacinto Street," the dude reads from his notes. "At ten fifteen, the perp entered the convenience store and demanded money. The only two people in the store were the cashier, Will Garfield, and a customer, Zafar Abdullah. The perp waved his gun to intimidate the cashier, who refused on the grounds that he was new and didn't know how to work the cash register. The perp shot Mr. Abdullah in what appears to be an accident, then fled the scene at ten twenty-eight. The victim was forty-two years old, South Asian descent, black hair, brown eyes. He received one gunshot to the chest, where the bullet lodged in the heart. . . ."

A big-screen TV behind the officer starts to show the gas station from inside. There's shattered glass and overturned shelves everywhere.

And get this. A body lies on the floor, covered with a cloth. There's yellow police tape around it.

Him! It should be *him*, not it. Because that body is definitely my uncle.

Rayyan's dad.

Rayyan makes a little whimpering sound. My head whips toward him. "Wait, we're not watching the whole thing, are we?"

He's staring at the screen, sweat dotting his upper lip. "Why not?" He sounds . . . dead.

"Um, because . . ."

Rayyan still doesn't look at me. "C'mon, you're brave, right, Mo? You box and fight with bullies. You can watch this. It's nothing worse than movies or video games."

Yeah, only movies and video games don't have your freaking uncle as the star of the show.

I lean forward and press stop. "How many times have you watched this?"

Rayyan shrugs. "I dunno. A lot."

"Why?" I'm seriously horrified. I can't get the image of that body out of my mind. You can't even see the face, but you know it's there. Someone dead.

A human being.

Rayyan finally turns to look at me. "I dunno," he repeats slowly, with zero emotion. "I just do."

I suddenly think of Bopoluchi and how many dead robbers she saw in her lifetime. Just lying there, killed by her own hands, no less.

Not to mention the old woman with her head bashed in.

Seriously, how awful.

Right there and then, on my cousin's bed, I revise my view of Bopoluchi. She didn't smirk or laugh as she killed. Maybe she didn't even live *happily* ever after.

Maybe she just lived.

Rayyan presses start on the video again.

Okay, this is officially enough.

I've had enough.

I grab the laptop and climb off the bed. "Not this time," I say firmly. "Let's go play soccer again."

15

Monday's music class is terrible. I spend the first half staring at Carmen's head, as always.

She's wearing another bow in her braid, this time white with red stripes.

It looks like a circus tent. But that's not the terrible part.

The terrible part is when Mrs. Nguyen makes us read this book online called *A History of Music for Children*.

It's seriously juvenile. At this point, I'd rather go through the trauma of playing the class recorder in front of everyone.

Frankie trips me as I'm leaving class. At least, he tries his best. I kick his foot at the last minute, and he ends up stumbling into the wall.

"Better be careful," I whisper as I pass him.

"*You* better be careful," he whispers back angrily.

I kinda smile, just a little, because these are the moments when I feel alive. Blood boiling in my veins. Ready to rumble.

In the hallway, I find Carmen. She's popping bubble gum and looking at her phone. We're not allowed to take those out during school hours, which means she's a bad girl.

I already know this. Hence my crush.

"What's up?" I say, trying to act cool.

She shrugs. "That book was so stupid," she complains. "What are we, in third grade?"

Oh! She's talking about the history of music book we read in class. To tell you the truth, once I got into it, I thought some parts were interesting. For example, the history of opera. That stuff is fascinating. It's basically storytelling, but in song.

There's no way I'm admitting all this. "Yeah, third grade, totally," I echo, acting bored.

Carmen looks up finally. I imagine that we have a *moment*, when our eyes meet, and the world stands still. Maybe there's the flutter of wings in the air, like she's my fairy Badri and I'm her human Prince Saif.

I stare. And stare.

Carmen pops another bubble. "Something on my face, weirdo?"

A hand slaps my shoulder. Hard.

"Yeah, weirdo, what are you looking at?" It's Frankie. Of course.

And get this, he puts his arm around Carmen and smiles at her. He looks like a shark with its teeth out. Or an ogre, also with his teeth out.

What I've learned from Patel Uncle's library is this: all villains have big, sharp teeth. It's very stereotypical, but also gets the reader up to speed very quickly.

Sharp teeth.

Evil smile.

Villain alert.

Here's what I want to do: rip Frankie's arm off my fairy princess, and use his face as a punching bag.

Here's what I actually do: scoff, shake my head, and walk away.

It's because the music teacher is standing right there in the doorway, watching us.

I dunno, that's my excuse. I'm definitely not scared.

Mo Mirza doesn't do scared.

* * *

Speaking of Prince Saif and Badri. Remember how he finds her after years and years of searching, and you thought that was the end of the story?

Well, not really. Here's part two.

When Saif sees Badri, he's ecstatic. He's finally found his love! And guess what? She recognizes him too, because (drum-roll please) she *also* dreamed about him.

Coincidence? I think not.

It's a match made in heaven. Fated mates. Blah blah.

Like I said, Saif is ecstatic. He and Badri can be together—although how he's planning on doing this when he's human and she's not is anyone's guess. He's just starved himself for forty days, and he's not ready for any negativity.

But.

Badri is more cautious. She tells Saif that she's not really free. She's enslaved by a giant called (predictably) White Giant. Imagine this: dude's tall as a mountain, white all over like the coldest snow. When he walks, the earth shudders.

Basically, the biggest, most terrible villain of all time.

What could be worse?

I'll tell you what's worse: White Giant is also in love with Badri and will never let her go.

Bummer.

Badri begs and pleads that Saif should run away before White Giant gets wind of this situation. She'll go back to her prison and try to forget the handsome prince, et cetera.

But remember Saif's goal-oriented mindset? Yeah, that comes roaring to life even though he's exhausted and weak. He's come this far, spent so many years searching for his crush. Begging on the streets. Doing the chilla business.

There's no way he's going back home without Badri.

He makes a plan, and they run away. Outside the town of Naran, there's a cemetery, and they hide there when it gets dark.

In the meantime, White Giant goes looking for Badri and can't find her anywhere. He thunders across the mountains to the lake where Badri visits each full moon. When she's not there, his fury erupts. He smashes a giant foot in the lake, which makes the entire region tremble and quake.

And that, my friends, unleashes a great flood. Actually, make that Great Flood.

In terror, Saif and Badri come out of the cemetery and watch the floodwaters rush toward them. It's like the apocalypse or something. There's no way to outrun the fast waters of the Great Flood, so they close their eyes and pray.

And pray. And pray.

Another drumroll, please! When they open their eyes again, they're in a cave on the highest mountain, far from the floodwaters.

How? Apparently, Saif still had Solomon's cap in his pocket. He remembered at the last minute and quickly pulled it on.

Moral of the story: magical travel comes in handy when escaping floods caused by giants. Speaking of giants, White Giant is so heartbroken that he falls down and dies. But before he does that, he cries. Like a lot.

His tears make another lake in the area, called Ansoo Lake. It's real; look it up on Google Maps. Ansoo is Urdu for *tear*, and the lake is shaped like a teardrop, I kid you not.

The original lake Badri used to dance on is called Lake Saif-ul-Malook (also real), and to this day, people say that the prince and his beloved fairy can be seen dancing there on full-moon nights.

*　*　*

"Mo, come up here!" Abbu roars as soon as I enter the house after school.

"Eat a snack first," Naila Phupo says quietly.

This lady. She comes home around four in the afternoon and goes straight into the kitchen to make snacks for me and

Rayyan. I mean, I get that her son needs to eat as much as possible, but still. It says something.

Today, she's got a tray of chicken nuggets (get this, home-made!) waiting for us like in those TV shows where moms welcome their kids home from school with smiles and food. The only difference is, instead of a checkered apron and a dress, she's wearing shalwar kameez.

It's a nice one too, yellow with white flowers. Cheerful, just like her.

I hug her before I know what I'm doing. She looks shocked, then that smile comes back, brighter than before. "Oh, mera bacha!" Oh, my child.

"Mo!" Abbu roars from his room. If there was ever an evil giant in my life story, he would be it.

"Er, I should go see what he wants first," I tell Phupo, biting my lip.

"Okay, go!" She shoos me away. "I'll keep this warm for you."

I hurry down the hall to where Abbu is pacing like a caged tiger. "Where have you been?"

"Um, school?"

Abbu glares at me, hands on hips. "What's the point of going to school? You're never going to amount to much. Just like your old man."

I beg to differ, because honestly, I'd rather jump into Lake Saif-ul-Malook before ending up like Abbu. But I stay silent and give him my I-don't-care look.

Listen, it's a classic look, and I use it seventy-five percent of the time.

One hundred percent of the time if I'm standing in front of Abbu. That's the only way to deal with his crazy. And by that, I mean the literal crazy that's in his mind.

Abbu resumes his pacing. "I don't know, I don't know," he mutters, pulling his greasy hair.

I look at him carefully. He's wearing sweatpants and a black tank top that's seen better days.

* * *

The shirt Abbu's wearing brings back an old, faded memory. There's a rip in the right shoulder from when he was trying to clean his car and snagged it on the wiper. I was nine, I think, and he was teaching me how to repair cars or fix engines or something.

I smile a little, because I'd totally forgotten this happened. We'd been hunched over the engine of this ancient car he used to have, a faded green Mustang that didn't start anymore, but he loved it because it was his first car. "I bought this with my first paycheck," he told me fondly.

"Oh, yeah?" I said. "Was it always this green color?"

Abbu frowned, but not angrily. More like confused. "What's wrong with the color?"

I decided not to say it looked like puke. He might lose his temper. I never knew what would set him off, so every word I said had to be perfect. "Nothing. It's nice."

He petted the side of the car like it was a cat or something.

"It was originally white, but I got a custom paint job with the package."

He picked up his tool bag and started talking about the engine. Horsepower and capacity and all that stuff.

I'd zoned out after a few minutes. But then he'd told me to help him with something, I dunno, fix a spark plug or whatever, so I did what he said. He explained everything slowly, and made me do it over and over until I got it right.

Made me feel all warm inside. Me and my dad, doing something normal for once.

* * *

I come back to the present to see that Abbu's still freaking out about something. He's walking jerkily and wiping his mouth, eyes darting around like he's seeing something that's not there.

Or maybe hearing something nobody else can hear.

It gives me the shivers.

I stand near the door, watching. Waiting. This scene isn't new. And it never ends well. "What's the problem?" I finally ask.

Look, I'm not sure I should've asked or stayed quiet. If Mama were here, she'd be giving him a lecture about his tank top and his greasy hair, and his pacing around.

And then they'd start screaming at each other.

I'm not doing that. Ever.

Abbu snatches his laptop from the desk and hurls it onto the bed. "This . . . thing! I can't get it to work!"

"Okay." I pick up the laptop before he destroys it. "Do you want me to help?"

"You?" Abbu glares at me. "You don't know anything! You're completely useless!"

I clench my jaw. "What. Do. You. Need?"

Abbu resumes his pacing. "I can't access my email. It's the government, I tell you. They've hacked into this computer. That's the only answer. That has to be it!"

It takes me a few seconds to get into his email. "The password has expired. You need to change it."

Abbu shakes his head violently. "No, it's not working. Why should I change the password, huh? That's what they want."

"Do you remember your old password?" I ask.

Abbu stops and thinks. His forehead crinkles. "Um, I think . . . Mohammad nineteen eighty-five. Capital M, and then the numbers."

My fingers freeze over the keyboard. His password is my name? And 1985 is Mama's birth year.

His password is all about me and Mama. Wow.

"What's the matter, it's not working?" he asks anxiously, leaning over me.

"No . . ."

"Try an exclamation mark at the end."

It works. I quickly change his password and write it down for him on a piece of paper. "This is your new password. Don't forget."

Abbu starts pacing again. "No use. I'm sure that will be hacked too."

I'm hardly paying attention. I'm in his email account, scrolling down, and the subject lines are . . . worrying. There's a bunch of medical emails with subjects like "Mumtaz, you're overdue for your appointment" and "Mr. Mirza, would you like us to refill your prescription?"

Is he not taking his meds again? Is he ignoring his doctors? That would explain his behavior. He's definitely worsening. I've never seen him this anxious. This quick to get upset. This . . . schizophrenic.

A few emails are from companies like shoe stores and furniture stores. I think they're ads, but then I see their subject lines. One says "Your recent job application." Another one says "Thank you for applying." So Naila Phupo was right. He's lost his job and is trying to find another one.

Not sure he's trying hard enough, but still.

Who knew Abbu's email would be the key to understanding him, at least a little bit?

I look up. He's gone to the bathroom, leaving the door wide open while he pees. I shake my head and try not to feel disgusted.

This is my abbu. No filter, in words or actions.

I go back to his emails. I know it's probably an invasion of privacy, but I need to know more. Knowing what he's up to is super important. It helps me be prepared.

And then my eyes pop. Right there is an email from Mama.

My heart pounds. For some reason, I never thought my parents communicated outside of our weekly video calls.

I scroll down, and yup, there are more emails from her. Not a lot, but still.

I tell myself to calm down. They're married. Of course. This is normal.

Only nothing in my family is normal, so seeing these emails makes me reel. Dude, is this jealousy? Not cool. It shouldn't matter what either of these people do. They're horrible to me, so why do I care if they're emailing each other?

For all I know, they could be devising new ways to torture me.

My hand moves on its own, and clicks on the latest email from Mama. It starts exactly like she talks: *Mumtaz, how are you?*

Ha. Even in email, it's obvious she cares zilch about how he is.

I hear the flush, so I know there's no time. I scan the email quickly. She's talking about not having time to manage his doctor's appointments all the way from Greece, so he's gotta do it himself.

Yeah, right. He'll never do that.

She's also reminding him to take his meds. The exact quote is: *Mumtaz, you have to take your meds. There's no getting away from it. You know what happens when you fall off the track.*

Yes, Mother. We all know. It's not pretty.

* * *

Here's how Abbu's fallen off the track in the past.

When I was seven, Abbu went away for two days. I didn't know what was happening, only that there was peace in the apartment for a couple of days. No shouting. No worrying. Mama told me he was sick, so he had to go to the hospital.

When I was ten, Abbu got so drunk that he fell down unconscious. I was eating dinner, a delicious chicken and broccoli with alfredo sauce. Mama screamed, "This is what happens when you stop taking your meds, Mumtaz!"

If you're thinking, *What do schizophrenia drugs have to do with alcohol?*, let me tell you the brief version.

You don't take your meds, so you start feeling bad. Really bad. Mentally, that is. All sorts of bad thoughts rush into your mind.

You drink to get rid of your bad thoughts. But drinking is bad for you, right? It makes you stop thinking clearly.

But schizophrenia also stops you from thinking clearly.

So you drink more. And more. And more.

You don't remember that you're a dad. And that your son needs you to be stable and not raving about aliens at dinner. He just wants to eat his favorite chicken dish in peace. And he'd rather not have his father drink until he drops unconscious right at the dinner table.

Mama sent him to a rehab place after that incident.

And me? I never ate chicken and broccoli with alfredo sauce again. It makes me feel sick.

When I was eleven, Abbu had an episode. He kept saying

there were people in the room with us, laughing at him. Watching him.

He had to go to the mental hospital for a week. Mama was furious. It's the week she was supposed to get an award from an environmental group, and she wanted us to be there as a family.

I couldn't sleep in the dark after that. I imagined those people from Abbu's imagination laughing and watching me. Waiting to make me crazy too.

*   *   *

Abbu is washing his hands in the bathroom.

I read the rest of Mama's email. *Nathan was asking about you again. Or rather, about Mo. I'm not sure what to say.*

My heart thumps hard. My uncle, Mama's brother. The one who lives close to me, yet I've never met him. Or heard from him.

Why have I never met him? Doesn't he want to get to know me? Am I that unlovable?

Before I can stop myself, I've hit reply. Then I type, "Becky, can you give me Nathan's contact info? I'll talk to him."

I know. I know.

I'm basically committing a crime at this point, impersonating another person via email. My guess, though? It's not really criminal. More like unethical.

That's okay. I left ethics behind a long time ago.

It's like swiping the banana from a local bodega. Uncool but necessary.

167

Once I send the email, I go into the sent folder and delete it. My hands are shaking, FYI. There's no way I'm letting Abbu find out that someone sent an email from his account.

His conspiracy theories will explode. Like, full-on detonate.

"Ho gaya?" Done? Abbu asks as he comes out from the bathroom.

I nod quickly. "Yes, done."

And guess what? My stupid heart is literally racing in my stupid chest.

16

Very cool facts about the human heart, as taught by Pigao:

1. The heart is made of muscle.
2. The average adult heart is the size of two fists.
3. There are four chambers in the heart.
4. The heart rate is also known as the pulse.
5. The heart pumps about two thousand gallons of blood every day.
6. During an average lifetime, a heart will beat 2.5 million times.
7. Electrical impulses control the heart's rhythm.
8. The human heart weighs less than one pound on average.
9. A female's heart beats slightly faster than a male's.
10. The heart can continue to beat even when it's removed from the body.

"The heart pumps blood around the body through a network of arteries and veins," Pigao says in biology. "Anyone know what this system is called?"

"The cardiovascular system," Rayyan and Frankie both call out together.

Pigao smiles and tosses Starburst candies to each of them. Frankie catches his with one hand. Rayyan misses, and the candy falls on his desk.

Pigao starts a slideshow on the smart board. The first slide is a picture of the heart. The cartoon one they have on Valentine's Day cards. The caption says Let's Have a Heart-to-Heart Talk.

"That's . . . not anatomically correct," Rayyan sputters.

Pigao chuckles. "You're right, but it's an important part of any discussion about the heart."

"Why?" Eli asks.

"The heart is a symbol of love," Pigao replies. "People put so much emotion into this organ. So much feeling and metaphor."

"Like, you're in my heart," I say. "Or the heart wants what it wants."

The class laughs. I think I just quoted a song lyric, but I can't be sure.

Pigao nods. "Exactly. People blame the heart for their actions. They think they're ruled by this organ, which is actually nothing more than a pump."

"A pump?" Monique repeats. "Wait, really?"

"Remember the circulatory system we talked about last week?" Pigao says. "The heart is at the center of it."

He clicks to the next slide. This time, it's the anatomically correct heart, with blood vessels coming out of it. One half is colored red, and the other side is colored blue.

It's kinda gross.

But also kinda beautiful.

Pigao explains how the heart pumps dirty blood from the body to the lungs. There, the blood gets an infusion of oxygen and becomes clean. The heart then pumps the blood back to the body.

Voilà! A transformation, thanks to a muscle that's the size of two fists.

The next slide has a video of the way the blood flows. I watch carefully, because I'm very sure there's going to be a quiz at some point.

Also, because this is fascinating stuff.

At the end of the class, while everyone is munching on snacks, we start talking about the hearts of other mammals.

"The fairyfly has the smallest heart of any creature," Rayyan tells us.

"It's not really a heart, though, right, Mr. Pigao?" Monique says. "Insects don't have hearts."

"Monsters don't either," I mutter.

Pigao looks at me sharply, but doesn't say anything. "Insects have hearts, Monique," he says. "Just different. Less complex."

"Which animal has the biggest heart?" a kid asks. I can't tell if he's asking Pigao or Rayyan.

"The blue whale, of course," Frankie calls out. "Four hundred pounds. Five feet tall."

The class gasps. Even Pigao looks impressed. About the giant whale heart? Or Frankie's knowledge?

Pigao's expression makes me mad. Why does nobody see Frankie for the bully he is? Just because he can spout facts he's obviously read on some world records website? "Duh," I mutter again, louder this time. "The blue whale is the largest mammal, so obviously it will have the biggest heart."

"It's actually the elephant," Rayyan protests. "If you only look at land animals."

"Who's looking only at land animals?" Frankie throws back. "Nerd."

That gets me all sorts of riled up. I'm halfway out of my chair before I can take another breath. "You don't know how to stay quiet, do you?" I growl.

Pigao holds up a hand. "All right, settle down, please." He looks from me to Frankie. "What's up with you two? You're always arguing in my class."

I sit back and shrug. Not sure what to answer here, honestly. This Frankie just . . . I dunno, gets my heart pumping, and not in a good way.

Frankie copies me exactly. Like, down to the shuffling feet and looking down at the desk combo.

Pigao's not done. "Do these two act the same way in all

their classes?" he asks the other kids.

"Yes!" everyone shouts back. Even Rayyan, the traitor.

Wow, my heart feels betrayed. You know, if it was the Valentine version, not the anatomically correct one.

* * *

Pigao takes us to the track field for the last fifteen minutes of class. "The weather is too nice to stay inside," he says.

What is it with Texas and outside classes?

On the other hand, it's the second week of November, so the weather *is* pretty nice. I hear summers in Texas are brutal.

Pigao calls us near the bleachers. "This isn't playtime," he says sternly. "We're going to do some practical work in biology."

Rayyan frowns. "What does that mean?"

"Well, I want all of you to have strong hearts," Pigao says. "Which means taking care of our cardiovascular health."

I already know what's coming. "Running laps?"

"Just one," Pigao says, smiling. "Come on, class! Start slow and then increase your speed."

"We need to stretch first," I interrupt. Frankie may be a gym rat (I highly doubt that), but I'm the one who knows about exercise. Zed and I used to jog around our apartment parking lot after school. Patel Uncle kept watch. It was . . . not horrible.

Pigao nods. "Yes, you're right, New York boy. Stretch first, everyone!"

Frankie gives me a disgusted look.

The rest of the class looks bored. Apparently exercising isn't cool or something.

I groan and decide to set an example, the good kind for once. "Heart health, people!" I shout, and get in position for stretches.

Rayyan follows, then Monique and Eli. Then the rest of the class, even Pigao.

Frankie and his goon stand watching us, but I don't even care. I finish my stretches and start jogging at the edge of the field.

Everyone follows me. Pigao is next to me, and Rayyan right behind me.

It's like the Pied Piper.

I'd be totally into that folktale, if it wasn't European. I stick to South Asian stories, thank you very much.

I keep a slow pace, mostly because I don't want Rayyan falling down at school. "Maybe we can talk about heart-healthy foods too, Mr. Pigao," I call out. "My cousin needs to eat more. Make his body and heart really strong."

"Good idea," Pigao says, panting. "I'll email everyone a handout."

My lips twitch. I want to burst into a big smile, but it's hard to let go of my image. The angsty boy who hates the world shouldn't be enjoying the cool breeze in his hair. He shouldn't find his biology teacher gasping for air at two miles per hour even mildly amusing.

And here I am, fighting a full-on belly laugh.

Who even am I?

Fortunately it doesn't take too long for me to go back to normal.

Here's what happens.

We finish our lap around the field. Then Pigao tells us to do push-ups to build muscle.

Ninety-nine percent of the class groans very loudly at this. One percent smirks.

Yup, that would be me and Frankie. We give each other ugly, knowing looks, and drop down onto the ground.

Somewhere between biology class and the running lap, we started hating on each other big-time. I mean, there's always this negativity between us, but right now, it's crackling with energy.

The kind that could light up the track field, if this was nighttime.

Reasons why I can't stand Frankie: he's a know-it-all jerk who hides behind his good grades. He bullies my cousin, which I'm not gonna tolerate.

Oh, and he put his arm around Carmen Rodriguez again on Monday.

She gave him a dirty what-do-you-think-you're-doing look, but still. I can predict that something is going to go down between Frankie and me very soon. And it won't be pretty.

Pigao counts out loud as we do push-ups. Most of the class collapses after five or six. Frankie goes up to fifteen. His face glistens with sweat (gross) and his arm muscles bulge. Okay, maybe he wasn't lying about the biceps.

On the sixteenth push-up, Frankie moans like he's in pain. And then, oh happy day, he falls to the ground, panting heavily.

Ha.

"Okay, I think that's enough," Pigao says. "Let's head inside."

My arms are mush, but I'm made of sterner stuff. Trained from birth to not show weakness. "No, keep counting," I whisper.

Frankie sits up, furious.

Rayyan starts to count.

I get to twenty, then gracefully lower myself to the ground. I almost say "Ta-da!" But then I decide I don't really need to rub it in anyone's face.

Everyone can see I'm the king of push-ups.

"Wow," Pigao says, shaking his head. "That was completely unnecessary, but very impressive."

He should see me box.

I stand up and grin. "Thanks."

Frankie, meanwhile, is looking mad enough to set the school on fire. I turn my grin in his direction, but it's not 'cause I'm happy. I'm feeding off his negative energy, and my insides are churning.

Something is about to happen. I just know it.

Living with Abbu has given me a kind of sixth sense about stuff like that.

The thing is, I'm so busy waiting for Frankie to turn on me

that I completely forget to watch out for my cousin.

The original bully magnet. The one Frankie's been messing with since before I came to Houston.

The dismissal bell rings while we're heading back inside, and Pigao is officially off duty. He waves goodbye to us and goes back inside. The rest of the class follows.

That's when Frankie makes his move. He shoves Rayyan into the wall. "That's for your elephant heart comment," he growls.

Rayyan doesn't reply, because one, who cares whether an elephant heart is bigger, or a whale heart? And two, he's trying to hold himself steady against the wall so he doesn't fall down or anything.

I freeze.

Fighting on school property is grounds for dismissal. Fighting on school property is grounds for dismissal.

How do I know this? I'd punched Jonah Wiley in third grade after he'd told everyone about Abbu. And the principal had called Mama to say exactly this: "Fighting on school property is grounds for dismissal."

Only Mama was well known and everyone loved her, so I got off with a warning.

Today, Mama isn't here. And I'm not in third grade anymore. So, no fighting.

I guess I have to handle this another way.

I stride up and hold Rayyan by the shoulder to steady him. "Thanks," he says quietly.

I turn to Frankie and walk until I'm chest to chest with him. Do we look like two gorillas ready to fight for the alpha title? Maybe.

Not sure if gorillas have alphas or something else. Anyway.

"What is the matter with you?" I snarl. "Didn't anyone teach you manners?"

He's stunned. I don't think he expected me to get in his face like this.

When he doesn't say anything, I grit my teeth and growl, "I am sick when I do look on thee."

Yes, ladies and gentlemen, I now know a single quote from Shakespeare. I'll be honest, I looked up the things Frankie said earlier, all that toad and knave business, and yup, it was the Bard. That's when I decided to fight fire with fire.

Or, ya know, insults with insults.

I'm not ashamed to admit I practiced in front of the mirror over the weekend. Making sure I had the line down pat, and also the expression of complete disgust and anger.

Judging from the look on Frankie's face, it worked. He's nervous.

Frankie's goon takes backward steps until he's at the door leading into the school. "Come on, Frankie," he yells.

Frankie stays where he is. He clears his throat and stands taller. "This is between me and Ryan," he says.

Oh, Ryan, is it? Mispronouncing someone's name is so 2020. I lean close enough to smell his onion breath. "Rayyan is like my brother," I say very slowly. "Anything you say or do to him involves me. And believe me, you don't want me involved."

He goes pale. "Who . . . who do you think you are?"

I'm guessing that's a rhetorical question. I reply, anyway. "I'm your worst nightmare."

"That's a cliché."

I don't even blink. Just because he uses French words doesn't mean he's not small and weak. Strength doesn't come from vocabulary. It comes from fear.

Abbu taught me that.

"My nightmares are not clichés, little boy," I say roughly. "They're very real, and they would tear you apart."

Frankie's eyes nearly pop out of his head.

I take Rayyan's arm and pull him away. When we reach the door, I turn to face Frankie. (His goon's long gone, and so are the other kids.) "Don't mess with my brother again," I snarl. "Or I will literally turn you into minced meat."

And here's what tells me this Frankie dude is actually highly intelligent, no matter how stupid he acts. He gulps and looks away.

Just like a scared little gorilla baby.

"You're insane," he whispers, just loud enough for me to hear.

"It runs in the family," I whisper back, just as low.

17

Once upon a time, in the village of Sonmiani, lived a fisherman named Aubhayo.

Sonmiani is a small town in Pakistan. It's close to the city of Karachi, where Abbu and Naila Phupo's parents—my dada and dadi—were born.

Anyway, Aubhayo the fisherman lived in Sonmiani with his seven sons. This is when Karachi wasn't a big bustling metropolis, but a small fishing village called Kolachi. Six of Aubhayo's sons were tall and strong, but the seventh one was Moriro, who was short and thin and weak. Every day the six strong sons of Aubhayo would go fishing, and every day Moriro would stay home.

You see, fishing was dangerous, and only the fittest people

went out on the fishing boats. So Moriro stayed home. Always.

Did he feel sad? Angry? Did he rail at the injustice of being left at home, or was he grateful not to put his life in danger? Nobody knows.

Another thing nobody knows: Was he friends with his brothers, or did they tease and taunt him? In other words, was there a good, brotherly relationship between them? Again, nobody knows.

It makes the story more interesting, because Moriro's motives aren't clear. Why did he do what he did?

But I'm getting ahead of myself. Here's the rest of the story:

Like I've said before, some distance from Aubhayo's village, Sonmiani, was the village of Kolachi. On its coast there was a dangerous whirlpool, which the people called Kolachi ju kunn. That means the whirlpool of Kolachi in the Sindhi language.

Yeah, I know, not very creative. What can I say? They were fishermen, not poets.

Anyway, this whirlpool was one reason why fishing in those waters was so dangerous. The boats that came from Sonmiani to Kolachi would sometimes get stuck in the whirlpool. Inside it lived a—wait for it—sea monster who loved eating helpless fishermen.

BTW, the story in Sindhi is titled "Moriro and the Magurmuch," which means crocodile. But other versions call it a whale.

Whatever. I like magurmuch better, so let's go with that.

One day, Moriro's brothers leave for their daily fishing adventures at dawn, but they never return. Again, we don't have details. Was Moriro upset? Did he fall down in grief? What did Aubhayo and his wife (did he have a wife?) do when six of their seven kids just never came back home?

It's not like just one disappeared, ya know. All six tall, strapping young men never came back from their fishing trip. That's a huge deal.

All I know for sure is that later the family gets some info. I'm guessing Aubhayo went around asking, or maybe even Moriro did. They make him out as a weak dude, just lazing around at home all day, but as you'll see, he ends up being pretty strong and brave.

What the family discovers is that the brothers' fishing boat was last seen caught in the Kolachi whirlpool. Yikes, that sounds horrifying, right? They deduced that the brothers were eaten by the magurmuch. This lights a fire under Moriro's butt. He's really, really upset, but not the normal kind when you cry at losing someone.

Nope. He decides to seek vengeance from the crocodile.

He goes to the blacksmith or whatever, and asks him to build a cage. This isn't an ordinary cage, though. It has to be big enough to hold Moriro, and it needs pointed spikes on the outside. Also, lots of sturdy ropes.

I'm sure the blacksmith has questions, but as long as he's getting the money, he doesn't care.

Or maybe he wasn't getting paid (Aubhayo's family can't

be rich, right?) and the entire village is just cheering on this revenge plan. Who knows?

Once the cage is ready, it's taken to the whirlpool. Moriro's friends fasten the cage to buffaloes, and lower it carefully into the water using the ropes. Moriro, of course, is inside. Ready for the role of a lifetime.

Killing the magurmuch.

Once the cage is in the water, it doesn't take long for the magurmuch to attack. It reaches the cage in a frenzy, opens its big mouth with sharp teeth, and tries to swallow Moriro. But lo and behold, the cage gets stuck in the beast's mouth.

There's a disadvantage to having too many pointy teeth, I guess.

Moriro tugs on the ropes, which is basically a signal to his friends waiting onshore. They pull the cage out, with the magurmuch still attached, thrashing and roaring. Someone kills the monster. It doesn't say who, but I'm going to go with Moriro.

What can I say? I'm rooting for him to be the strong and brave hero in this story.

When the magurmuch is dead, they cut open its stomach and find the remains of all six brothers. Gross. But also poetic in a way, right? The remains are brought back to Sonmiani, and they get a decent burial.

And Moriro is forever the guy who battled the sea monster for the sake of his brothers.

I'm guessing they let him go fishing after that.

* * *

"You called me brother," Rayyan says.

We're sitting on the floor in our room, notebook between us, working on our science fair project.

We've got to submit our idea on Monday, and we have zilch right now.

Typical me.

Poor Rayyan, super student, having to deal with me and my lazy attitude about academics.

"This afternoon in school," Rayyan adds, "you told Frankie I was your brother."

"Yeah, so?" I raise my eyebrows. "Aren't you my brother?"

"Not really. We're cousins."

I shrug. "Same thing. We're blood. We have matching eyes. That's what matters."

"Yes, but cousins," he repeats. "Not brothers."

I chuckle. "Sure. You just don't wanna adopt my dad."

Rayyan doesn't think this is funny. "That's not the reason!" he cries.

I definitely think that's the reason, but I'd rather not press the issue. "We may be cousins, but look at us. We share a room. A bathroom. We spend all day and all night together. In school. After school. The other day you were brushing your teeth while I peed. It's like we're joined at the hip. Brothers."

He flushes. "You were in the toilet room. It's not like we could see each other."

He's right. The toilet has its own room, as tiny as a closet.

Chalk that up to another strange Texas thing. Or maybe it's just a house thing. I'm used to apartment living, where there's no privacy.

"What I'm saying is, we're practically brothers, since we spend so much time together," I say.

Except when he goes to the doctor. I stay home then.

Listen, I'd go in a heartbeat. Anything's better than staying at home and listening to Abbu rant and rave. But Rayyan doesn't want me going.

He's weirdly protective about his health issues. My guess, he's embarrassed. But it's okay; who am I to judge? I have my own problems.

The good news: he's put on some weight since I moved here. Like, seven pounds, but Naila Phupo is happy, so I'm happy.

Anyway, Rayyan isn't done with the brother conversation. "You didn't have to come between us, you know. Me and Frankie have a thing. It's okay."

"You and Frankie have a thing?" I stare at him. "You mean a bully and victim thing?"

He flushes again. "He's harmless, as long as you don't make eye contact and do whatever he says."

"See, that's what I don't like," I reply. "You should look wherever you want and do whatever you want. He's not your father."

Rayyan blinks and looks down.

Wait, was that insensitive? Because he doesn't have a dad?

Ugh, what's wrong with me? I'm so clueless, especially when I'm trying to be nice. "I didn't mean . . ."

"It's okay, I know what you were trying to say." Rayyan looks up, and I'm shocked—*shocked*—to see that he's grinning. Like, full teeth display and everything. "I suddenly imagined Frankie as my dad! It was too funny."

"Whoa." I rolled my eyes. "That went south fast."

"Yeah, I know!"

I shake my head. "Hope he gets a personality transplant when he grows up. Otherwise he'll be a dad like my abbu."

Rayyan's grin fades. "Come on!"

"No, I'm not kidding," I say. "He reminds me of Abbu sometimes. Like, the same anger, the same aggression."

"Well, lots of people have anger management issues."

I wish that was Abbu's only problem. I sigh and tap on the notebook. "Let's choose a topic," I say.

Rayyan reads from the paper. "Well, we have three options left, because *somebody* keeps shutting down every idea I get."

I wag my eyebrows. "That's right. I'm the boss."

Rayyan continues. "We could test heart rate recovery after different kinds of exercises. . . ."

I start to say something, but he puts up a hand. "No, be quiet and listen!"

"Okay, I'm listening," I grumble. Look, I'm pretending to be grumpy, but this is heaven to me. This hanging out, talking about stuff, being normal.

It's heaven.

"Or we could test sound localization," he continues. "You know, blindfolded, and then figure out where various noises are coming from."

"You and your blindfolds," I joke.

"Or we could make a model of the eye," Rayyan ends.

I sit up. "Ooh, I like the idea of a model. Hands-on, you know? No testing shesting. No graphs. That's boring."

"Okay, but a model of the eye?" He looks uncertain, and I know why. We haven't studied the eye in biology. Pigao's syllabus says the focus is on the blood, heart, muscles, and the digestive system.

I can't wait for that last one. Rayyan is gonna get schooled about healthy diets.

"Maybe another model?" I'm still thinking when the door opens and Naila Phupo waltzes in. She's holding a tray with snacks and juice boxes.

What are we, six?

Rayyan grabs the mango juice box. "Ooh, Shezan, my favorite."

Phupo sets the tray down on the desk. "You boys study too hard," she says. "It's Friday evening. You should be having fun."

I take some papar. It's light and crispy, fried to perfection. "Like what?"

"Watch a movie?" she suggests.

Ha. What would she say if she knew we'd just finished

watching the press conference of her husband's death *for the third time?* Freak out, probably.

Rayyan has a problem. Think of it like scratching at a scab or pulling at a loose tooth. There's no reason for it, but you do it anyway. Just to hurt yourself.

Or maybe to prove it's not hurting anymore.

Anyway, like I said, my cousin has a problem called the press conference video. And now that I know about it, he's dragging me into it too. It's a metaphorical whirlpool like the one in Sonmiani. Only instead of a crocodile, it's got a beast called grief.

They both have sharp teeth, let me tell you.

"Oh, you could play a board game!" Naila Phupo continues. "I'm an expert at Clue, you know."

My eyebrows shoot up. "You? Really?"

She nods. "Yup. Used to play with Rayyan all the time when he was younger. Now he's a teenager and apparently doesn't need his mama playing with him anymore."

Rayyan protests, but it's obvious they're joking around. She's got a happy look on her face, as if hanging out in her son's bedroom talking about board games is the most fun thing in the world.

Don't think about Mama. Don't think about Mama.

Especially don't compare Mama to your aunt, or anyone else.

Rayyan goes to the closet and brings out a battered old box of Clue. Okay, so I guess we're doing this?

"Look at you two!" Phupo clasps her hands together like a

Disney princess. "Just like brothers."

I shoot Rayyan an I-told-you-so look. "I'm your Moriro," I say.

"What?" they both ask together.

"Never mind," I mutter. "Start the game."

Naila Phupo sits down on the floor with us. Then she looks up. "Should I ask Mumtaz bhai if he wants to play?"

I laugh. "Don't bother."

She pats my hand. "He's stressed out these days. Moving your whole life and not having your wife with you isn't easy."

Not to mention the schizophrenia, which, as I've said before, is getting worse.

We start playing, and it's okay, I guess. Rayyan is taking it way too seriously, but that's just his style. It's another form of heaven, playing a board game where the weapons are little tiny metal thingies.

After a while, I notice Naila Phupo looking at me. "You're happy here, aren't you, Mohammad?" she asks gently.

I nod. "Yes, I really like it here, Phupo."

"Good." She smiles that happy smile she has. The one that makes me feel warm inside. It's like a hug without hands.

"I'm grateful to you, for letting us stay here," I say softly. "I know Abbu doesn't always act like it, but we're both grateful."

Well, I don't know this for a fact. For all I know, Abbu could absolutely detest our current living arrangement. But it doesn't matter.

I'm gonna pretend he's happy to be with his sister. His family.

Naila Phupo sighs. "I thought he was getting better, your abbu," she says hesitantly. "But . . . I don't know. Sometimes he scares me."

"You and me both," I mumble.

"Worries me, I mean," she corrects herself with a little laugh. "That's what I meant."

I guess we're both good at pretending. I look at her, and she looks back at me. What would it feel like to tell someone all your secrets? Share all your burdens?

I mean, sure, I've told Rayyan a lot of things. But he's a kid, so it's not the same. He can't do anything.

She's still looking at me, with this soft expression that I've never, ever seen on Mama's face. How lucky Rayyan is to have a mom who can make that expression.

Judging from the way he's smiling, he knows it too.

Finally, I crack. I'm gonna try giving her a burden, see what she does with it. "I don't think Abbu's taking his medication," I whisper. "The ones for his . . . mental issues."

Her eyes go round. "Oh, I didn't realize."

I shrug. "Yeah, well. It's easy to hide."

That's the thing with mental health, you know? It's easy to fake that you're doing well. Like the indigo jackal, you can act like the king and everyone will take your word for it.

And when you start feeling bad, people think it's normal stuff, like anger or stress. They don't see the delusions, the hallucinations. They don't understand that when Abbu isn't well, he makes bad decisions or forgets to take care of himself.

Or he doesn't care, period.

That's the worst part. His brain makes him think he doesn't care. About himself, about Mama.

About me.

Naila Phupo bites her lip. "Maybe I can talk to him. He'll listen to me."

I shoot her a disbelieving look, but because she's so nice I don't say anything. I pick up a card from the board. I don't want to spend this little slice of heaven talking about *him*. "Tell me about Zafar Phupa," I say. "I wanna know all about him."

Rayyan comes alive. He talks and talks about his father. How he was kind and smart and always gave money to charity. How he took Rayyan to the Astros ball games and also helped him with homework. How he told the best bedtime stories and cooked the best lamb chops.

Naila Phupo mostly listens, smiling to herself. "His lamb chops were famous," she agrees.

And me? I'm silent. Struck dumb with a festering jealousy, living in a world where my father is nothing like Zafar Phupa and my mother is nothing like Naila Phupo.

Hating, hating my cousin—my brother—for having a perfect family. Yes, it's perfect even though one of them is dead, because their memories of each other are good.

Hating myself for hating him, because he sure doesn't deserve it.

Turns out I'm more like Moriro than I think, feeling all kinds of things for his brothers, none of them good.

The only difference is, I'm never going to slay the magur-much.

18

"So how are you?"

Mama looks at me through the screen with narrowed eyes. She's wearing another T-shirt, this time beige. I can't see the necklace, but I know it's there.

I've got bleary eyes and I'm yawning, because I was up last night after one of my nightmares. They wake me up and then I'm too freaked out to go back to sleep. In Queens, I'd just switch on the light and read, but now I'm sharing a room with Rayyan, so I've got to lie in the darkness and stare out the window.

Just to be clear, this is not a good way to spend the night after scary dreams. One hundred percent do not recommend.

"Mo?" Mama repeats impatiently.

I wonder what she'd say if I told her about the nightmares. Would she worry?

Let's not get carried away. Of course she wouldn't.

* * *

This is how my nightmares always go:

I'm in my Queens apartment, hanging out. It's always different. Sometimes I'm listening to music. Sometimes I'm eating at the kitchen table. Sometimes I'm doing my homework.

I'm always alone. Always happy.

Or at least, not unhappy. There's a difference. Think about it.

Then somebody calls me from the other room. Shouts my name urgently. Loudly. Mostly it's Abbu's voice, but sometimes it's Mama's. Or my friend Zed's. A couple of times it's been Patel Uncle's.

I go looking for whoever calls me, and there they all are, my family, my friends, teachers. Whoever I meet, they're laughing and talking, but there's a dark undercurrent. A stealthy vibe in the room, like they're all pretending. Like they're not really who they say they are.

The uneasy feeling grows and grows in me as I walk around the apartment. The rooms get darker and narrower. The people sit alone now, one in a room. Sometimes they're skulking in shadowy corners.

I'm still walking around, still trying to shake off the empty, dark, heavy mood. Then I catch sight of someone—anyone, doesn't matter—and it's very clear they're not a real person. They're a copy. They wear a mask that makes them look normal, but they're the opposite.

Cruel. Haunting. Monster.

That's when I look around me and realize they all look the same—my mother, my father, my friend, whatever. But they're also not. They're the monstrous copy. The heavy, shadowed version.

I run, but they're after me. Not sure why? I think they want to kill me, or make me wear a mask too, but there's no way I'm stopping long enough to ask what the heck they want from me.

They chase me, still laughing, still talking. From room to room to room. In my dreams, my Queens apartment is bigger than Buckingham Palace. I tell myself I have to escape the monsters and find the real people.

Find the real Abbu and Mama, the ones who love me and care for me, and don't want to kill me. The ones who don't wear masks.

It's not my imagination. It's not wishful thinking. In some of the rooms I find the real people. The good people. The ones who don't need masks because they're whole and real and *good*.

But those people never come to me. I always lose them. I know they're around, maybe in the next room or around the corner. Yet they disappear like smoke. Just out of reach.

If I only run fast enough, I'll catch up to them.

And then the monsters in the masks will have to let me be.

"I'm fine," I tell Mama. "Busy with school."

"That's great," she replies. "I'm glad you're fitting in. I didn't think this move would be good for you, but I guess I was worrying too much."

Okay, hold up. Two things. First, she wasn't on board with the move? She's the one who stopped paying rent on the apartment, and we were kicked out. Asked to leave, the landlord's email said.

Yup, I've been reading Abbu's emails, ever since I changed his password and got access.

I think we all know I'm a bad kid. No surprise there.

Second, she was worrying about me? Clearly that's a lie. A wave of anger clutches my throat. "If you worried so much, you wouldn't have left me," I choke out before I think.

Mama's eyes widen. "I didn't leave you alone," she protests. "You're with your father."

I'm ashamed of my outburst now. "You know what he's like," I mutter.

"That's no excuse! He should take responsibility."

I shake my head. What does it matter? We've been having the same arguments since I can remember. "He should, but he won't," I remind her glumly. "He can't."

"That's not my problem, Mo. I have a job. A mission. I can't keep holding myself back because he won't take his meds."

"What about me?" I ask brokenly.

Listen, I try to make my voice strong, but it's not possible.

Sometimes, my voice is weak and low and trembling. It sounds like I'm gonna cry, even though I won't.

Ugh.

Mama leans in until she's almost touching the screen. "Mo, my boy! You're a piece of my heart. I love you. But I *have* to do this. It's important to me."

I steel my heart, make it strong. "Sure."

She sighs. "It's not permanent. You know that."

I do. Her UNESCO fellowship is only two years long. By the time she gets back, I'll be in tenth grade.

Mama must have seen the hard look in my eyes, because she changes the subject. Sort of. "Where's your father?"

I look at the bed, where Abbu's sleeping off his alcohol and high blood pressure and intense emotions. She can't see him from her angle. "I don't know," I say.

It's such a small rebellion, but it gives me a thrill. What can I say? I'm bad to the core, just like everyone thinks.

She sighs. "Well, tell him I emailed him."

My hand itches to open a new tab and log into Abbu's email account right this second. "Okay, I'll tell him."

She smiles. "Now. Have you made any friends at school?"

*　*　*

Rayyan finds me in the backyard. It's become our regular Saturday afternoon hangout, after my video call.

I've just finished round seven. My fists are aching. My face is sweating.

In one way, I'm sorta happy. Abbu's window looks out into

197

the backyard, and I heard Naila Phupo come in and wake him up a little while ago. They chatted about things that happened when they were teens. I dunno, some beach party they both went to, had loads of fun.

Abbu and Phupo having fun as kids. Who knew?

When Abbu was nice and relaxed, Naila Phupo brought up his meds. Just like she'd said.

Finally, a grown-up who showed up for me! I'd stopped boxing and jumped up and down with a stupid grin on my face.

Of course, the grin dissolved pretty soon because Abbu acted like he was A-okay and didn't need any sort of treatment. "I'm in perfect health, Naila," he'd scoffed. "You're being ridiculous."

She'd left soon after. Who wanted to be called ridiculous to their face?

And I'd boxed until my arms grew weak.

"You okay?" Rayyan asks, staring at my hands.

"Mama emailed back with Nathan's contact info."

Rayyan leans against the tree. "Where does he live?"

"It's an area called Cypress."

His eyes widen. "What? That's, like, only half an hour from here."

I let out a rusty laugh. "Yup."

"How strange that Mama didn't know," Rayyan says.

"What makes you think she didn't?" I say, stung. "You think she tells you everything? Adults always have lots of secrets."

Rayyan rolls his eyes. "Oh, she keeps secrets, all right. Like how my doctor thinks I'll never get better. Or how she cries herself to sleep because she still misses my dad. Or . . ."

I straighten up. "You need a new doctor. You'll get better, you'll see."

A ghost of a smile passes over his gaunt face. "Oh yeah? How do you know?"

I show him my gloved hands. "Because I'm your protector now. I'm taking care of you."

This, he likes. I can tell by how his eyes crinkle at the corners and he ducks his head in embarrassment. "Gee, thanks," he mumbles.

I grab my water bottle and chug.

Rayyan goes to the patio to sit down. Dude is so weak he can't even stand up for too long. I remember some of the muscle stuff we learned about in biology this week.

Protein. That's what he needs. Chicken and beef and all the other foods that will make him strong.

And a new doctor.

I wasn't kidding. He needs me, and in a weird way, I need him too.

Just like Moriro needed his brothers, but in the end, the brothers needed Moriro too. If only to avenge their deaths or whatever.

"So what are you going to do about your uncle?" Rayyan asks.

"I don't know yet," I reply. "Maybe I'll go meet him."

"Or?"

I shrug. "Or maybe I'll ignore him, like he's ignored me all my life."

From the disapproving look on his face, I can tell what my cousin thinks of the second option.

* * *

"Be careful with those paints, you hear me?"

I'm handing out construction paper and watercolors to the kids in Sunday school art class.

Also, I'm yelling.

Unlike Imam Shamsi, we do *not* have these little pests under control. They chatter loudly throughout the class, and have to be told constantly to simmer down.

Today, the excitement level is higher than usual. This may be due to the fact that we've graduated to paints, at least for the older kids.

See, Rayyan and I had a little lesson plan discussion on the drive over. I mean, if we have to teach these kids, then we might as well do it properly.

The first thing we did when class started was to divide them into two groups based on age. Rayyan got the younger kids and the tubs of crayons. I got the older kids and the watercolor paints.

Rayyan's finished handing out his supplies, so we get started on the lesson plan. This is how it's supposed to go:

1. Wiggle time. Ya know, get your wiggles out, et cetera.
2. Group projects. The younger kids draw a house with a

yard and people. The older kids paint a beautiful scene like the beach or a farm. If it was me, I'd draw the Queensboro Bridge or the New York City skyline, but hey, these kids can do whatever they like.

3. Time to show your projects to the class. This part is interesting, because they all want to go together, like a big wall of art held up at the same time. Not sure what's up with that, but it's cool.

4. Snack time + chat time. This is where Rayyan likes to insert his little Islamic lesson, as he calls it. Something small and easily understandable. Today, it's all about when to say *bismillah* versus *alhamdolillah*. It's funny, really. Rayyan calls out an action, and the kids decide what to say. For example: "Before you start eating?" "Bismillah!" And "After a sneeze?" "Alhamdolillah!" Then someone starts pretend sneezing, then coughing, and pretty soon, it's pandemonium.

Yup. Loud and happy, that's Sunday school art class for you.

It seems a world away to me, like I'm watching it all on the TV screen. Like there's a veil between me and the rest of the class.

I want to laugh and talk, but it feels wrong. Too heavy. The thoughts that weigh me down are too heavy.

Mama. Abbu. Nathan. Rayyan. Frankie.

Ugh, why do I even bother with these people? I know better than to care about anyone or anything. It only hurts later.

Because no matter what, people disappoint you. One day

you peel off the mask, and there's an ugly monster behind it.

Well, except for Rayyan and Naila Phupo. They're genuine. And maybe the imam. He seems like an okay dude.

When the bell rings, Rayyan makes the kids help clean up. Even the toddlers. That was another thing we'd decided before class began.

The kids are happy to help. True, they make a mess of cleanup too, but it still goes a lot faster.

Soon the classroom empties out. Sana the Pigtail Girl is the last one to leave. "Why are you so sad, Mohammad bhai?"

I try to smile. "I'm not sad. You're sad."

She giggles. "No, you are. Your lips are pouting."

I pull a pigtail. "Having fun in art class?" I ask, hoping she'll be distracted.

She jumps a little. "Yup. So much fun. Art is my favorite subject."

"That's good." It wasn't my favorite before I came to Houston, but now it feels like a lifeline.

"You know why?" she asks.

"Why?"

She gives a beautiful smile. "Because of you and Rayyan bhai."

Look, I could believe her and smile back. She's a kid. She's got no reason to lie. But she doesn't know me.

Abbu knows me, and he thinks I'm completely useless. No good. Stupid.

I'll take my chances that he's right.

Sana's still smiling at me, though, and I don't wanna break her heart. I'm not a total villain. "Thanks," I say, smiling a little.

She waves at us and leaves. Rayyan stands by the door. "Let me guess. You're sticking around?"

I'm already turning toward the storage container in the back. "Yeah, just a few minutes," I say. "I'll see you soon."

* * *

My painting this week is inspired by the muscles of the human body. Long lines, tough and sleek. Maroon paint, dark and glowing. Some pinks and purples mixed in, but not enough to take the image out of darkness.

I start out smooth, but the tracks become barbed and rough as they move down the canvas. One, two, three, seven, eleven, twenty.

Up, down, round and round.

Secrets. Lies. Pain.

You know when you've boxed too long, or run too fast, and your muscles ache so deeply? Yeah, that pain. It's not really pain, it's more like a never-ending throb that makes you lose your mind.

I paint and paint. Everything I do, the colors I use, the movements of my hand, all make the painting harsh. Ugly.

Wretched.

19

Carmen is absent on Monday, which means I can focus in music class.

"We're going to learn about different genres of music," Mrs. Nguyen says. She hands out a paper with a list. Blues. Rock. Hip-hop. Punk. Classical.

I pounce on the last one. "When they say classical, what do they mean?"

She turns to me with a smile. "Well, that's a good question. What do *you* think it means?"

Oh, she's that type of teacher? The one who wants you to answer your own questions? Well, then I'd like to know what she's being paid to do?

Okay, deep breaths.

Guess I'm still salty about my life.

I tap a finger on my desk. "Ballet, opera, symphonies . . ." I pause. It's all I remember from that history of music book.

"That's a good start," Mrs. Nguyen says, smiling again.

She's always smiling. She reminds me of Naila Phupo, even though they're different. Mrs. Nguyen is very thin and has silky black hair like a cap around her head. She usually wears pantsuits; today she's wearing one that's cream colored, with navy blue trim and buttons.

Too bad I'm in a grumpy mood and want to wipe her smile off her face. "I'm guessing it doesn't include classical music from the East."

The smile stays on. "Like?"

I scoff. "Like, uh, classical music from the Indian subcontinent. Qawwali. Sitaar. Raag."

Okay, I'm basically throwing out words I've heard from Patel Uncle and Abbu. It's not like I'm an expert. But these Texans seems to live in their own world, where New Yorkers are called Yankees and anyone different is protested with signs.

I'm gonna enjoy shocking them, angering them, smashing their stereotypes and assumptions.

Like I said, I'm in a grumpy mood today.

"Is that all, Mohammad?" Mrs. Nguyen says, her eyes glinting. She pronounces my name perfectly, so I don't correct her or ask her to call me Mo.

"What do you mean?" I ask.

"Eastern music isn't only from India and Pakistan, you know. There's all sorts of classical music in Asia. Quan Ho or Ca Tru in Vietnam, for example."

My muscles lose some of their tightness. She's right, obviously. Asia is huge. Like, almost fifty countries huge. They all have different cultures and food and dress.

And folktales.

"Quan Ho is related to folktale songs, right?" Frankie asks, leaning forward. "I heard it in a lunar festival last year."

My jaw drops. Folktales are my—I dunno, forte. Turns out Frankie knows about them too? Why? How? I crumple the genres of music worksheet and close my mouth tightly.

Mrs. Nguyen's smile is bigger than ever. "What a perfect segue to our current discussion, Frankie."

She goes back to her desk and fiddles with her computer. The smart board in front of her comes to life with a video of a group of singers in long, colorful robes.

"This is an example of the Quan Ho style of singing," she continues. "It's my favorite. We used to listen to it in Vietnam as children."

Melodious singing fills the air. It's sharp and heavy, like the sounds of a bell.

I sit back and breathe deeply again. The sounds of the Quan Ho seep into me, relaxing me.

I turn slightly to see Frankie. He's got a peaceful look on his face too.

* * *

One time, when I was eleven, Abbu decided to take me on a walking tour of New York City.

"The tourists all pay good money to do it," he said, "but we'll use Google Maps and make a route. It's easy as that, and completely free."

I didn't want to go anywhere with him, but also I did, because he was in a good mood and when he was like that he was a lot of fun.

Mostly.

"It's all about supply and demand," he told me as we headed outside. My ears perked up, because supply and demand was one of those things Patel Uncle talked about a lot. Mostly in connection with Mama. "Your mother has the skills to provide clean water, which is a basic need," he'd say. "So people will pay good money to have her come work for them."

This was when he first started kid-sitting me. I may have complained about her working at a fancy new organization when the old one near our house was perfectly fine.

Supply and demand sent my mother to Greece, so it's a concept I'm familiar with.

Abbu led the way, his cheeks flushed with the cool air, and probably with his happiness. Like I said, it was one of his good days. He was having F.U.N.

Me? Not so much.

Let me tell you, the walking tour was stupid. I don't know why tourists do that sort of thing. I don't want to walk around looking at a bunch of old buildings or parks or whatever. The one good part, though? Street musicians.

If you've ever been to New York, you'll know what I'm talking about. The street musicians are mostly in the subway stations, sitting on the ground with instruments around them. Guitar, drums, flutes. There's even a lady who plays on a saw.

Yup, that's right. A musical saw.

Oh, and a dude named Mohammadu from Gambia who plays on this big brown African harp. He's cool, because of his name and because of the harp.

"Did you know you have to audition for some of these spots?" I said to Abbu. "It's called MUNY. Music Under New York." I'd read this in a pamphlet in my school library.

He nodded to a Black girl sitting on the corner, wearing drab clothes and ragged shoes. His lip curled into that sneer that had been absent all day, but now was starting to show. "I doubt she's auditioned for anything."

"It's just for the subway program, not the entire city. . . ." I stopped. There wasn't any use trying to convince him anyway.

I crept closer to the girl. I dunno, her music was magnetic. She wasn't singing, only playing this haunting melody on a beat-up violin.

I stood and listened for a long time. Like, really long.

I don't know what was keeping me there. It was still a bit chilly, and I'd forgotten my jacket. Plus, we hadn't eaten lunch yet. But none of that mattered right then.

Only the music mattered.

Abbu stood next to me, eyes distant like he was remembering something. After a while, he disappeared, and then came back with a bag of doughnuts and handed me one. I took it without looking.

Also ate it without tasting.

Yeah, the music was that good.

Finally the girl packed up to go. I found a crumpled dollar in my pocket and gave it to her. "Let's go!" Abbu grunted as he walked away, leaving me scrambling after him.

That was the last time I felt such peace in music.

Until Mrs. Nguyen put on the Quan Ho in class.

*　*　*

My peace is shattered pretty quickly.

Frankie pushes a bunch of kids around at lunch. I search for a teacher or parent volunteer. Nope, there's no one.

I grit my teeth and stand up.

"What . . . what're you doing?" Rayyan whispers. He's sitting next to me, safe and sound, munching on his egg salad sandwich.

Frankie shoves another kid, right behind the trash can, and my temper soars.

Listen, I know that none of the citizens of Alice Walker are my responsibility. Still, I feel obligated.

You just wanna fight, says a voice inside me.

Yeah, that too.

It's wise, that voice. Usually warns me when I'm about to do something stupid. Like now.

Too bad I hardly ever listen to it.

I go to Frankie and pull his arm. "Go back to your seat," I growl. "Stop bothering people."

Frankie whirls away from me, teeth bared.

What? He thinks I'm scared of him? I bare my teeth too. We can both be wild animals together. The indigo jackal and the . . . I dunno, something less strange but equally vicious.

A tiger. Or a magurmuch. Ha.

"All right, break it up!" A teacher comes running. *Now* the adults are concerned? When I get involved. Sheesh.

I let go of Frankie's arm and turn back to Rayyan.

The teacher's not having it. His name's Mr. Stanton. He teaches us algebra, and not very well, I might add. "Not so fast," he says. "You need to go see the principal."

My mouth drops open. "Me? Why me?"

"I saw you," Stanton insists. "Bothering Frankie here."

Bothering? My gut burns, and it's not the cafeteria food. It's that Frankie's the star student in Stanton's algebra class, never gets less than a hundred on any test.

From the corner of my eye, I see Frankie deflate like a popped balloon. His face smooths out and looks calmer. "It's okay, Mr. Stanton," he says. "We were just goofing around."

Stanton shakes his head and leaves. The entire cafeteria is silent, watching me and Frankie.

Okay, I'm officially furious. Like, ready to box furious. "I don't need any favors from you, understand?" I say, deathly quiet.

Frankie shrugs. "No worries, you get 'em all the same. It's our southern hospitality, Yankee boy."

The bell rings, and everything erupts into noise and chaos.

The horses in the cowboy mural look down at us like they do every day.

Frankie walks away, whistling.

Whistling, I tell you.

And this is what I realize: not only is my peace shattered, but there's now a different kind of burn in my gut.

Revenge.

* * *

The day passes in a blur. I am all clenched fists and tense muscles.

"Today's the last day to tell me your science fair project," Pigao calls out in biology.

"I emailed you two weeks ago, Mr. Pigao," Frankie says.

"Yes, Frankie, I remember," Pigao replies. "I was very happy to see you follow directions."

I close my eyes. Why won't this day end? I just want to get away from Frankie before I do something really bad.

Something that will make people say "He's just like his father."

Rayyan taps my shoulder. "What should we say? We haven't decided yet."

"I dunno," I mumble.

"Is there a problem?" Pigao asks.

Frankie snickers. His goon snickers even louder. In fact, he downright laughs.

Ugh.

"Er, we don't have our topic yet," Rayyan says nervously.

I can hear it in his voice. He wants so hard to be the perfect student, and not having a topic for the science fair is making him freak out big-time.

I sigh and raise my head. "We have *some* ideas. . . ."

Pigao claps his hands in glee. This guy, always having fun in class. What's his problem?

"Everyone, let's help Rayyan and Mo. Like a brainstorm!"

Um, what?

Even Frankie looks disgruntled.

"How about a simple juice versus electrolyte experiment?" Pigao says. "Since we're starting the digestive system today?"

I shudder. Gatorade tastes like medicine.

"How about tap versus filter water?" Eli says.

Oh lord. I don't want anything to remind me of my mother today. "Nothing to do with water," I mumble.

Other kids throw out ideas. They're all boring. Or stupid. One is both boring *and* stupid.

"Turn a potato into a battery," Frankie says. I perk up because that actually sounds cool. Like, seriously cool. Then he adds, "Oh wait, I already took that one."

I shoot him a glare hot enough to sizzle his socks.

"Um, we wanted a model of some kind," Rayyan inserts. "We talked about it on Friday."

We really did. I'd totally forgotten.

Pigao straightens up. I think his patience is gone. "We don't have more brainstorming time, but if it's a model you want to do, how about a model of the heart?"

I don't hate it. "What kind?" I ask slowly.

"It doesn't matter. You can use balloons, or straws, or clay, whatever you like. There are lots of resources online."

Rayyan and I look at each other and nod. "Okay, we'll do that," Rayyan says, smiling faintly. "A heart model sounds great."

Happy. He's happy.

That makes me happy. Or at least less mad.

So I guess we're making progress.

Pigao makes a note in his computer. "Done." He stands up. "Now let's get back to the digestive system. How much do you kids know about the stomach?"

20

Two things happen on Friday.

They're both bad.

*　*　*

One, Abbu has an episode.

Look, it's not his first time, and it won't be the last. That's not the problem here.

The problem is that I'm the one dealing with it.

Does that make me selfish? Maybe.

I wish I could be the good, kind, self-sacrificing son my parents need. The one who can take care of Abbu when he hurls himself off the track. The one who smiles at Mama through the video screen and tells her she's brilliant.

The one who turns a blind eye when Frankie bullies the

entire student body of Walker Middle School, and then spouts poetry or Civil War facts like he's a savant or whatever.

But news flash: I'm not that kid.

I stopped being that kid when I was eight years old and Jonah Wiley and Company ganged up on me.

Or maybe I still had some goodness left in me then. Maybe I became the real villain when Mama left me.

It doesn't matter. When and why and how don't matter.

What matters is that today, Friday after school, Abbu has an episode and I'm the one who has to deal with it.

I don't want to, but I do.

Because I may be bad to the core, but I'm still his son, and he's still my father. Some things are just basic biology.

Anyway, here's what happens.

When Rayyan and I get home from school, things are quiet. Naila Phupo feeds us snacks—beef samosas and some of that sweet Shezan mango juice—at the kitchen table.

"Where's Mumtaz Mamoo?" Rayyan asks.

"In his room," his mom replies. Then she looks at me. "He's been upset all day. Something on TV set him off."

I scoff, because it's not the TV that sets him off. It's his own inner demons.

"Was he angry?" I ask, trying to not care.

But who am I kidding? I care. It comes out in the wobble of my voice, like I'm a baby. Ugh. Get a grip, Mo. Maybe it's nothing. He's always upset about something, isn't he?

Maybe it's not a big deal.

Naila Phupo shrugs. "Angry, sad, scared, who knows? All of it." She bites her lip. "He kept looking around, talking to himself."

Rayyan makes a shocked sound. "Really?"

I grip the table. Yup, this is a big deal. "Er, don't worry about it," I say. "He gets like that sometimes. It'll be fine."

Naila Phupo looks me straight in the eye. She knows this isn't something that will just *be fine* one day. "I tried to convince him to take his medications the other day, but he didn't listen to me."

I nod helplessly. I'm just a kid. If none of the adults in my life can do something to fix this mess, what can I do?

I'm just a stupid kid.

Rayyan gets up. "I'm gonna run to the bathroom."

I hardly notice as he leaves the kitchen. I sit at the kitchen table, chewing a samosa. Trying not to throw up.

The anticipation is what hurts the most. Waiting for something to happen.

Waiting for the monster to come and eat me up.

"I have to take Rayyan to the doctor," Phupo tells me. "Will you be okay by yourself?"

I nod. I'm always okay by myself. It's my specialty. Alone but not lonely.

Well, okay, a little lonely. But nobody needs to know that.

"It's a nutritionist this time," she adds. "She's got some good food plans for Rayyan."

I know she's trying to distract me, but it's not going to

work. Like I said, I'm in waiting mode.

I wait until Rayyan and Phupo leave. Then I tiptoe up the stairs (tiptoeing is another one of my specialties) and go into my room.

I could lock myself in here, but Abbu may come looking for me. If the door's locked, he won't like that.

I grab my boxing gloves and head out to the backyard. Abbu's window is open, and I can hear him talking to someone on the phone. Shouting, actually. Saying he totally deserved some job he was kicked out of. Complaining that it was unfair, that he's gonna call the Department of Labor on them.

He won't, but the guy on the other end is worried. I can hear it through the speaker.

Abbu hangs up and calls someone else. It's an old coworker in New York. Abbu shouts about the job there, how he was kicked out, how he's going to talk to the news. He accuses this man of knowing about it. Of being a part of the conspiracy.

Cause, you know, there's always a conspiracy.

The coworker sounds tired, like he's heard all of it before.

Me too, dude. I've heard it all before too.

I'm exhausted.

"I'm going to seek revenge!" Abbu yells. "I have deep connections, you know. All the way to the secret service."

The man sounds downright weary now. "Yaar, I'm telling you the truth. I don't know anything about it."

"We'll see," Abbu says, grunting. He's finally losing steam. "I'll think of a way to test your truthfulness."

"You do that."

Finally Abbu falls silent. I box for another half an hour. The sun is setting, so I go inside, wash up, and pray Maghrib.

Yeah, I know. I don't do it often enough. But I'm praying in the Islamic center on Sundays now, and it's keeping me in the habit. When things are daunting, I feel the need to pray.

Even though God isn't listening.

Nobody is listening.

Maybe that's why I let go in prayer. Nobody can hear me lose control. Just give up all my fears and worries. Cry. Scream. Pray for miracles I don't believe in.

It's completely dark outside when I raise my head from prostration. My eyes feel swollen, and my face feels wet with tears.

My chest feels lighter than it has in months, though, so that's something.

I fold up the prayer mat and tiptoe into Abbu's room.

He's lying on his bed, arms spread wide. The phone is on the floor near the wall, broken in half. There's also other broken stuff. A coffee mug. A vase. Dishes. Did he eat in here last night?

I come closer.

Abbu's sleeping. His snores are loud, but my heart is thumping even louder in my chest.

I'm not sure what's going on. Is he drunk? Is he on something else? Is he just pretending, and will he spring up to grab me by the throat?

Like my nightmare.

I watch and wait. Ten minutes. Twenty.

When my legs get tired, I slide down the wall to the floor and close my eyes.

* * *

Once upon a time, there was a sparrow couple. The female sparrow was nice and friendly and hardworking. Let's call her Saadia. The male sparrow liked flying around and having fun. Let's call him Nasir.

The names are just random, by the way. I don't actually know any sparrows named Saadia and Nasir.

The sparrows fly around all morning, looking for food. Grain, worms, what have you. One day, Saadia brings home a few grains of rice. Nasir brings home some grains of moong daal. They realize that's a winning combination and cook some khichri. They're working well together, enjoying their moment.

Here's where it gets tricky. Once the food is cooked, Saadia goes out to get some water. Nasir decides he's too hungry to wait for her, and he gobbles up all the khichri. Then he covers his eyes with a strip of cloth and pretends to go to sleep.

When Saadia comes back with water, she finds the bowl of khichri empty and Nasir sleeping happily in the corner. She asks him, "Who ate up all the khichri?" even though she probably knows. Like, who else is there besides Nasir, with a full belly and a smirk?

But get this. Nasir replies, "The raja's dog ate it."

How random, huh? He probably thinks she'll never be able to prove him wrong.

But Saadia's determined to get to the bottom of this. She goes to the raja's court, and says, "O raja, your dog has eaten up my khichri. I demand justice."

The raja is shocked. His dog eats juicy steak, not poor man's rice with daal. He tells Saadia, "Prove what you say, so that justice can be done."

Nasir is still confident, thinking there's no way anyone can find out the truth of this matter. The raja, however, knows of a way. He leads them all—the dog included—to a well in the palace grounds. There he stretches a string of flimsy thread across the well's opening and says, "Each of you must swing from this string. The one who falls inside is the one who has eaten the khichri."

Is it just me, or does this sound unscientific? There are so many variables. Does the raja have a magical thread? Does a witch live at the bottom of the well, waiting to pull the culprit into her clutches? It's all very unclear.

Anyway, Saadia trusts the raja (she also trusts Nasir, so this doesn't say much about her). She grabs one end of the thread and starts swinging from it. She swings and swings until she's tired, but the thread doesn't break. Hooray!

Then it's Nasir's turn. No sooner does he grab the thread than it breaks, and he falls into the well.

Now, I'd say he's guilty, based on the raja's criteria. Also because we know he's actually guilty.

But Saadia and the raja have no clue. For all they know, the thread could've weakened because of all the swinging Saadia did.

The raja claps and shouts, "Justice has been done!" and the dog barks happily now that he's not under any suspicion. The two go on their merry way, totally done with this sparrow couple and their problems.

But Saadia, poor sparrow, quite likes Nasir. Sure, she's mad at him for eating the khichri all by himself, but she'd never wish he would fall into a well. That's just awful.

She starts to cry.

A cat passing by hears her and asks what's wrong.

Now you might be thinking, Why does a cat want to help a sparrow? Maybe she's a nice cat. Kind and helpful.

Or maybe she's trying to get close enough to eat Saadia.

In any case, when Saadia tells the whole story, the cat offers to jump into the well and get Nasir out. Not that he deserves it, but still.

Here's the kicker, though. The cat wants something in return.

"I'll make you rice pudding," Saadia promises. And in her heart, she knows she'll have to stand guard to make sure Nasir doesn't steal that too.

The cat loves rice pudding way more than scrawny sparrows, so she agrees. She jumps into the well and brings a wet, bedraggled Nasir out. He flies away, not even thanking her.

"Now make me the rice pudding," the cat says.

"It will take me some time," Saadia says. "Come back when you see smoke rising out of my chimney."

A few days later, Saadia makes a big fire in her house and heats an iron plate on it. When it's hot, she puts a covered dish next to it. She totally acts like there's rice pudding inside the dish.

When the cat sees smoke rising out of Saadia and Nasir's chimney, she's excited. She runs in, ready to eat. I'm guessing she's also excited to eat the two sparrows for dessert.

Saadia says, "Welcome! Welcome! How happy I am to see you, my friend!" She points to the hot plate. "Please sit here!"

Of course when the cat sits on the hot plate, her butt gets burned. She leaps up in the air and runs away yowling.

Saadia and Nasir have a good laugh and hope they never see the cat again.

* * *

Rayyan finds me in Abbu's room, half asleep. He looks at me, forehead tight. "Come on," he whispers.

I stand up and follow him back to our room. On his desk is a bag with Shake Shack's green logo. The aroma fills my nose, and I realize I'm starving.

Emotional upheaval will do that for you, I guess.

"I got you a shroom burger," Rayyan says. "And a milk-shake."

"And fries?" I ask, my voice cracking.

"Duh."

We sit on the floor again, just like last time, and eat. He

puts on music, and I recognize Nazia Hassan's "Disco Dee-wane."

I know what Rayyan's doing. He's trying to make me feel better.

I want to scoff and tell him everything's fine. I don't need pity. I don't need anything or anyone.

But it's not true.

I don't want to be alone anymore. I want someone to help me. Being bad is no fun anymore. I'm ready to try something else.

"So the nutritionist thinks I need to up my calorie intake by, like, two hundred percent," Rayyan tells me.

I look at him. Food in his mouth, fingers so thin the knuckles look translucent. "Oh yeah?"

He nods. "Lots of burgers and fries in our future, I guess."

I chuckle at his disappointed face. I've never met a kid who genuinely didn't like to eat. I wave a fry in his face. "Bring it on, brother."

*　*　*

The second bad thing that happens on Friday goes like this.

After Rayyan and I binge on Shake Shack, we watch the murder press conference video again. You know, the one that makes Rayyan crumple up inside his own body.

"Why do you even want to watch this?" I ask as he finds the link.

He doesn't answer.

I groan, but then sit down next to Rayyan and watch the

video. He's my cousin (and brother and friend). He deserves my support.

The video doesn't get better the fourth—fifth? Sixth? I've lost count—time around. It's still horrible. It's still infuriating. The police giving speeches from the lectern instead of going out to find the killer.

Yeah, that's making me see red all over again.

But it's not even the bad thing that happens. That comes later, when Rayyan's gone down to get a glass of water, and I decide to check Abbu's email again.

You know, just in case there's something I need to know.

And yup, there is. It's a new email from Mama. Subject line: "Saturday."

It's like a cold finger down my spine. I know something bad is coming before I click.

But stupid me, I click anyway.

Mumtaz, how are you? I wanted to let you know that I'm very busy this next week and won't be able to video chat. Please extend my apologies to Mo.

Please extend . . .

Please extend . . .

Apologies to Mo . . .

I keep reading the words over and over. I think I hyperventilate at some point. I can hear myself panting like a dog. Rayyan comes back and taps me on the shoulder. "Are you okay, Mo?" His voice is concerned. Worried.

But it's all fake. If my own mother isn't concerned about

me, why should anyone else be?

My blood is boiling. My heart is pounding.

My muscles are wound so tight it takes effort to move.

Slowly, I go back to the inbox and go through Mama's pre-vious emails. I find the Cypress address I need. "You want to help me, brother?" I croak.

"Anything."

I clench my jaw. "Then come with me tomorrow. I'm gonna visit Nathan Eckert."

21

Rayyan's the one who comes up with a plan.

Sort of.

"Mo and I want to hang out," he tells his mom at breakfast the next day. "Just the two of us."

Naila Phupo is cooking parathas at the stove. She turns sideways to give him a puzzled look. "Sara waqt to tum dono saath hotey ho." You two are together all the time.

This is true. So true.

"That's boring," Rayyan says. "School and home, all boring."

She smiles as she puts a steaming paratha on my plate. "So, what is not boring?"

This is exactly the segue Rayyan's looking for. "The science

226

museum!" he says loudly. "It's got a new human body exhibit, and that's exactly what we're studying in school, and it will be educational. . . ."

Naila Phupo holds up a flour-covered hand. "Acha acha, samajh gaeey." Okay, okay, I understand. "How will you get there? I'm not driving you; it's my one day off."

Only here's the thing with Naila Phupo. She's so nice, she will easily sacrifice her day off to drive us halfway across the city.

Which, you know, would be awesome on any other day.

Today, when we're not actually going to the science museum, it's a problem.

And yes, I realize we're lying. The whole plan is a dishonest, stupid mess. I'm aware.

Here's the other thing. When most adults in my life have let me down, kept secrets from me, and lied over and over, then I'm not going to keep to the straight and narrow either.

I'm gonna fight fire with fire.

Lying, cheating, stealing . . . it's all on the table.

(Well, maybe not stealing. I'm not a thief, usually.)

Oh, and beating up bullies if they cross me. That one's definitely on the table. Basically, Mrs. Whatsit would be shocked by how long my list of faults is at this point.

"No need to drive us on your day off, Phupo!" I say. "We'll go by ourselves." This is what Rayyan and I agreed on. He'd talk about the museum, and I'd talk, lie, whatever, about the transportation.

We knew Naila Phupo wouldn't let us go alone. So I had a plan. "We're taking the bus."

Naila Phupo looks horrified. Big eyes, pursed lips, the whole look. "Bus? No!" Then she thinks of her day off, probably, and dials it down. "Are you sure?"

"I used to go everywhere on the bus in New York," I say confidently. "The subway too."

And that, ladies and gentlemen, is no lie.

I start my laptop, which is lying on the table, cued up to the Houston Metro site. I turn it slightly toward her to show her the map. "There's a bus stop next to the park, on San Jacinto Street. The number sixty-five leaves every hour, so the next one will be at ten o'clock. It will take us directly to the museum district." I tap a finger on the screen. "The science museum is right there, in front of the bus station."

Naila Phupo inspects the map on the screen. "Hmm, you boys have really planned it out, eh?"

Rayyan nods eagerly. He knows he's got her. "Yes, Mama."

She turns to me, still hesitant. "Maybe we should ask Mumtaz first."

I shrug. "He won't care. Like I told you. I used to go all over the city with my friend Zed."

Rayyan jumps in. "And New York City is way more dangerous, Mama. Criminals on every corner."

Whoa. Let's not get carried away.

I give Rayyan a dirty look. He makes a "Sorry!" face. He knows not to mess with my beloved New York.

Naila Phupo sighs. "Acha theek hai. Chaley jao." Okay, it's fine. You can go.

She starts rolling dough into balls for more parathas. "But be back by afternoon. I'm making biryani."

Rayyan squeals.

I act a little less childish and just smile.

Nobody knows it's a fake smile, because inside I'm nervous as all heck.

* * *

We didn't lie one hundred percent. The bus stop is on San Jacinto. The number sixty-five does leave in an hour, and we're right on time to catch it. It takes us on the route we need, but we'll get off three stops before the museum district.

Sidebar: San Jacinto is the street with the gas station where Rayyan's abbu was killed. I'd totally forgotten that. Not the killing, but the street name.

Rayyan stares at the gas station the whole time we wait at the bus stop. No words. Blank face. Fists at his sides.

Well, actually, you can see the grief on his face if you look hard enough. I don't think anyone else would notice, but I'm not anyone.

I've got grief and anger on my own face too. I can recognize these things.

I stand real close to him, so our shoulders are touching. It's my way of showing support without getting all sappy.

It takes us forty-five minutes to get to Nathan Eckert's neighborhood, thanks to a bunch of stops on the way. The bus drops us off at a fancy collection of high-end shops called—you guessed it—the Collection. These aren't your average strip-mall shops, mind you. They're the ones you visit if you've got serious money. There's a boutique with a bored-looking mannequin in the window. She's wearing a white feather dress that looks very itchy.

There's also a home decor shop, and another boutique, this one for bored-looking kids. Oh, and a few restaurants with names in French.

Look, I try not to judge people based on looks. But the look of the Collection is making me judge Nathan Eckert quite a bit.

Rayyan tugs me toward the back of the shops. There's an entrance to the neighborhood with high arches and rose bushes. "What's the address?" he asks.

"Twenty-three Rosehill Court," I reply. What a bougie address, seriously.

We find the house three streets over. It's brown stucco with dark green shutters and a balcony on the second floor. A big front yard with a row of tall trees. There's a sleek black car in the driveway. "Is that a Lamborghini?" Rayyan whispers.

Yes. Yes, indeed it is.

I'm the one frozen now, staring at the house like it's alive. I tell myself that the man who lives here has no power over me. No matter how many Lamborghinis he owns.

I'm Mo Mirza, son of a monster.

"What if he's not here?" Rayyan suddenly says. "What if he's on vacation? Or out visiting friends?"

I scowl. "You couldn't have said this before?"

"I didn't think!"

I sigh. It doesn't really matter. I can come again, anytime. I think I just wanted to take this trip to become less freaked out about the whole I-have-an-uncle-right-here-in-my-city situation. Even if I don't meet him today, it will still mean I took a step.

One that I controlled. One that I decided on.

I ring the bell.

* * *

My uncle is, in fact, home. He opens the door and stares at us with blue eyes just like Mama's. His blond hair is also just like Mama's. "Can I help you?"

Rayyan nudges me.

"Ahem, I'm, er, Mo. Er, Mohammad," I stammer. "My mom's Becky. Your sister?" I say the last part like a question, because technically, I'm not sure if this is Nathan Eckert or some other dude who looks eerily like my mom.

But actually, I'm sure.

You know that feeling you get when you meet someone who's part of you? That sense of home? Belonging?

Yeah, that's how I know this is Mama's brother.

Nathan Mamoo.

He breaks out into the biggest smile I've ever seen. In this, at least, he's not like Mama. She never smiles this big. "Mo! Oh my god, I can't believe it! I asked Becky if I could see you, but I never thought your dad would agree."

I don't say anything. I don't think it's wise to admit Abbu has no clue where I am.

Nathan Mamoo opens the door wide, still smiling. "Come in, come in."

"Er, this is Rayyan, my cousin," I say as we're led down a hall to a sitting room. It's very fancy, with delicate wooden chairs and a glass coffee table, and silk curtains on the windows. And paintings. Lots of paintings.

"Nice to meet you, Rayyan. You must be Naila's son." He pronounces it Naa-ee-la like it's a delicate flower.

Rayyan nods. He's starstruck by the room, the house, the car. He's probably still thinking about the Collection.

"Sit, please!" Nathan Mamoo sinks down on a chair, and we follow. "Tell me everything! How are you? What are you doing here? When did your dad decide to let you come? I've been waiting ever since I found out you two were moving here."

I take deep breaths. Tell him everything? What does that even mean? How much does he know? Should I start from the year I was born? Or from our move to Houston . . . ?

I feel a touch on my hand. It's Rayyan's hand, gripping mine.

Giving comfort. Telling me he's here with me.

I'm not alone.

What finally comes out of my mouth is this: "Um, I didn't know you lived here. I don't know anything about you except your name."

Nathan Mamoo stops smiling. He blinks rapidly. His face, which is already pale, loses even more color.

And he looks hurt. Like, someone shoved a fist into his stomach hurt.

"She . . . Becky never talked about me?"

I shrug, bad-boy style. He's just reminded me that he's *her* brother. Therefore, not automatically my friend. "You know Mama," I say. "She only likes to talk about herself."

He slumps in his chair. "I'm sorry, Mo. I had no idea. We're not very close, just hellos and happy birthdays."

Same, dear uncle. Same.

We're silent for a while. I don't really know what to say.

Actually, there's a lot I could say, but I don't know how to form the words. Like, I needed you to be there for me, but you weren't. I needed you to help me. Maybe you could have made my mom see sense and convinced her not to leave.

Maybe my life would've been different if you'd been a part of it.

"Have you lived in Houston for long?" Rayyan asks. I think he got uncomfortable with the silence.

Nathan Mamoo nods. "All my adult life. Becky and I grew up in New Jersey. Then she went to New York for college, and I stayed behind. I moved to Texas when I got a job here about ten years ago."

"What kind of job?" Rayyan asks. He's always asking about college and work. A true nerd, my cousin is.

"I design IT systems for big companies."

"Cool," Rayyan says. "Isn't that cool, Mo?"

I scoff. Am I supposed to act like everything is normal? Like I didn't just devise an evil plan to secretly visit a relative who's never been a part of my life? "What's cool about IT?" I say. "In our family, you have to save kids in poor countries if you want to be anything special."

Rayyan gasps at my rudeness.

Nathan Mamoo barks in laughter. "You're funny, Mo! And absolutely right!"

"I don't joke," I say shortly. But inside, my heart is fluttering at his laughter. *He thinks I'm funny. He thinks I'm funny.*

* * *

Here's the story of why I never joke.

On my twelfth birthday, Mama took us to a work event. Abbu and I were dressed in our best clothes. Ya know, khaki trousers and white button-down shirts.

"You look like twins," Mama had cooed, amused.

Abbu just grunted.

I tried not to react. It was the worst insult you could give me, and I think she knew that.

It was an outdoor event, but fancy. No carnival-style games for these people. There was a buffet table laden with food. There was a stage for a band that hadn't arrived yet. Their drums and guitars were waiting for them.

And there were speeches. At least half of them were praising Mama in some way. Her amazing research. Her dedication. The water systems she'd designed.

234

Ha. Seriously, ha.

Abbu was jumpy and antsy throughout. At one point he pulled my hair and told me I looked terrible. I should have dressed better. Then he grabbed my plate and spilled food all over the ground. I'm pretty sure it was an accident, but still.

Everyone turned to stare at us.

Soon a man came to the stage and announced that the band would be late. "In the meantime, let's have some of our kiddos come up here," he said. "Maybe sing a song or tell a joke."

Abbu's face lightened up. Here was his chance to show his importance. He wasn't just the husband of the brilliant researcher. He was also a father. "You go up," he said to me. "Go up and tell one of your jokes."

"What jokes?"

Abbu ignored me. He raised his hand and waved it around. "Over here, my boy will tell a joke."

The man on the stage beamed. "Ah yes, Dr. Eckert's son, Mohammad. Come on up!"

Abbu beamed too.

Mama looked . . . blank. No expression. No hint of what she was feeling as I dragged myself up to the stage and stood there.

And stood there.

Everyone was staring at me. Half smiling, expecting the perfect funny joke to fall from my lips. Waiting to laugh.

"Young man, you want to begin?" The man grinned. "Any time now. Today."

The audience snickered. Abbu too.

I racked my brains. I knew lots of jokes—I was sure. Zed and I had borrowed a joke book from the public library just the other day.

But as I stood there in front of a bunch of rich, haughty people, my mind was completely, totally blank.

I stood there for the longest two minutes of my life. The man looked annoyed. "I can't remember," I finally choked out.

"Okay, then, off you go!" The man turned away. "Dr. Nanjiani, how about your daughter? I heard she's got a great voice."

I crept off the stage and went to Mama and Abbu.

He was still smiling, but his jaw was clenched, so I knew he was grinding his teeth really, really hard. "Never mind, these things happen," he said.

Mama just looked at me, her face still blank.

We left five minutes later, just as the band came onstage.

* * *

Rayyan and I stay at Nathan Mamoo's house for an hour.

He's got a wife called Tina and a three-year-old daughter named Olivia. They've gone to some Gymboree class (don't ask, I have no idea), but he shows us pictures on his phone. They're all the same. White skin, blue eyes. Blond hair.

All like Mama. Nothing like me.

When I see Olivia, I realize something. Mama has a girl to pass her grandmother's gold necklace to. It may not be a daughter, but a niece is close enough.

A niece without the schizophrenia genes.

Awesome.

Nathan Mamoo talks about his childhood in New Jersey. I nod and even smile a little, although every breath is fire inside my lungs. But I don't pretend too much. Just because I'm talking to this guy doesn't mean I'm his best friend.

He seems to get that. He talks with a humble look, serious and sad.

When we get up to leave, he grabs my arm. "Please come again," he begs. "I want you to meet Olivia. Get to know her."

"Sure," I mumble. I'm actually not sure, but whatever.

"What's your number?" he asks. "We can talk and message."

Rayyan snickers. I roll my eyes. "I don't have a phone."

Nathan Mamoo frowns, then reaches over into a side table and takes out a phone. "Here. I bought a new phone last month, so you can have this one. The service is still active."

My mouth drops open. It's not one of those cheap burner phones you get at gas stations. It's a nice one, sleek white with a gold stylus. "Th . . . thanks."

He texts me, so I have his number. "Call me anytime you need me."

I want to tell him I'll never need him. I don't need anyone. But something keeps me quiet. Maybe it's the phone in my hand, or the sadness in his eyes.

I want to hate him, but I don't.

I nod and we leave. When we reach the end of the street, Rayyan exclaims, "Dude! You got a phone!"

22

It's Thanksgiving week, and I am far from being thankful.
Here are all the reasons why.

* * *

Sunday
Islamic School is closed, because many people go out of town.
This means I don't get my weekly dose of laughing, talking
children who always take my mind off my issues.

It also means no secret painting.

That's when I realize I'm sort of obsessed.

I never thought oil paints would give me so much . . . actually I don't know the word. It's not comfort, or happiness. It's
more like . . . a cleansing.

I don't wanna sound gross, but it's like when you've got a stomach bug and your entire body is in pain, but then you vomit and feel so good. You're still sick, but for a few minutes after that vomit spews out, everything feels incredible. No stress. No pain. Just relaxation.

That's what oil painting does to me.

And today, I can't paint. I make do with reading my library book all day.

* * *

Monday

I miss Carmen's braid. I wonder what color ribbon she's wearing today. Or maybe she leaves her hair loose when she's at home. I jump from Carmen to music class in general. I start thinking about the song Mrs. Nguyen played in class. Quan Ho.

It was nice. Maybe I should find it online and listen to it. Maybe.

In the meantime, I find a classical song by Ravi Shankar. It makes me feel closer to Patel Uncle, I guess.

It also makes me realize, that now, with my new phone, I could call Patel Uncle. Like, actually talk to him on the phone.

Hearing his voice would be another form of cleansing. Like I could have a reset from the last few weeks.

That's another maybe. If I ever found his number.

Rayyan tells me it's time to work on our science fair project. "What kind of heart model should we make?" he asks from across the room.

He's sitting cross-legged on his bed, looking at me as if I've got all the answers.

"How should I know?"

He scowls. It looks weird on his face, because he doesn't do it often. "You *should* know. It was your suggestion. Let's make a model, you said. Something big that will take lots of time."

"Okay, first of all, I never said that last part," I protest, sitting up. "And secondly, why are you all . . . upset?"

It's true. Rayyan the Chill Dude is gone. Rayyan the Stressed-Out Guy has taken his place. "Wait, is this about NJHS?" I ask. "Are you worried about that again?"

"No!"

"Because the application isn't even due until February. You can relax. You'll have lots of volunteer hours by then."

Rayyan throws up his hands. "There are other things on the application, like grades. Which is why we need to do an amazing science project. It's twenty-five percent of our grade."

I shake my head. Fixing a quarter of a grade on one single assignment is a bit much. Still, this is Rayyan, and no matter how mad and sad and everything else I am, he's my responsibility. I promised I'd look after him.

I groan. "Okay, fine."

We check out some videos and science blogs. There are all sorts of models, using all kinds of materials. Rayyan wants to go shopping and buy everything. I insist we use what we find around the house.

We decide on a cool project created by some kids in Nepal. There are step-by-step directions, and it uses everyday items like balloons, PVC pipes, tape, and a stress ball. We take notes and plan a few things.

Finally I stand up and stretch. "Okay. Who wants some food?"

Rayyan doesn't look at me. He's still looking at the screen, but not like he's really seeing it.

I tap his head. "Hey, what's up?"

He shrugs without looking at me. "Nothing. Everything."

"NJHS would be stupid not to choose you," I tell him firmly.

"It's not that." His voice is thick and trembly. "It's . . . this week is my abbu's death anniversary."

I sink back down. "You mean, he was killed during Thanksgiving week?"

Rayyan nods.

Whoa. That's messed up. Here I am, thinking of my own problems, wondering what I have to be thankful for. And my cousin has an actual tragedy marking this holiday.

I decide I hate Thanksgiving.

It's one more thing on my list of things and people I hate. No biggie.

I watch as Rayyan starts that stupid press conference video again. "Nope!" I say, pushing the laptop away. "I forbid you to watch that!"

He pulls it back. "What's your problem?"

"I'm your protector, remember?" I say. "This is me protecting your, uh, mental health or whatever."

"But I watch that to remember him."

"Well, find a better way," I growl, and pick up the laptop so he can't reach it. "This isn't good for you, dude."

Rayyan's shoulders slump. He looks so lost. "Like what?"

"I dunno. Anything with good memories. Do you have pictures?"

He does. They're in the cloud. I give Rayyan his laptop back, and he shows me the pictures. Him as a kid, riding on his abbu's shoulders. Him older, at some amusement park, holding his abbu's hand. Him and both his parents, standing outside in front of the yellow door.

The whole family on Eid, dressed in nice clothes and big smiles.

I should be happy for him.

But there's a different kind of cloud on me. Something dark and heavy and made of tears.

* * *

Tuesday

Rayyan and I collect materials for the science project.

"We'll need to go to a dollar store for some of these items," I say, looking at our list.

"There's no dollar store close by," Rayyan replies. "But the gas station on San Jacinto has a big convenience store."

Nope, not happening. "I'll go by myself," I tell him sternly.

Yes sirree, I take my bodyguard duties very seriously.

I walk to the gas station, buy the things we need, and also buy a bunch of other things we don't need. Spicy jalapeño chips. Soda. Ice cream cups. Chewing gum.

Where do I get the money from? That's a story for another day. It involves Patel Uncle and his ridiculous system of paying for chores like organizing his books and making his chai and reading to him.

Basically, I've got a lot of allowance money saved up. It's in a secret place Abbu can never find.

My plan is to replace Rayyan's bad associations for this store with delicious ones. I could make it a weekly thing.

Smother him with snacks.

* * *

Wednesday

There's a big fight between Abbu and Naila Phupo.

I don't see it coming.

Recently, the siblings haven't been hanging out together as much. Some of it is because Naila Phupo is always at work. When she's not at work, she's cooking. Or cleaning.

Rayyan and I help, but she keeps saying things like "Studying hard is your only job!" and "You'll be too tired for school if you spend all your free time on chores."

Abbu, on the other hand, prefers to hide out in his room doing god knows what. Yelling on the phone. Job hunting (debatable). Drinking (nondebatable).

The last two are what the fight is about.

Rayyan and I sit on the stairs and listen. The adults are in the kitchen, just like a few weeks ago when Abbu was arguing about Area 51.

This time, there's no mention of the aliens.

Only of beer.

"Bhai! You know we are Muslim! How could you bring this into the house? What kind of example are you setting for the children?" Naila Phupo shouts. How her voice can be loud and heartbroken at the same time is beyond me.

Abbu goes into this long rant about Islam. How it's all fake. How religious fanatics have changed everything. How a little alcohol never hurt anyone. Blah blah.

Naila Baji gives out a screech at this. "A little? You're drunk! Drunk! Astaghfirullah!" God forgive you.

There begins Abbu's next rant. How he's forced to drink because of his troubles. What else is he gonna do, stuck at home with no wife, no job, an ungrateful son who's bound for juvie.

I grit my teeth. This last part is nothing new, but it still sends a zing to the middle of my chest.

Like my heart's—what did Pigao call it?—electrical impulses are wonky.

"Don't you dare say anything about that sweet boy!" Naila Phupo says. Sorry, she shouts. She's still shouting.

My cheerful, soft-spoken aunt is gone. In her place is a warrior, fighting the monster.

The monster isn't pleased. He yells and yells, then stomps out of the house with a loud "If I'm not welcome here, then I should just leave!"

Naila Phupo's response: "Take your beer with you!"

Incredible.

Once he's gone, I go into the kitchen and hug my aunt.

She's got tears running down her cheeks, but her face is fierce.

She hugs me back so tightly I can't breathe.

Which is the best kind of hug in the world.

*　　*　　*

Thursday

After breakfast, Naila Phupo tells me to go check on Abbu, make sure he's showered and dressed and everything.

I know what she really means. Make sure he's sober.

I grit my teeth and go into Abbu's room, but he's not there. Everything looks just the same as the day before. I realize that he never came home.

"Where do you think he went?" Rayyan asks, peeking from behind my shoulder.

I shrug.

"Today is Thanksgiving," Rayyan continues, like I need a reminder.

I say, "He'll be back."

We go to our room and work on the science project. It's coming along nicely, even though it looks strange with tubes extending from a cut-up stress ball.

The stress ball is supposed to be the heart, which is, well, appropriate.

I don't know how much more stress my actual heart can take.

It feels weak and trembly, like it will shatter any day now. Maybe I need to do some of those cardiovascular exercises we talked about with Pigao to make sure my heart stays strong.

Boxing, that's what I'll do.

I go to the backyard and do some heart-strengthening punches. I'm sweaty and tired by the end, and there are tears on my face.

Naila Phupo puts on some Urdu music in the kitchen while she cooks Thanksgiving dinner. It's lively, but I can tell by her pacing that she's not into it.

She calls Abbu's cell phone over and over, but it goes to voicemail each time. In the evening, we eat halal turkey and aaloo ka bhurta (mashed potatoes, desi style). Phupo puts her phone next to her on the table, and keeps looking at it. But Abbu doesn't call her back.

The turkey is delicious.

You know, I'm guessing. I can't really taste anything.

See, my emotions are all tangled up. I'm worried about Abbu, and I'm also annoyed that I'm worried about him. Why can't I just forget him? Why can't I feel happy that he's gone? Why am I wondering where he is, or what he's doing, or whether he's been hit by a bus or he's drunk out of his mind in a ditch somewhere?

That's not the only thought swirling in my mind either. I'm wondering if Mama is eating turkey. If they even celebrate Thanksgiving in Greece. Those refugee kids definitely have a lot to be grateful for, so maybe yes?

And so, all this *thinking* is making the turkey Naila Phupo cooked all day taste like sandpaper.

Ugh. Thanksgiving should be banned in the Mirza house. We have no use for it.

"Take some more bhurta." Phupo pushes the dish toward me. I scoop some onto my plate and stare at it miserably.

After my last mouthful of sandpaper turkey, my mood starts shifting from worry to anger. How dare he? After all his sister has done for him, how can he walk out and not even eat the meal she's cooked? What sort of brother is he?

Naila Phupo looks down at her plate. "We're Muslim. We don't drink," she finally says. "It's a sin."

I pat her hand. "Nobody's blaming you, Phupo."

She sniffs. "If something happens to him, I'll blame myself."

I can't stand her glassy eyes. Something *should* happen to him. Maybe then he'd learn his lesson. Start taking his meds and see a therapist and stop treating people so badly.

The rest of the meal passes in complete silence. "Let's share what we're grateful for," Rayyan finally says.

I stare at him like he's grown two heads.

Naila Phupo sighs. "You're right, beta. We have so much to be thankful for."

I can't help it. "Like what?" I ask in a grumbly voice.

She leans sideways and gives me a one-armed hug. "Well, I'm thankful for you, my dear nephew."

Rayyan nods quickly. "Yes, I'm thankful for you too. You're my brother, and you hang out with me, and you protect me from bullies."

I have to smirk at that. Rayyan does have a way with words.

"Bullies?" Naila Phupo gasps. "Has anyone been bothering you at school?"

"Don't worry," I reply. "I have it all under control."

Rayyan waves a fork at me. "Your turn. What are you grateful for?"

I look down at my plate. How do I answer this? Saying nothing will make them feel bad, because they both chose me as their reason.

Surely, there must be something I'm grateful for.

I close my eyes and think. Try to get out of the tangle of emotions suffocating me. I picture driving across highways and cities and towns, then coming to a weary-looking house with faded paint and a bright yellow door. "You and Phupo," I whisper. "I'm so glad I came to live with you."

Naila Phupo makes a soft sound, like a hum.

"Art class," I add. "Painting."

"Yeah," Rayyan says.

"My new phone." I open my eyes to see both of them smiling at me. They're little smiles, full of worry, but still.

And when I smile back, it's not fake at all.

23

Friday

Abbu still hasn't come back.

I try not to let it bother me.

I wake up way too early—thanks, nightmares!—and pace the hallway outside his room. Naila Phupo's door is half open, and I can hear the rustling of fabric inside.

I take a peek. She's an early riser, but it's not even dawn yet.

Phupo is praying, and that's when I realize it's Fajr time. That early morning prayer before the sun rises and the birds wake up. She's standing with her hands folded on her chest, head and shoulders covered in a brown shawl I've seen her wear countless times.

It's familiar.

The whole scene is familiar.

Her sobs aren't, though. She's obviously crying, low-pitched and heart-wrenching. I watch, transfixed, as she bows, then kneels and prostrates, and finally completes the prayers. I know what—who—she's praying for.

Her son.

Her brother.

Maybe even me.

When she finishes, she turns her head and sends me a watery smile. "Best start to the day, eh, beta?"

* * *

Mama emails again, saying she can't do a video call tomorrow. Something about one of the refugees getting a knife wound.

Okay, whatever. I'm over her. I'd been serious about what I'd said at the Thanksgiving table. I've got Naila Phupo and Rayyan; they're more than enough for me.

I'm mad at my mom, and that's okay too. I'm allowed to be mad.

Right?

Right.

Nathan Mamoo calls to say happy Thanksgiving. "I'd invite you to our house, but we're in California to spend the holiday with Tina's parents," he says apologetically.

"That's okay."

"Maybe we can meet next week?"

My heart jerks in my chest. "Maybe."

"So how was your Thanksgiving?" he asks. "Do anything fun?"

I feel my eyes burn. What would he say if I told him how not fun my week has been? Would he be concerned? Or would he act like his sister?

I clear my throat. "Um, why don't you and Mama talk?" I ask in a rush. "Like, how come I'd never heard from you all my life?"

He sighs so loudly, it's like a gust of wind in my ear. "Your mother . . . my sister . . . is a difficult person to get along with."

I scoff, but it's watery and sniffly. "Yeah."

"We had an argument a while back, when we were younger, and then never really got close again." He pauses. "I . . . I wish I'd apologized. So many years passed, and neither of us made an effort."

"Do you . . ." I swallow. "Do you want to make an effort now? With me?"

I can hear his smile across all the miles. "Yes, definitely. I don't care what Becky says. I want to get to know my nephew. Forgiveness is easy with family, or at least it should be."

* * *

Once upon a time, there was a king. He had three beautiful daughters. Let's call them Princess A, Princess B, and Princess C.

What? I'm not in the right frame of mind to think of three girl names that befit royalty.

Anyway, the king loved his daughters very, very much.

Although, pardon me if the idea of a parent loving his kids

unconditionally is a bit of a tough swallow for me right now.

Turns out, it wasn't unconditional love. The king had a mean streak. Or maybe he wasn't completely sure of their love. He decided to test them.

If you're wondering, who does that? Let me tell you, lots of parents test their kids in different ways. Sometimes the tests are so difficult the kids fail.

So the king calls the three princesses to the throne room to ask them a question. "How much do you love your father?"

What a question, right?

Anyway, the girls aren't fazed. Maybe they're used to their father saying such things.

Princess A replies, "Father, I love you more than all the diamonds and rubies of this world."

The king smiles proudly. It's a good answer. There are lots of diamonds and rubies in the world, and they're very expensive.

Then it's Princess B's turn. She says, "Dear father, I love you more than all the precious gold and silver in the world."

Okay, so she copied her sister's answer. But that's okay, it's still a good answer. And the king is happy, which is all that matters.

Now it's the youngest daughter's turn, and let me tell you, she's always been a little different. Maybe she's the reason the king thought of this test in the first place.

Princess C says, "Dear father, I love you as much as all the salt in the world and more."

Obviously, this is a strange answer, when the other girls talked about diamonds and rubies and gold. It's downright insulting. The king is furious. He doesn't think salt has any value, not when compared to jewels. "Your sisters love me as much as diamonds and gold, but your love is like salt!" he shouts.

Princess C tries to explain, but the king is not listening. He banishes the poor girl from the kingdom.

Yeah, some parents are evil, what can you do?

Princess C hides in the woods for a while. She's tired and hungry and scared. She doesn't know what to do.

Just then, a handsome prince from a neighboring kingdom passes by. And yes, lots of folktales have handsome princes, duh. He meets Princess C and instantly falls for her. Maybe there's a song and dance here, like in those Bollywood movies. By the end of it, he's decided he wants to marry her.

Princess C doesn't mind. What else is a banished princess to do? It's not like girls in those days could become water experts and save people's lives or anything. She agrees to the marriage, but she has a condition. She won't marry him until her father comes to see her. I guess she still misses him.

Or maybe she just wants everything to be back to normal, even if he's a dad who takes her love for granted.

The prince agrees. He takes her back to his palace and arranges for a feast. Then he invites the king from next door. Princess C orders the cooks to make the most delicious foods. But there's to be no salt in any of them.

The king arrives, not knowing that his daughter is in the palace somewhere. He thinks this is a state meeting or an interkingdom summit or something. He's welcomed into the dining hall by the prince, and all those delicious foods are brought out. The king takes a bite of one dish, but it's awful.

He tries another dish, but it's the same. Terrible.

It goes from bad to worse, and finally he spits on the floor. "These dishes are so bland!" he shouts. "Where is the salt?"

That's when Princess C flounces into the room with a salt-shaker and a smile. She doesn't even have to say anything. She's taught her lesson with a bunch of bland, tasteless dishes.

There's no flavor without salt. Basically, it's an essential ingredient.

The king realizes his mistake. And he probably misses his daughter. He hugs her and begs her forgiveness.

Princess C forgives him, and they all live happily ever after.

Well, the prince and princess do.

The king goes back to his kingdom, to his other two daughters. He's probably thankful his bad temper and rash decision didn't have a bad result after all.

24

"Who wants to go for Jummah prayers?"

Naila Phupo peers into our room, where Rayyan and I are working on the science project. Yet again.

Look, I think it's finished. Rayyan thinks there's more to be done, like painting the stress ball red, and writing the labels in calligraphy.

I really doubt that's going to make a difference, academically speaking.

He obviously doesn't agree.

Phupo wags her eyebrows. "Chalo na!" Please let's go.

Here's what I've learned about my aunt and her relationship to God. It's everything. Literally her whole world revolves around this unshakable trust in God. Allah ki marzi. What

255

God wills. She cries while she prays, then smiles through her tears and makes a joke.

It's weird, because how on earth is Abbu her brother? The guy who sneers at believers and thinks religion is a conspiracy or something.

Just to be clear, I like Naila Phupo's attitude way better. I jump up. "Great idea. Let's go!"

I may not be a huge religion nut, but Friday prayer at the mosque sounds perfect right now. It's what my fractured soul needs.

We can't just get up and leave, though. Prepping for Jummah is a whole thing. Shower. Wear nice clothes. Perfume or cologne if you're into that sort of stuff. There's no time for lunch, so Naila Phupo promises we'll eat something on the way back.

I take my wallet. If we're eating out, I'm treating.

The Islamic center parking lot is full. Everyone is home for the holidays, I guess. There are still a few minutes before the adhan, and people are hanging out on the grass. Imam Shamsi sees me and Rayyan and strides over with arms wide open. "Ah, my precious volunteers!"

Rayyan ducks his head. "Salaam alaikum, Imam."

I murmur the same.

"Walaikum assalam!" the Imam replies. "Your art students have given me the best feedback."

"Oh yeah?" I say. I can picture Pigtail Girl talking his ear off.

He nods. "They think you're the best artists they've ever seen. Subhanallah."

I think about my oil paintings, hidden in the storage container in the art room. What would he say if he knew about them?

"We're just hanging out having fun with the kids," Rayyan says. "Thank you for giving us the opportunity."

Imam Shamsi gives us a stern look. "When you do something for the masjid, it should be to gain Allah's pleasure. Not for any other reason."

Rayyan, whose sole reason for teaching art is the NJHS application, nods enthusiastically. "You're absolutely right, Imam sahib."

I look at the ground. Most days, God and His pleasure are far removed from my mind. It's like I'm battling a bunch of demons, and God is standing there watching me, doing nothing.

Okay, rationally, I know that's not true. I'm a Muslim. I know what God's power is, even if I don't feel it in my everyday life. As Zed would say, that's a you problem.

As in, not feeling the presence of God is *my* problem. I'm the only one who can fix it.

It's just . . . I don't know how.

The loudspeakers outside the building crackle, and then the adhan sounds. Deep, melodious, spine-tingling.

It's the same call to prayer I've heard countless times, but today, my arms get goose bumps. Rayyan heads inside. So does everyone else.

Me? I'm rooted to the spot, wondering what I'm doing here.

"Everything all right, son?" I look up to see Imam Shamsi

still standing in front of me.

My eyes burn, and I blink. "Y-yes, everything's fine."

He obviously doesn't believe me. "The sermon today is about courage in the face of adversity."

Well, that's appropriate. Here's a person who needs some courage in the face of pretty adverse circumstances.

Me, I'm that person.

"I'll be listening," I say weakly.

* * *

Remember the wise man Watayo Fakir?

Once upon a time, on a very cold winter night, Watayo's mother says to him, "Oh, Watayo! You're so close to God, aren't you?"

Watayo's a humble man, so he doesn't really accept how close he is to God. It's the way of good people; they always think they're not good enough or something.

So he doesn't say anything to his mother. Just listens.

Watayo's mother continues. "Oh, it is so cold tonight! If you're so close to God, why don't you do something about this horrible cold?"

Watayo is bewildered. "What am I supposed to do?" he asks.

His mother thinks. "Why don't you ask God to give us a bit of fire from hellfire? It will most definitely keep us warm in this atrocious weather."

Now Watayo is a good son. He's respectful and courteous, so he can't really tell his mother what a stupid idea this is. And not really possible, since hellfire isn't real.

It's more metaphorical, or otherworldly, or whatever. Different people have different opinions.

So what does Watayo do? He calmly tells his mother, "Amma, dearest, I already talked to the angels about it."

"And what did they say?" the mother asks eagerly.

"They said there's no fire in hell," Watayo explains. "Everyone has to bring their own."

* * *

Imam Shamsi's sermon about adversity is pretty good. He talks about the Prophet Muhammad going through some awful situations.

Here's a synopsis.

In the early years of Islam, the enemies of the Prophet boycotted him and his tribe. No trade. No food. No homes. The Prophet and his family were driven out of Mecca and had to live for three years in a shabby place on the outskirts of the city. Nobody outside the tribe was allowed to associate with them.

They had to survive with very little, obviously. Poverty became the norm. When they ran out of food, they ate leaves.

Leaves. I kid you not.

The imam gives other examples too. I sort of become fixated with the leaves issue, so I don't listen to the rest of it really well.

As a kid who loves burgers and fries and pizza and so much more, it hurts me to hear of someone eating leaves to survive.

And when that someone is from my prophet's family? Like I said earlier, I may not be a religion nut, but some things make you *feel*.

Imam Shamsi wraps up his sermon. He looks straight at me and says, "Sometimes we feel weak and helpless. Like we can't do anything, can't change anything. But please remember, my friends, that the strongest heart is the one that keeps beating. Keeps going on, day after day, hoping for a better tomorrow."

Imam Shamsi starts the Jummah prayer, and we all follow. I breathe deeply as I listen to his voice, standing in a row shoulder to shoulder.

Quiet.

Reflective.

I think of everything that's happened since I moved to Houston. The ways I've been angry and desperate. Also the ways I've been happy.

The happy parts aren't many, but I'm holding on to them fiercely.

The angry and desperate parts? They're the ones that burn inside me like the fire in Watayo's story. It's the emotion that swirls like darkness in my brain.

And like Watayo said, it's the fire inside us that makes our own personal hell.

The imam leads us into prostration. I pray with all my might. I pray for Mama to come home. To put me first for once in her life.

I even pray for Abbu to come home, because his absence is

messing with my mind.

I pray for Rayyan to get healthy. To forget his father's death and focus on his life instead.

I pray for my heart to be strong. The strongest heart, still beating. Still hopeful.

I pray and I pray and I pray.

When we finish, the prayer mat is wet with my tears.

*   *   *

After Jummah, Naila Phupo says she's got to clean out a file cabinet in her office. "Just give me thirty minutes, okay?" she says.

I nod. I'm so angsty after that prayer session, I need some alone time.

Rayyan looks at me with a frown. He was right next to me on the prayer mat, so he probably knows about my sobbing.

Okay, I wasn't sobbing, but still. The tears are embarrassing.

"I'll help you, Mama," Rayyan finally says.

We agree to meet back in the parking lot in half an hour. I practically run to the art room, hoping it's open.

It is. Fist pump!

I close the door and head to the storage container. My hands are trembling with a . . . how do I say it? A craving to eject all my despairing thoughts onto the canvas. Just get them out of me, somehow.

Quickly I set everything on the art table. The paintbrushes fall on the floor, and I grab them. Tell myself to be quiet or someone will come to investigate. Tell myself to calm down, it's only art.

Finally I'm ready. I take some dark brown oil paint and slash it across the canvas. No plan, no outline. No idea what I'm painting or what's it gonna look like when I'm done.

I paint.

And paint.

Or whatever this frenzied activity is. Throwing paint down, jabbing brushes into the canvas. Splattering. Eviscerating.

Everything out in the open. Abbu's drinking. His disappearing. Mama's . . . I dunno, researching. Giving water to kids across the world when her own offspring is thirsty for her affection.

Rayyan's lost face as he describes his father's murder. God, I can't even imagine. Going out for gas and getting gunned down because you're in the wrong place at the wrong time.

What is this life?

When I'm finished, I'm breathing hard, and my eyes are wet. Again.

I blink about fifty times and breathe in and out slowly, carefully. Patel Uncle taught me breathing exercises called pranayama. They come straight from some ancient Hindu text or something. He used to do them with me whenever I'd get upset.

Which, honestly, was a lot.

Listen, that was before I got tough. Before I stopped hurting and started hating. Before I hardened my heart into a stone that only pretended to beat.

Because guess what? If you can't feel, you can't get hurt.

And I'm done being hurt.

*　*　*

Naila Phupo takes us to a halal Mexican restaurant. "They make tortillas just like my roti," she says happily.

We talk about silly things that don't matter. Pigao's lab coats. Classical music. When we'll play Clue again. TV shows we like. TV shows we can't stand.

We don't talk about the things that matter. Where my father might be. When Mama might come home.

Rayyan's fixation with the press conference video.

Frankie. Ugh, stupid Frankie, the thorn in my side at school.

It's all good, to be honest. I'm fine pretending everything is okay for a little while.

Today's painting sesh took a lot out of me.

Which is, ya know, A-okay.

We hang out at the restaurant for a long time. When I say I'm going to pay for our meal, Naila Phupo surprises me. Instead of saying no, she beams. "That's my good son!"

My eyes burn again, and I practically run to the cashier to pay.

Seriously, what is up with all this emotional nonsense? I just want this day to be over before my bad-boy rep is shot for good.

When we leave, it's almost sunset. Rayyan climbs into the

passenger seat and looks back at me. "What's that?" He points to the cardboard box I hauled out from the Islamic center.

It's supplies from the storage container. Canvas. Oil paints. My four paintings. The one I did this afternoon is still wet, but I put it carefully on the top.

It doesn't matter if it gets smeared. It's not pretty or anything.

And no, I didn't steal this stuff. I went by Imam Shamsi's office and asked him if I could take a few things home. I told him it was for practice.

In reality, I'm worried someone will think my canvases are trash and throw them out. That one day, I'll come to class and find everything gone.

Or worse, I'm worried that someone *will* see the paintings. Like, really look at them, and wonder what kind of person paints such a horror show.

Me. I'm the horror show. The canvases are just a reflection of the inner me.

It's better to get rid of the evidence.

"Well?" Rayyan asks, raising his brows.

"Nothing," I mutter.

Obviously, he knows that a box of *something* isn't nothing. But he sits back and doesn't say anything else.

Naila Phupo starts driving. "I think we should eat some ice cream when we get home," she says. "It will be the perfect end to a perfect day."

25

Abbu slinks home on Sunday morning.

We're eating breakfast when he appears at the table, looking like something the cat dragged in.

Dirty clothes.

Swollen, red eyes and stubbly chin.

Ruffled hair. And is there a bald patch on one side? It looks like he grabbed a handful and pulled it out.

Naila Phupo pushes back her chair when she sees him. "What happened to you, bhai?" she gasps. "Where have you been?"

He mutters something and sits down. He's not making eye contact with anyone, which is weird. He always looks at people straight on, like they are nothing, and he is everything.

Today, he doesn't look like everything.

He looks small and—how is this possible?—scared. He keeps muttering, looking around and shaking his head.

At one point he waves his hand around like there are bees in his ear.

I stare. I've seen him act like this before, but it's been a while. Is he having another episode? The bad one with hallucinations?

Is that why he disappeared?

Or is that why he's back?

Naila Phupo stands up, then sits back down. "You don't know how worried I've been!" she almost shrieks. "I called the police and all the hospitals! I went around to the nearby shelters, asking if they'd seen you. . . ."

Wait, she did all that? I had no idea.

I imagine her driving around the city, searching for my father. And here he is, pulling dishes of food toward him like he doesn't care.

I forget his strange behavior. I forget everything except how he's not even looking at us. At her.

This man doesn't deserve her.

He doesn't deserve me either. To think I was praying for him just two days ago.

All my anger and fear and worry explode as I look at the monster sitting across the table. I take in my aunt's tearful face. She's slumped back now, twisting her hands together.

"It's okay, Phupo," I say harshly. "It's not the first time he's done something like this."

Everyone looks at me. Even Abbu looks up.

His face is blank, like he's frozen. His eyes are cold like ice. I wonder what's going on inside his body, you know, anatomically. Are his bones aching? Is his blood sluggish? Is his heart pumping *dum-dum-dum*? Or is he, like I suspect, nothing but cold, hard stone?

"Mohammad!" Abbu warns. His tone is gritty, like he's got gravel stuck in his throat.

I stand up. "What? You think you can just disappear for days without letting anyone know where you are, and then come back to eat breakfast with us?"

"Mohammad!" he thunders.

Ah, now his eyes aren't ice. Now they look like they're on fire.

Perfect. I feel like *my* entire being is on fire.

"Mo, calm down," Rayyan whispers. "We shouldn't be fighting right now. Your dad doesn't look well."

I can't bring myself to care. Not about anything.

Because guess what? Nobody cares about me. And it's time I return the favor.

I back away from the table on unsteady feet. Abbu returns to staring at his plate and shaking his head at something only he can hear or see.

"Mo, please!" Naila Phupo calls pleadingly.

"I'm sorry," I tell her, because I know my manners are atrocious. But like I said, there's a fire inside me, and I don't care about anything or anyone right now.

When I reach my room, I realize I'm trembling.

With rage.

I'm trembling with rage.

For the first time, I feel like Abbu. Not the scared man at the table, but the one who shouts and threatens and throws things around. The aggressive, destructive one.

* * *

With frenzied movements, I open the box I brought home from the Islamic center. Paints and canvases spill out on the floor.

I ignore the mess. Grab a blank canvas and black paint.

Black like the monster's soul.

I don't bother with a brush. I just squeeze the paint on my fingers and slap it onto the canvas.

One slap. Two slaps.

I strike the canvas with my hand over and over. Black splatters everywhere, like an explosion of ugly thoughts and feelings and actions.

Tears are streaming down my face, but I don't even care.

"What are you doing?" That gritty voice startles me so much I whirl around. Paint spots appear on Abbu's face and chest.

"What do you want?" I ask shakily. Like, seriously, I'd like to know what he wants from me.

He's wiping at his face, but his eyes are fixed on the snarl of paints and brushes and canvases on the floor. "Art?" he shouts. "My good-for-nothing son is painting like a common laborer?

How long has this been going on?"

I try pranayama, but I already know that breathing exercises aren't going to help me.

You can't bring a paintbrush to a fight. You need to use your fists.

"There's nothing wrong with art!" I shout back. "It . . . it helps me. It makes me feel better."

Abbu comes closer and looks at the paintings I've done at Sunday school. He sneers at them.

Literally sneers.

"This ugly mess? This helps you?"

I take a deep, sobbing breath. "Yes," I whisper.

He comes closer. Leans right into my face. "This ugly mess helps you?"

Enough.

I've had enough.

I open my mouth and become the monster. "Yes!" I scream. "This ugly mess is me! It's me! It's my heart, it's what I feel, what I am!"

Abbu shakes his head and waves his hand around. He looks sideways and hisses, "Shut up! Shut up!"

I know—I know—that he's not talking to me. It's his hallucination, whatever it is.

But like I said, I've. Had. Enough.

"You shut up!" I yell at the top of my voice. "You're a horrible father. A . . . a tyrant! I hate you. I really, really hate you."

And then, ladies and gentlemen, I run out.

*　*　*

Once upon a time, there was a tyrant king named Shri Badat. He was a total baddie. He ruled over the area of Gilgit with an iron fist.

He was known for a lot of horrible things. Murder. War. You name it. But the worst of Shri Badat's cruel habits was cannibalism. His nickname was Adam Khor, which means someone who eats human beings.

Like I said, he was a horrible dude.

The story of how he got into eating people is really gross, so I won't mention it here. Just know that at some point in his life, he decided he was going to eat a person a day.

Not just any person, but a child. A baby. Cooked in his kitchens and served to him on a platter.

Yup, he was a monster.

The citizens of Gilgit loathed Shri Badat. They wanted to get rid of him, but they also feared him. They suspected he wasn't human himself, but a demon.

You see, Shri Badat had mysterious magical powers. Nobody knew where they came from, only that they made him strong and cruel and able to do whatever he wanted. Including cannibalism, apparently.

So the people of Gilgit complained about him and his awful eating habits, but didn't really do anything. They wanted to revolt, but they didn't have any power. Or money.

Shri Badat kept them poor and weak. He wasn't only cruel, you see. He was smart as well.

One day, though, the citizens' luck changes. A prince named Azur Jamshed wanders into their kingdom with his entourage. Some say he's fairy born, others say he's human. Who knows?

Doesn't really matter. All that matters is that he's handsome, because guess who falls in love with him? Shri Badat's daughter, Noor Bakht. She's willing to go against her father's wishes to be with this dude. When the people of Gilgit see this, they realize something important: if Noor Bakht is rebelling against her dad to be with this human outsider, then maybe she'd rebel in other ways too.

Like, getting rid of him, perhaps? Killing him? Sending him away? Whatever can be done to make him stop eating their children.

So they make a delegation and go to Noor Bakht and Azur Jamshed to ask for help in defeating the demon king.

Noor Bakht isn't stupid. She's Shri Badat's daughter after all. She knows better than anyone how powerful her father is. Nobody's been able to defeat him before. Why would she and her husband be any different?

Noor Bakht and Azur Jamshed realize they need inside information. Some weakness of the king's that they can use. They hatch a plan. Noor Bakht goes to her dad, acting all freaked out. She's crying and looking scared, saying that she's worried for his safety because the citizens of Gilgit are out to kill him.

Shri Badat starts laughing. "Oh no, daughter. Don't worry.

Nobody can kill me. My body is immune to bullet, arrow, or sword."

Noor Bakht is horrified. If he can't be killed, all their plans will backfire.

The king continues. "Only fire can kill me. So it has been told by fortune tellers."

Noor Bakht comes back to the delegation and tells this huge secret. Now they have a plan that could actually work! They bring all the menfolk of the kingdom together, weapons and horses and everything, and surround the palace.

With shouts and screams, they attack.

And best of all, the attacking army has burning torches. They light fires around the palace. Huge, hot fires.

Shri Badat can't tolerate it. Weak, exhausted, and scared, he climbs onto his horse and rides away as fast as he can.

The people of Gilgit celebrate for days. They crown Azur Jamshed the new king and Noor Bakht their new queen.

*   *   *

I leave Naila Phupo's house and walk on the streets the whole day.

Listen, I realize I'm doing the same thing Abbu did, disappearing without a word. I want to feel guilty, but I just can't make myself. I've left without telling anyone. Without thinking that someone will be worried about me. Scared for me.

Whatever. Right now, my heart is barely even beating. What would Imam Shamsi think about that? I don't feel strong. I feel like the weakest of the weak. The way Gilgit's citizens probably felt when faced with Shri Badat's cruelty and power.

I stay away until the evening. Just walking around the neighborhood. A couple of times I find myself standing in front of the gas station on San Jacinto. I wanna know . . . am I better off than my cousin, who doesn't have a dad at all?

Sometimes the answer is easy.

Sometimes the answer is hard.

When I get home, Naila Phupo is sitting in the living room. She sighs deeply when she sees me come in, like she was waiting for so long.

Like she'd been worried.

"Tum theek ho?" Are you okay?

I shrug. Like I said, sometimes the answer is hard.

"I know you are angry, beta," she continues. "But don't hate your father. Please."

I blink. Who else am I supposed to hate?

I mean, yes, there's my mother. But at least she's gone away and not come back. She's not here today, gone tomorrow, leaving me wondering, calling my art ugly. At least she's doing something with her life, not sitting at home drinking beer and yelling at people on the phone.

Who else is so hate-worthy?

"Mo?" Phupo says softly. "Are you listening?"

I close my eyes and lean against the door. I never thought Naila Phupo would be the one to torment me. "I have to hate him," I finally say. "There's no one else."

"It's not his fault," she replies. "He's sick. He's not in control of himself."

I shake my head over and over. No. I refuse to believe that the man who's in control of me isn't in control of himself.

That makes no sense.

"Sure," I mutter finally. There's no way I'm gonna argue with my angel of an aunt.

She sighs heavily again. "Acha choro. Kuch kha lo." Okay, leave it. Eat something.

"I'm not hungry."

I go to my room and crawl into bed. Rayyan is sitting at his desk, working on something. Homework, maybe? I don't ask.

"You okay?" he asks, like always.

I grunt.

Look, I'm sorry, but it's been quite a day.

Quite a week. It's the last day of this horrible Thanksgiving break, and I suddenly cannot think of a single thing to be grateful for. To be happy for.

Life is too much, sometimes.

After a while, the light switches off, and I hear rustling as Rayyan gets into his bed. "You'll feel better when you go to school tomorrow," he says.

This time I don't even grunt.

26

"Wake up, you're going to be late for school!"

I'm buried under my blanket on Monday morning. The next thing I know, a pillow lands on my head. Stupid Rayyan.

Stupid room I have to share with someone who is always excited about education and learning and all that.

"Leave me alone," I groan. "I'm not going to school."

"What, like ever?" Rayyan asks in a squeaky voice.

I close my eyes. "I wish."

He stands next to my bed for a few minutes. I know, because I can hear him breathing. (Rayyan is a mouth breather. How did I never notice that before?)

Finally, finally, he leaves and I relax. Now I can go back to sleep and forget that yesterday ever happened.

The next thing I know, my bed moves and settles, and a cool, gentle hand strokes my head. That's definitely Naila Phupo.

"Mo beta, what's the matter? Why aren't you getting up?"

I don't turn around. I can't face anyone right now. I've still got so much pent-up frustration and sadness and anger whirling inside me.

If I keep my face buried in my pillow and my eyes tightly shut, none of that can escape. I don't need any more outbursts. I'm tired.

Exhausted, I tell you.

"Mo?" Naila Phupo asks again. She sounds really worried.

"I don't want to go to school today," I mumble. "Can I stay home, please?"

I mean, it's not a real question. She's not my parent. I don't need her permission. Still, she's the only adult I feel any respect for, so I guess it makes sense.

She hums. "Acha, theek hai." Okay, it's fine.

"But . . . ," Rayyan begins.

The bed shifts as Naila Phupo stands up. "Let's leave him alone, Rayyan. He's not feeling well."

Rayyan waits until the door closes, and then comes close enough to hiss in my ear. "It's Monday. You're gonna miss music class. You'll miss seeing your beloved Carmen."

"I don't care," I say fiercely, turning around. "I don't care about anything right now."

His face softens as he looks at me. "I know what you're

going through, you know. I was a total mess after my abbu died."

"I'm not a mess," I protest, but it's weak. I know I am. A complete and total mess. A jumble of tangled feelings and weakened spirits.

I wonder if Abbu feels the same way.

Then I tell myself to stop thinking about him. He's horrible, mean, cruel, et cetera et cetera. If he could get some human babies, he'd gobble them up, like that Shri Badat dude.

Rayyan shakes his head and picks up his backpack. "I'll see you later. Get some rest."

I put my head back under the covers and close my eyes.

*　*　*

An hour later, Naila Phupo brings paratha and eggs to my room. "Kuch kha lo, beta." Eat something, son.

How can I tell her this simple act makes me furious all over again? I've never had anyone bring me food, even last year when I had the flu and was puking every two hours.

I don't move, so she leaves it on the desk I share with Rayyan.

I only move when I'm sure the food is cold and unappetizing. That's my punishment for being a bad boy.

The worst boy.

*　*　*

For lunch, Naila Phupo delivers chicken soup and homemade garlic bread to my room.

I'm still under the covers.

I don't want to move.

I should feel bad for making my aunt come up and down the stairs with trays. For worrying about me.

She's got enough on her plate, worrying about Abbu.

God knows what he's been up to since his outburst yesterday. How's he feeling? Is he also in bed like me? Is he still waving his hands and talking to invisible people?

Ugh, why do I keep thinking about him? It's obvious that he never thinks about me. Plus, I told him I hated him yesterday. That pretty much destroyed all lines of communication between us.

Right?

I grab the garlic bread and chomp on it. There's no use crying over spilled milk, as that folktale says. What's done is done.

And that's why I'm a total mess. I can't even decide whether I'm happy or sad that I said what I said to him. On one side, I feel relief. He finally knows.

On the other side, I want to box my own face. What kind of son says that to his father?

The worst kind.

* * *

At two o'clock, I drag myself to the bathroom and wash my face. Brush my teeth (thanks, garlic bread).

Then I change my mind and do the full ablutions. Hands, mouth, nose, face, arms, head, neck, ears, feet.

It's refreshing. Comforting.

Then I go pray my Zuhr prayers.

Let's not mention the crying. I am so sick of crying.

* * *

Rayyan comes back in the afternoon.

Well, he stomps up the stairs and pushes open the bedroom door so hard, it crashes into the wall.

I'm back in my bed, huddled under the covers, trying to sleep.

"I hope you're happy!" he says harshly.

I don't move. Happy? What makes him think that emotion has ever really touched my life?

Listen, if I'm sounding miserable and pathetic right now, that's because I am. Nobody gets to judge me until they've walked in my shoes.

Rayyan, though. He's in a very judgy mood today. "It must be nice, sleeping in bed all day. No school. No worries. NO BULLIES!"

The way he shouts the last part makes me open my eyes. It seems personal. What . . . who . . . is he talking about? "Frankie and his goon?" I mumble.

Rayyan throws his backpack onto the floor with great force. "Frankie and his goon!"

I pull myself out of the depths of despair. Or, ya know, the bedcovers. "What happened?"

Wait.

Wait just a second.

Rayyan looks awful. The split lip and bruised knuckles say

it all. "Oh my god, you got into a fight?" I scramble out of bed and toward him. This is one way to get all the sadness out and my heart pumping again, I suppose.

Rayyan tells me the whole story. Like, play-by-play.

The day was going well, but he was nervous. He was used to me by his side. His protector, his friend.

His brother.

(I already know this is going to be my fault. You know, based on the looks he's giving me, but also based on the way he starts out by listing all those things about me. Like he's listing betrayals to come.)

Everyone was talking about their Thanksgiving week. What they did, who they saw. What they ate. Rayyan kept quiet, because our Thanksgiving week was straight out of a horror show.

Again, my fault. I get it.

At lunchtime, Frankie sat next to him. "Where's that loser cousin of yours?" he asked.

Me, a loser? Stahp.

Rayyan tried to ignore him. When that didn't work, he lied. Said I was finishing up an assignment and would be there soon.

Rayyan lied, people! I'm still processing that, when he moves on to how Frankie looked around nervously, then got up and walked away.

So basically, Frankie was behaving because he thought I was around.

I cringe. I know what's coming next. I know.

By the end of the day, Frankie has wised up. I'm not in school. I mean, he should have figured it out sooner, since we share a lot of classes. Maybe he was too busy reading poetry, or staring at Carmen Rodriguez.

Who I don't care about anymore. Like, at all.

Anyway, after school, Frankie grabbed Rayyan in the hall with all the lockers. "No protector today, eh, Ryan boy?" he said with an evil grin.

I can visualize that grin so well. "So he hit you?" I gasp.

Rayyan shakes his head. "He pushed me, and I fell. That's how I got this bruise and lip wound."

Lip wound. What a baby.

Then I look at Rayyan's tearful eyes, and the way he's glaring at me, like he can't stand me.

Not a baby. My brother, who I failed to protect because I was feeling sorry for myself.

"And your hand?" I ask, nervously.

"I got mad, so I stood up and tried punching his face like you showed me."

Hold the phone. Like *I* showed him?

I realize he means the boxing. "You . . . you don't know how to box! You don't even practice with the pillow and tree."

Rayyan closes his eyes. "I know, dude. That's when it got ugly."

I don't think I can take any more. "Meaning?"

"Meaning, he hit me back, right in my stomach." Rayyan rubs his middle. "I'm so gonna get a bruise, and it's all your fault."

Yeah, yeah, I get it. "Then what happened?"

"Mr. Trent saw us. He ran over and separated us. Gave us a lecture."

I try to smile reassuringly. "Okay, Trent's not too bad. At least it wasn't the principal. Then you'd be in hot water."

Rayyan opens his eyes and gives me a disgusted look. "Mr. Trent is the NJHS coordinator. He said he was disappointed in me. Student behavior is part of the decision model. Service, leadership, citizenship, CHARACTER!"

Oh.

Well.

"Did he actually say he was going to put this in your record?" I ask. Maybe Trent is that unique teacher who understands that kids have problems, and doesn't punish them.

"*Of course* he's going to hold it against me, Mo!" Rayyan sinks down on his bed. "I can't believe it! Everything I worked for, gone! NJHS, Van Meter, college. All ruined. Just because of you."

"Hey now," I protest. "It's not . . ."

He looks at me, and whoa, that whole can't-stand-you look is multiplied times ten now. "Yes!" he shouts. "It's because of you! I was fine being low-key bullied by Frankie. It's the way of the jungle, the strong prey on the weak, whatever. You're the one who came in like a hero, told him to stay away, acted like you were my bodyguard!"

I'm feeling a little attacked now. "How is that a bad thing?"

Rayyan throws up his hands. "Because it's Frankie! I've

282

known him since kindergarten. He's tough. No dad, and his mom is always sick. He took it as a challenge, this whole Mo's-gonna-protect-Ryan thing. He was just waiting to strike when you weren't around."

"Two things," I say carefully. "One, don't call yourself Ryan."

He scoffs. "You never take anything seriously."

"Two," I go on. "He didn't really strike, it seems like. He was just messing with you, and you're the one who punched him first."

Rayyan looks at me in complete horror. "Are you defending him?"

I swallow. "What? No!"

"Yes, you are! You just said he didn't strike, I did!"

"But . . . that's the truth."

Rayyan jumps off the bed. "I can't believe it. You're supposed to be on my side. No matter what."

My heart sinks. He's right. Making excuses for monsters is a habit, I guess.

Rayyan stomps back to the door, then turns around. "This is all your fault. I never said I needed a bodyguard, but you inserted yourself anyway."

"I'm not just a bodyguard . . . ," I begin brokenly. After all this time, is that how he thinks of me?

He narrows his eyes. "I never said I needed a brother, either. I was fine before you came to live here."

And then he slams the door shut and leaves.

27

I am livid as I walk into Walker Middle School the next morning.

Livid, I tell you.

Also, strangely, I'm gloomy.

How can both things be true at the same time, you may ask. Let me explain.

I'm livid because of what Frankie did to Rayyan. Yes, his goon was also there, but that dude is just a sheep. All he knows is how to play follow the leader.

Case in point, I still don't know the goon's name.

Moving on.

Besides being livid, I'm also sad because of, well, everything that happened on the weekend. Plus, Rayyan has made it clear he doesn't want me to do anything to avenge him. He literally said it in the morning as we got ready for school. "I don't want you to do anything, Mo!"

"Do anything?" I tried to school my face into innocent Mo, which, let me tell you, isn't easy on normal days. Today, it's next to impossible. I worry that the whole world will be able to see my broken, livid feelings.

And gloomy feelings. Let's not forget those.

So, armed with all these conflicting emotions I wouldn't wish on my worst enemy—well, maybe I'd wish 'em on Frankie, because he totally deserves them—I enter the school.

Please note that Rayyan is walking as far away from me as possible without bumping into a wall. I guess his emotions are not at all conflicting.

He hates me. Period.

Wonder how he'll react when I give in to my anger and do the "something" he told me not to. Because, c'mon, this is me. I'm a master of doing what I'm told not to.

Just another item on Mo Mirza's list of faults.

Frankie's standing in front of his locker, which is perfect. I walk right up to him, so close that I can see the zit on his nose.

If this was any other day, I'd make fun of his zit and be done with it. But this is today, and I have bigger, badder things to talk about.

"What're you doing?" he says, shocked. "Personal space, dude."

I lean forward. "Did you think of personal space when you hurt my cousin yesterday?"

Rayyan has reached us by now. "Mo, I told you not to do anything," he whisper shouts.

I ignore him. I ignore the kids around us. I ignore no-name goon. I just keep my eyes on Frankie.

Frankie backs up a little. "Uh, I didn't actually . . . he started it."

Wrong answer. I take another step forward. "I warned you. To stay away from him." My voice is harsh and low. Basically unrecognizable.

Frankie takes in a sharp breath. Rayyan does too.

I am feeling much more livid and much less sad now.

I like it. I hate feeling sad most of all.

There's no action in being sad. Nothing you can do to make it better. With anger, you can fight and punch and box and scream until everything is gone.

Until not a drop of feeling is left.

Until you're numb.

I want that feeling. The numbness.

The bell rings, and there's a rush of movement in the hall. Frankie steps back again, then whirls around and, get this, literally runs away.

What a loser.

I want to run after him, but I don't. Rayyan is giving me a very disappointed look. Shaking his head. Pursing his lips. The whole drama. "I don't need your help," he tells me, very prim and proper.

My shoulders slump. The sadness is coming in waves now. "Rayyan . . . ," I begin.

He shakes his head and turns away from me. "Don't wanna hear anything."

I'm left behind in the crush of students trying to get to class. Alone, furious, and now, also blue.

Perfect. Just perfect.

* * *

Frankie is smart, I already knew this.

He manages to avoid me almost the entire day. We're in four classes together, plus lunch, and in each one he's as far away from me as humanly possible. No eye contact. No smirks. No snide comments.

He's scared, obviously. But that doesn't make me happy. I want him to get in my face and argue. Or shove me, which is his signature move.

Or call me a loser or whatever.

I just want a spark so I can set it ablaze into a fire. My own personal hell, only I'll take him with me.

Frankie knows this, probably. Which is why he keeps away from me and Rayyan. Who, let's not forget, is also keeping away from me.

Ha.

It's like me, Rayyan, and Frankie are three planets orbiting around the universe. Never meeting. Always the same distance away from each other.

In PE, Coach Andrews divides us into teams and makes us play basketball. Frankie and Rayyan are on one team. I'm on the other.

I play terribly. I hit the wall behind the basket so many times the coach removes me from the game.

I jog to the side of the gym and sink down to the floor. Everyone stares. Rayyan too. He looks worried, or is that just wishful thinking?

When he catches me staring, he looks away quickly.

"Water break!" Coach Andrews calls out. When the other kids are busy, he comes and squats next to me. "You okay, Mo?"

"I'm fine," I mutter. "Just sick of everything right now."

He nods. "I understand, my man. Sometimes life gets too heavy."

I wonder what he'd say if he knew that my life's been too heavy for years. That I'm cracking under the burdens, and I'm not sure how long I'll keep standing.

*   *   *

When sixth grade started in New York, I thought about talking to someone about everything at home.

I mean, I wasn't a snitch or anything. It just gets to be too much sometimes, you know?

This was right after the worst summer vacation of my life.

Oh, did I not tell that story yet?

Imagine being stuck at home all summer. Nothing to do except watch TV and read books. Mama's busy with work, as usual. Plus, she keeps going away. She attends three long conferences that take her away for a week each. One time, she goes to Oman, which is a country in the Middle East.

She's gone for two whole weeks that time.

Abbu is angry all the time. And he talks to himself a lot.

I wouldn't call it an episode per se, because it's just low-key talking. No outbursts or anything.

I guess he doesn't realize how spooky I find it. Imagining there are people around I can't see.

Or maybe they're ghosts or evil spirits.

The fact that there may be invisible spirits around me, not just my dear father, keeps me awake most nights.

There are good things that summer too. Zed comes around a lot, and we do a bunch of free stuff together. Library visits. Walks to the park. Feeding the pigeons near the subway entrance. Rating our top-ten favorite TV shows. Rating our top forty songs of all time. Rating our school friends (and enemies).

It all gets boring really fast, but we still keep doing it, because what else are we going to do?

Patel Uncle is another nice thing that summer. Zed and I hang out at his place a lot.

Mama comes back from Oman just before summer ends, and soon school begins again. I think about telling someone in school what's going on with Mama and Abbu. Don't get me wrong, I doubt anything will change. What's anyone going to do, scold my parents? Ha.

After that, Abbu would be even meaner and Mama would be even more disappointed in me.

No thanks.

But wait, what if I could just talk to someone, let it off my chest, tell all the secrets that burn my heart . . . what then?

Could I do it?

I think and think and think. All the thinking paralyzes me. One day I wake up and decide I'm gonna do it. Tell my homeroom teacher, Miss Gomez, who's really nice. Or the school counselor, Mr. Shabazz. He's really cool.

Maybe the nurse. She'd want me to be safe, right?

Then I realize that no, I can't tell the nurse, because she worships Mama. One time Mama came to pick me up from school, and the nurse asked for her autograph. There's no way she'd think anything was wrong.

Actually, most days, I don't know for sure if anything *is* really wrong, or it's all in my mind. Abbu's told me so many times that I'm stupid, so maybe it's all in my head. Maybe I'm imagining it.

So I change my mind and decide not to tell anyone.

Nobody will care, anyway.

When kids are stuck in refugee camps, getting sick and dying, who cares about a boy in America who has everything?

* * *

Indiana Bones has a new look. He's not wearing clothes or a wig. Instead, his skull is open like a box with a hinged cover, and inside sits a gray lump.

"Let's discuss the brain, you brainiacs," Pigao says cheerfully as we enter the classroom.

For the first time since I came to this school, I'm not

interested in biology. I've got bigger worries than the human body systems, I'll have you know.

The other kids start talking about the brain. You know, the stuff everyone's heard of.

It's gray. It's covered in wrinkles. It's like a computer. It's in charge of all the other functions of your body.

Yada, yada, yada.

Pigao hands out some candy (I don't get any because I didn't say anything in class) and then starts a slideshow on the smart board. "The brain is part of our nervous system," he explains. "It connects to all the nerves in our body through the spinal cord."

The slide he's showing has a human body with all the nerves mapped out. "Cool," I whisper. "It's like a spiderweb."

Pigao hands me a Hershey's Kiss.

I frown. "What's this for?" I ask. "I didn't answer any questions."

"I'm just happy you're participating," he replies with a wink. "Thought you were asleep today."

I shake my head. "I'm awake."

"Good." Pigao goes back to the smart board. The next slide has a diagram of the brain, with three big sections marked out. They're blank, so I'm predicting homework.

Pigao leans against his desk and crosses his arms. "The entire human body, all its systems, is amazing," he begins.

Rayyan nods at my right. I know this because I've been peeking at him throughout the day.

"But if you ask me my favorite system," Pigao goes on, "it's the brain."

"Why?" Monique asks.

Pigao smiles like he's got a secret. "You'll spend the next few days answering this question. But I will tell you this: the brain is the incredible mission control center of your entire body. It interprets information from the outside world, and then ensures that each part of the body reacts in appropriate ways. All those other systems you've been learning about? Blood and bones and muscle . . . they're all ultimately controlled by the brain."

It's like he's speaking my language. "This means," I say, "if some part of the brain isn't working properly, then our body can become affected? What we say or how we behave?"

"Yes, exactly!" Pigao tosses me another Hershey's Kiss.

I lean back in my chair. I remember Naila Phupo's words. *It's not his fault. He's sick. He's not in control of himself.*

"Wow, that's . . . wow," Frankie says.

I look to my right. Rayyan is looking straight at me, for the first time since the day before. And this time, his face isn't angry. He looks . . . understanding.

Accepting.

Sorry.

28

Things seem to improve. Barely.

The rest of the week passes like a slow breeze. Nathan Mamoo texts again, asking how I am. Wants to know my grades, of all things.

At first I scowl, because who is he to come barreling into my life and acting like he cares?

Then I realize that I don't have a lot of people in my life who ask about my grades. So I send him a screenshot of my student portal, which is all As and Bs.

He texts back "we have to celebrate" in all caps.

I roll my eyes. He's like an adult version of Rayyan.

It's December now, so everyone in school is in a happy mood. There are posters for the winter party on the walls.

Trent gives me a library book titled *Fairy Tales from Around the World*. It's got folktales from Iceland and New Zealand, and even Persia. That's modern-day Iran, which gets me excited because it's so close to South Asia.

Frankie is Frankie, but from a distance. He's still shoving other kids and demanding their lunches, but he keeps far, far away from Rayyan and me. I'm counting that as a huge win.

Speaking of Rayyan, he's okay for now. I mean, he hasn't brought me back to best friend/brother status, but at least he's talking to me. He keeps to himself, studying even though winter break is almost here.

Nobody can tell that kid not to study. He loves his books.

In biology, Pigao talks about the brain a lot. He puts on videos about brain development and stuff. It's cool.

I'm starting to get why the brain is his favorite part of the human body. It's the most important, most powerful organ. The one that can make or break you. The one that can turn you into the best or the worst.

The best human. The worst monster.

* * *

What doesn't seem to improve?

Abbu.

Mumtaz Mirza is even worse than usual. If I thought his outburst on Sunday was bad, I was wrong.

He's now officially on DEFCON One.

This means the highest level of alert. The most dangerous situation. Expectations of nuclear war.

For Abbu, this means the worst symptoms he's ever had.

He sits in his room, talking to himself. Rocking back and forth. Sometimes shouting, sometimes whispering.

Sometimes crying.

It's the crying I can't stand. I'm not used to it.

He starts on Thursday evening, just after dinner. I can hear him from the hallway outside his room. I stand outside his door, listening. Stomach churning. Should I go in? Should I do something?

Then the anger pushes in. Why should I do anything? How many times have I hidden in my room for a good cry and he never cared?

This was in Queens, of course. If I hid in my Houston room and cried, Rayyan and Naila Phupo would descend on me like a pack of concerned hens. Bringing me plates of food and stroking my hair and telling me everything was going to be all right.

There's no way I'm doing that with Abbu.

I finally open the door and creep inside. It's dark and still, like a storm is coming but nobody knows yet, not even the meteorologists. Like a secret. Heavy and horrible.

He's only a lump on his bed, shaking with sobs.

Okay. I have no clue what to do.

I switch on the lamp on the desk, and look around. His closet is open, and everything is dumped on the floor. Clothes, shoes, boxes of stuff we brought with us from New York.

One of the boxes is smashed open. I can see a CD player

inside. It's ancient, but the paint gleams. Abbu doesn't take care of most things, but this one is different. He loves this thing. He plays songs on it sometimes when he's in a good mood.

Well, he used to. He hasn't played it since Mama left.

I pick it up, then look for the CDs. There's one with Indian classical music from the 1920s. Seriously old.

I put in the CD and switch it on. There's a fifty percent chance it won't work. Does it even have batteries?

It gives a whir, then music fills the air.

Soft, trilling music.

I breathe deeply. It's like a hand stroking my hair, this music. It's like a hug I didn't know I needed.

Abbu stops sobbing. "What's that?" he says, his voice cracked.

I don't reply. I place the CD player on his side table, and leave.

Or at least, I try to leave. In the end, I don't go anywhere. I close the door and stand in the hallway listening.

The only sound is the classical music. No more crying.

* * *

On Friday morning, Naila Phupo tells us she's staying home. "I don't want to leave bhai alone at home in this state," she explains as she butters Rayyan's toast.

Please note that Rayyan isn't a mama's boy who needs his toast buttered.

His mama is desperate to put calories in him, so she does

things like this. Little acts of love that he shakes his head at, but that squeeze my heart with envy.

"You can't do anything," I say. "Being here isn't going to help."

She shakes her head. She's looking haggard. No smile. Forehead wrinkled with worry. For the first time in, like, ever, I wish she'd be more like Mama. Not worrying so much about everything.

But then she wouldn't be my beloved phupo, would she?

I leave my eggs and go to hug her. Tight.

Okay, it's not my usual thing, but she brings out the hugger in me. I'll take it.

She takes it too. She hugs me back like she's scared and stressed out, but it will all be okay in the end. "Anything from your mother?" she asks quietly.

I shake my head, still holding on tight. I don't wanna think about *her* right now.

Naila Phupo pushes me away gently. "Can you please email her? Tell her what's going on with your abbu? Tell her how you feel?"

I go back to my eggs even though I'm no longer hungry. "She won't care."

"She will," Phupo insists. "Jo me keh rahee hoon woh karo." Do what I'm saying.

I clench my jaw. If she's so worried about Mama, why doesn't she send an email herself? Then I sigh. How can I say no to this woman? "Okay. After school."

At school, Friday turns into Fri-yay, and not because it's Pizza Day.

For the first time, Carmen talks to me like I'm more than dirt on her shoe.

"You missed music this Monday," she says to me in the lunch line.

Wait, she knew I was absent? My mouth drops open, and I quickly shut it. "Um, yeah. I wasn't feeling well."

She pops her gum and looks at me with narrowed eyes. "You're the one talking about that Vietnamese folk music, right?"

I nod like a bobblehead. "Yup, that's me." I gulp down my nerves—Carmen Rodriguez is talking to me, ah!—and ask, "Why, did you miss me?"

She makes an are-you-kidding expression. Then lets out a little laugh like I'm an adorable puppy. "Mrs. Nguyen mentioned you in class. We listened to classical music from South America, and she asked where you were, because you would've liked it."

I gulp again. A teacher asked where I was? Knew what I liked and wanted me to enjoy it? What universe is this?

And another first here. I'm glad I'm in Texas now. This is some next-level southern hospitality.

"Well?" Carmen says, putting her hand on her hip.

"Well, what?" I ask, confused.

"Are you going to be there next Monday?"

My face breaks out into my familiar bad-boy smirk. I lean forward a little. "Sure, I'll be there. Will *you* be there?"

She rolls her eyes. "Good. If there's a group project or something, make sure you partner with me, teacher's pet."

The line moves forward, and she turns away like she was never talking to me. "Teacher's pet?" I whisper in horror. That's, like, the complete, utter opposite of bad boy.

"Har har!" Someone laughs behind me. "You, teacher's pet? More like school delinquent."

It's Frankie. Of course it is.

"Did you forget I told you to stay away from me?" I ask. But there's no teeth in it, because I'm still high from talking to Carmen.

Also because this is the lunch line, and he's not doing anything wrong.

"Music was great because you weren't there," he taunts. But weirdly, he has no teeth either. In fact, we're both in a strange, calm mood.

Huh.

Maybe things are starting to look up after all. Maybe everything will be okay, at least in school.

Right then and there, under the cowboy mural, I have—what's it called? An epiphany. A bright idea. Here's what I tell myself. I decide that if this whole week goes okay, then it's a prediction of a good year.

Fingers and toes crossed. Prayers uttered. All that good stuff. I just need to get to the end of the day. And then things will be better.

"You know," I tell Frankie pleasantly, "one day, you'll eat crow."

Frankie doesn't even pretend he doesn't know what that means. "Nope, that'll never happen," he replies, just as pleasantly.

I tap my finger on my chin. "Look at us, all friendly. Like pals. Talking about crows."

"You're nuts," Frankie grunts. "Move."

I step to the counter. We get two slices of pizza each, plus a small salad with wilted lettuce and one single cherry tomato. I grab my tray and Frankie grabs his.

I start back to my table. Rayyan's already there, eating while reading. His usual style. "See you later, my friend," I tell Frankie cheerfully.

Get this, I even wave. That's how relaxed I am.

* * *

Once upon a time there was a great Mughal emperor named Akbar.

Well, his full name was Jalaluddin Mohammad Akbar, aka Akbar the Great, aka Akbar I. But I'm gonna call him Akbar cause that's the easiest.

Akbar's court had nine amazing dudes who formed, like, his advisory council or something. They were called nauratan, or the nine gems. One of the gems—sorry, dudes—was named Birbal. He was an adviser and also a commander of one of Akbar's armies. Oh, and also a poet.

Poetry and violence. Brain and brawn.

Kinda like Frankie.

Now, Akbar and the Mughals were real, obviously. Birbal

and the other gems of the nauratan too. There's a lot of historical info about all that. But there are tons of folktales about Akbar and Birbal too. They're called Akbar and Birbal stories, where the two have a really fun, friendly relationship. Ya know, playing pranks on each other, asking each other tough questions, working together, et cetera.

This is an Akbar and Birbal story.

Once upon a time, Akbar and Birbal were taking a walk in the palace gardens. Imagine the scene: beautiful gardens in the royal palace. Trees, shrubs, pretty walkways or whatever. Birds singing in the trees. Maybe a fountain or two.

Akbar and Birbal used to spend a lot of time together, so this was totally normal. Also normal: Akbar wanting to test Birbal's quick and smart thinking. A lot of these stories start like that, by the way.

So Akbar decides to ask Birbal a tricky question. "How many crows are there in my kingdom?" he asks. I'm not sure why crows specifically. Maybe there were a bunch of them flying around, or maybe he heard a *caw caw caw*. Anyway, that's what he asks, and guess what? When the most powerful emperor of the most powerful kingdom asks you a question, you better answer.

Birbal knows Akbar, though. He can tell this is just the usual banter they always have together. He realizes that the emperor wants a funny slash clever reply. He pretends to think, then says, "My king, there are ninety-five thousand four hundred and sixty-three crows in our kingdom."

Now, this number is different in every source for the story, but it doesn't matter. The main thing is that Birbal gives an actual, very specific amount. If it was me, I'd say, "There are a lot of crows," but not Birbal. He's got to be specific, because obviously Akbar is trying to trip him up. Trying to make him confess that he doesn't know the answer.

Because let's face it, who knows the correct answer? Nobody, that's who.

When Akbar hears Birbal's response, he's shocked. But he's also smiling at the way Birbal has given the quick response. That's what he was hoping for. "What if I were to count them, and there were more than ninety-five thousand four hundred and sixty-three?" he asks.

Birbal just shrugs. "Then the crows from the other kingdoms must be visiting us," he replies.

"And what if there were fewer crows?"

Another shrug. "Well, then some of our crows must be visiting other kingdoms."

Akbar grins, and Birbal grins back. That's what their relationship is, back-and-forth witty banter and stuff.

29

When Rayyan and I get home in the afternoon, nobody's there. No Naila Phupo in the kitchen. No Abbu in his room. There's a pile of carrots and potatoes on the kitchen table, half chopped. The knife is still on the cutting board, peels sticking to it.

Naila Phupo went somewhere in a hurry, obviously.

The living room is a mess. It's like someone had a full-on temper tantrum. Everything's thrown around—cushions, books, knickknacks. A bowl of cherries lies on the floor, smashed to pieces.

Rayyan looks around, eyes big as saucers. "What do you think happened?"

I shake my head. My stomach is churning, and I feel queasy.

I should go to the bathroom just in case I puke.

I mean, we all know there was only one person who'd do this.

Abbu.

But not knowing what happened, and when and why and all that, is messing with me big-time. "Let's get my phone, so we can call your mom," I tell him shakily.

"Yes, good idea."

We're climbing the stairs when the front door opens and Naila Phupo trudges in. Slow movements, shoulders slumped, eyes red.

Rayyan rushes to her. "Mama, what happened? Where were you?"

Naila Phupo looks up at me. I'm still on the stairs, gripping the banister like I'm gonna fall. "Mumtaz bhai had a really bad episode. I had to take him to the hospital."

The mental hospital. That's what she means. Not the regular hospital where regular people go when they have regular illnesses. Nope, this is the mental institution. The real deal.

For some weird reason, I can't breathe properly. Both Phupo and Rayyan are staring at me with pity and grief.

I don't need that. "Okay," I reply in a clipped tone. "Thank you for taking him."

Her lips tremble, and I realize she's trying to smile that signature happy smile of hers. Only it comes out all wobbly and weak. "Of course. It's my responsibility."

I blink. I don't think anyone has called Abbu their responsibility before. It's like he's a kid, and he needs someone to take care of him.

"How long will he stay there?" Rayyan asks. "Can we see him?"

I grip the banister harder. The stretch of my knuckles reminds me it's been a couple of weeks since I boxed.

"Maybe tomorrow," Naila Phupo replies. She sounds exhausted.

I relax my fingers and start down the stairs. "You go sit down," I tell her. "Rayyan and I will make you some hot chai."

Rayyan raises his eyebrows. He's so used to being served. "Er, sure."

Naila Phupo sinks down on the couch. "This place is a mess," she mutters.

"Don't clean up!" I tell her sternly. "We'll do it after we make chai."

Rayyan and I hurry up to our room to change and wash up. Then we go to the kitchen, where I teach him how to make chai. While the water is boiling, I chop the rest of the vegetables on the table and sauté them in a pan. I can toss them with some pasta later.

Rayyan watches me. "How do you know all this stuff?"

"What? Cooking?"

"Well, yeah," he replies. "I guess just . . . overall, taking care of things, knowing what needs to be done."

I shrug. "I dunno. I've had to do it all my life. I don't have parents who take care of me, like you do."

Rayyan stiffens. "Only one parent."

I bump his shoulder with mine. "You know what I mean."

"Yeah." He relaxes. "Mama is more than enough parent for me."

"She takes such good care of everyone," I say, smiling. "Your mom is incredible. I hope you realize that."

"I do."

The kettle whistles, and I get back to making the chai. I put some ginger cookies from the pantry on a plate, and everything on a tray.

"Are you okay?" Rayyan asks softly. "With your dad in the hospital?"

I don't look up. "Of course," I mumble. "It's not like it's the first time."

Here's what I don't tell him: every time is like the first time. I'm scared and worried. I'm feeling powerless and weak. Also angry, but that one is less focused.

After all, who do I feel angry at? Naila Phupo keeps saying it's not Abbu's fault. I'm not sure I believe her one hundred percent, but I trust her.

And I am so, so tired of being angry at Mama. She's not even here for me to throw the anger at.

She doesn't even know about Abbu.

Oops. That's when I remember I didn't email her like Phupo told me to. I hand Rayyan the tray and run upstairs. "You take this in. I have to send a message to my mom."

* * *

Mama's email to Abbu, dated the day before:

Things are busy here. I'm not sure when I'll video call again. Hope you had a great Thanksgiving.

She doesn't even mention me this time.

That's fine, because I don't mention her to anyone either. Not even in my thoughts.

My email to Mama, dated now:

Mama. This is Mo. I'm letting you know that Abbu is in the hospital. Hope you had a great Thanksgiving.

* * *

When I'm done emailing, I sit back on my bed. The chances of Mama responding are about zero percent. This is based on other times I've emailed her.

For example, when I emailed her three months ago saying I missed her and I wished she hadn't left, there was no reply.

When I emailed her two months ago, telling her we were leaving New York and I didn't want to go. Guess what? No reply.

So yeah, I'm not holding my breath.

Even if she does respond, what's she going to do? She's too far away to help.

My gaze connects to the side table. Inside the drawer is the phone Nathan Mamoo gave me. I haven't really used it much, except to reply to his texts. I've never contacted him first. Never really known what to say.

Now I do.

With shaking hands, I power up the phone. It's out of

charge, so I connect it to the cable and wait for a few minutes.

Waiting is agony.

I go back to my laptop and browse for a bit, but it's too boring. Don't ask why, but I search for schizophrenia. Lots of hits come up. Like, a ton. Most are links I've already visited: symptoms, old therapies, even videos of people in mental hospitals.

I guess I'm like Rayyan with his press conference videos. Pulling on the old scab, ya know? But I'm looking for something specific now.

I change my search and try schizophrenia + brain. Specifically, what happens to the brain when someone has this horrible illness? Is it all about anatomy? Or is it something else?

In seventh grade, our technology teacher, Mrs. Crenshaw, taught us about this thing called media literacy, and how to choose good sources. I make sure I click on medical sites only. Hospitals and mental-health facilities.

I read and read. There are a few videos, so I watch them too. There's so much about the brain in here, I start to take notes. Maybe Pigao will be interested. Maybe I can do a presentation in class.

Ha. Let's not kid ourselves.

I'm reading this for myself, not anyone else. To learn a little more about the monster inside my father.

When my back starts to hurt because it's been hunched up for so long, I look at the time and realize it's almost sunset. Just the right time for Maghrib prayers.

I wash up and pray. Thoughts circle in my head. There's a raw pain in my mind. All the worry squeezes my heart tightly. All the new . . . what's it called? Perceptions about Abbu, swirling in my mind, thanks to my research.

I think of what Imam Shamsi said. "The strongest heart is the one that's still beating." Well, right now, my heart is a thundering mess inside my chest.

Still beating? Definitely.

When I finish, I send a message to Nathan Mamoo.

Abbu is in the hospital. Can you please tell Mama I need her?

* * *

Naila Phupo takes me to visit Abbu the next day.

I'm so nervous my armpits are swimming with sweat. Gross.

In the olden days, people used to call this place all kinds of names. Loony bin. Asylum. Crazy house. Funny farm. Now people are nicer. They don't call it all that, at least out loud. It's a regular hospital, but the patients are sick in the brain, not the body.

I mean, the brain is also part of the body, but whatever. It's just something people say. Sick in the brain.

"Now don't be scared when you see him, all right?" Phupo says as we park the car outside a big white building.

Alarms blare in my head. "What do you mean? Why would I be scared?"

"Oh no, don't worry, it's nothing bad!" She pats my arm. "Just wanted to prepare you."

Don't worry? Don't be scared? Obviously now I'm both. Plus, the sweating.

Perfect.

She gives me another pat, then we go inside. The lobby is bright and open. Pictures of smiling people hang on the walls.

I can't imagine Abbu smiling in a mental hospital. He'd be scowling and growling, telling them he was perfectly fine and wanted to go home.

Somehow, weirdly, the image of a scowling, angry Abbu settles my nerves. I may not like his behavior, but it's familiar.

After we've checked in, Naila Phupo takes us up in the elevator to the third floor. Abbu's room is at the end of the hallway. When she opens the door, my breath catches in my throat.

There's no scowling, growling Abbu.

There's only a man lying quietly on a bed, covers up to his chest, eyes closed. He looks so peaceful. I've never seen him like that.

"Is he sleeping?" I whisper.

"No, he's sedated," Naila Phupo whispers back. "That means they've given him some medicine to sleep. He can't wake up until the medicine wears off."

I don't like that.

I stare at him for a while. "Why are we here, then?" I finally ask. I think I'm annoyed. Or maybe it's stress that's causing me to speak harshly.

I never speak harshly to Naila Phupo.

She pulls me into a sideways hug. "I thought you'd want to see him with your own eyes. See that he's okay. He's got a whole crew of doctors and nurses making sure he gets better."

"I don't . . . I didn't want to see him," I mutter.

But that's a lie. I did, even if I didn't realize it.

The door opens, and a nurse peeks in. "Ma'am, we need you to fill out some more forms," she says apologetically.

"I'll be right back, Mo." Naila Phupo smiles and leaves with the nurse.

Okay then. I'm not sure what I'm supposed to do, so I sit on the chair next to Abbu's bed.

At first I look at the floor. It's made of white tiles with a black diamond inside each square.

Then I look at his hands. Medium-size nails, because he always forgets to clip them. He's made me so many Nutella sandwiches with those hands.

He's helped me with homework so many times, holding a pen or pencil with those hands.

Picked up boxes, luggage, mechanic's tools. Scooped soil for the flowerpots in our little balcony in Queens.

He's held the steering wheel with those hands every time he drove me places. Took me shopping. Brought us to Texas.

He's held my hand with his so many times, even when I didn't want him to. My first day of kindergarten. My first time walking across the busy street near our apartment. Every time we entered Mama's office, wherever she worked.

Every single time, like we both needed that extra boost.

I blink. Weird how I never remembered these things before now.

I move my stare to his face. His closed eyes. The stubble on his jaw. There's so much I want to say to him, but he's just lying there, not listening.

I want to wake him up, but what would I even say? I'm sorry?

I forgive you?

Please forgive me?

Maybe when he wakes up, he'll be normal. No schizophrenia. No anger.

Ha. If wishes were horses, beggars would ride.

* * *

Once upon a time, when gods and demons battled ferociously, there was a brave and powerful king named Muchukunda. Even Indra, the king of the Hindu deities, was impressed with him.

During a battle with demons, Indra's army comes to Muchukunda for help.

He gives them shelter and general military help. Whatever is needed to fight off a demon army.

Many yugas pass. (In Hinduism, a yuga is an age, or a very long time period.) The battles rage on. With Muchukunda's help, Indra and the other gods finally win.

Indra is really grateful, but he can't send Muchukunda back to Earth because, ya know, yugas have passed. All his family and friends have died long ago. Nothing is the way it used to be. Even if Muchukunda could return, what would he do? Where would he go?

Instead, Indra offers Muchukunda any boon he likes. A boon is like a favor, or a gift. An ask-and-ye-shall-receive sort of situation. Muchukunda is exhausted after all the battles, and sad about his family, so he asks for undisturbed sleep.

Like, nobody should bother him, he shouldn't wake up, et cetera.

Some versions of the story include a punishment for whoever disturbs him—burning to ashes. I like this version a lot.

Anyway, the gods grant Muchukunda his boon, and he goes into a deep sleep inside a cave.

More yugas pass. Lots more. Muchukunda sleeps undisturbed.

Then the age of Krishna arrives. He's a very famous Hindu god. Like, celebrity-level famous. Everyone knows him.

Of course, Muchukunda's been asleep all this while, so he's not aware of Krishna or what's going on the world.

Spoiler alert: there's another war, this time between Krishna and this great king/demon dude called Kalayavana. This war is so epic, Kalayavana brings in thirty million barbarians to fight with him. He battles it out with Krishna, and they enter the cave where Muchukunda is sleeping.

Inside the cave, it's pitch-dark. Krishna hides. Kalayavana can't see anything. He attacks Muchukunda thinking it's Krishna, and of course the slumbering god wakes up.

And he's mad. Like, MAD. Ready to burn the world to

313

the ground for being disturbed.

Instead, he burns Kalayavana to ashes.

Krishna is extremely happy at this turn of events. Imagine having an enemy vanquished without lifting a finger! He sets Muchukunda free from the cave life and blesses him to eternal bliss.

You know, the Hindu god equivalent of living happily ever after.

30

I think it's a stupid idea to go to Sunday school, but Rayyan insists.

"The kids must be missing us," he says. "It's been two weekends since we had class."

I grumble under my breath.

Look, I'm not proud of it. He's right, our little students expect us to show up. It's just that I'm so tired. The visit to the mental hospital was, like, mentally draining. And then when we came back home, Nathan Mamoo showed up.

He'd asked me for Naila Phupo's address, but I thought he'd send a card or something. I'd never expected him to actually show up.

I don't really have a lot of people show up for me.

He sits in Phupo's living room for a long time. It's mostly the adults who talk, while Rayyan and I listen.

How Houston traffic sucks. How the weather sucks. What the doctors say about Abbu.

I perk up my ears at the part about Abbu's doctors. What *do* they say? It's always a mystery. Something nobody wants to explain to kids.

Here's what the doctors say.

Abbu's psychosis (that's the episodes) is worse than before because he had stopped taking his medicines entirely. He needs to be on regular medication and also see a therapist. In time, he will become better.

That's the thought that helped me sleep last night. A better abbu.

One where he's not ruled by schizophrenia, but where he rules it.

Kind of.

Naila Phupo drives us to the Islamic center on Sunday morning before heading to the hospital. "I need to talk to the doctor," she says, but I know the real reason she's going. She wants to sit in that chair near Abbu's bed, watching over him.

At least, that's what I would do.

I'm a little nervous as Rayyan and I walk to the Sunday school building. It's only been two weeks since I was here, but it seems like a different time. A different world too. This is where I painted those ugly windows into my soul. The ones Abbu trashed. The ones I hate and love equally.

Can I go back to the room where I painted? Act like everything's fine? That my father isn't sleeping—sorry, sedated—in a hospital for crazy people?

So yeah, I'm nervous.

And yeah, I know you're not supposed to say *crazy*, but so what? Sometimes the word fits.

Imam Shamsi meets us in the lobby. "Assalamo alaikum! I heard about your father, Mohammad," he says. "I'm praying every day for his recovery."

"Thank you," I reply awkwardly. I wonder if he knows what Abbu is sick with.

My guess: yes. Here's why.

One, he's not asking any questions. Most people will ask things like, "What happened? What do the doctors say?" But the imam doesn't want to know anything, which makes me think he knows everything.

Two, he's looking at me with this cringey sympathy that makes me want to run away. But his eyes are also warm and friendly, so it's not too bad, I guess.

Imam Shamsi continues. "Please tell us if you need anything. Our meal train volunteers are always ready to help. They can give Sister Naila some assistance."

My jaw drops. I'd never thought about asking the mosque for help. A meal train would be such a good surprise for Naila Phupo. So much help too. "Er, sure," I stammer. "How do I . . . ?"

The imam pats my shoulder. "Don't worry about it. Consider it taken care of. I'll drop the first meal off myself tonight."

"Thank you," Rayyan and I say together.

Okay, I may have tears in my eyes, but let's not mention that.

* * *

"What are we going to paint today?" Pigtail Girl asks with a cheeky grin.

"I wanna paint too," a little boy next to her grumbles.

"No crayons!" a toddler shouts.

Rayyan shakes his head. "The older kids paint. The younger kids use crayons. Those are the rules."

"It's a stupid rule," the first kid complains. "Who made this rule?"

"We did," I reply. "Your teachers."

The class erupts. The older kids are happy, the younger ones are angry. Rayyan groans. It's low, but I hear him because he's right next to me.

"Let's do something else," I tell him.

"Like what?"

I open the supply closet and search inside. I remember seeing boxes of craft supplies. Glue, construction paper, beads, stickers . . . so many stickers. I take everything out and set it on the table. Then I hold up my hand and say loudly, "Everyone will use crayons today!"

The older kids look at me in dismay.

The younger kids cheer. They're happy with crayons now that the injustice has been corrected. They've all been equalized into crayon users.

"Why would you do that, Mohammad bhai?" Pigtail Girl asks, shocked. "I can paint really good!"

I waggle my eyebrows. "I know, but today we're doing crafts instead."

Within minutes, the class is quiet. Everyone focuses on their crafts. Rayyan gives them a few different choices from the internet, and looks up instructions. Like, how to make a masjid with felt, or how to make a Five Pillars of Islam chart using glitter and Popsicle sticks.

But most of the kids don't want instructions. They're just doing their own thing, having a good time.

I pick up a piece of construction paper and start coloring with crayon. Just squiggles and lines, stars and swirls, over and over. Instead of my usual dark colors, I use bright yellows and greens.

"That's nice," Rayyan says, looking over my shoulder.

"Yeah?"

"Well, it's not like your oil paintings," he replies. "Those are awesome."

I look up, startled. I know he saw the mess of paints and canvases on our bedroom floor the day Abbu came home. But to call the paintings awesome? Seriously?

Rayyan is looking at me with a bright, open face. Truthful. There's a warm glow in my chest. "Thanks, dude."

He grins. "You're welcome."

* * *

On Monday, a lot of stuff happens.

That's good in a way, because it keeps me distracted from Abbu.

Carmen waits for me in music class, an empty seat next to her. "Sit here, Mo!" she calls.

Everyone turns to look at her. She's got her hair in a tight braid this time, with a little rubber band instead of a pretty bow.

"I'm okay here," I reply, and slide into my regular seat at the back of the class. I know why she's being so friendly. I still remember the teacher's pet comment.

"Nice to have you back, Mohammad," Mrs. Nguyen says. "We've been listening to classical music in the last ten minutes of every class. I think you'll appreciate it."

Again, everyone turns, but this time they're all looking at me. "Um, sure," I mumble, looking at my desk.

We study musical notes, which is super boring. Mrs. Nguyen is a good teacher, though. She explains things in a way that makes the lesson interesting. I slump in my seat, eyes closed, because, ya know . . . my reputation. But I'm listening, believe me.

When ten minutes are left in the class, she starts a video on the smart board. "Today I've cued up some classical music from India and Pakistan."

My eyes pop open. Um, what?

The sounds of raag fill the air. The video is of a group of people sitting cross-legged on a stage covered with white cloth. In the middle is a woman with a microphone in front of her. Next to her is another woman. She's holding a sitar in her arms, lightly strumming it. They're both wearing orange-and-brown saris and have bindis on their foreheads.

The other people onstage are guys. They're dressed in white

kameez and pajamas, and have white caps on their heads. One of them has a small drum set, the tabla. The other guy has a harmonium.

How do I know the instrument names? Thank Patel Uncle.

The music begins, and it's all lyrical and sweet.

Mesmerizing.

I don't look at my classmates, or Mrs. Nguyen. I just listen. At some point I close my eyes again, but my ears are alert. My heartbeat? Smooth and calm. *Dum. Dum. Dum.*

I listen and think.

I think of Patel Uncle. Of Abbu. The long line of desis in whose souls this music lies, ready to soothe and bring joy.

*   *   *

"Only a week left for the science fair," Pigao reminds us. "Please use this period to work on your projects."

Rayyan raises his hand. "We already finished."

Pigao taps his chin. "Who else has finished their project?" he asks.

Five other kids raise their hands. I look around. Besides me, there's also Monique, Eli, Frankie, and his goon (whose name is Aiden, apparently).

Frankie gives me a disgusted look.

I wink at him.

Look, I'm trying to forget how he called me the school delinquent last week.

Pigao claps his hands. "All right then. You six, pack your bags. You're going to the library."

Aiden groans like going to the library is worse than going to the dentist. I grab my backpack and stand up. "Ready," I say. I can't wait to see what other books Trent has saved for me.

The six of us head to the library and settle in. Rayyan starts on his homework, and the other kids browse the shelves. Trent is alone at the librarian desk, so I put down my backpack to go talk to him. "Hi, Mr. Trent."

He smiles. "Hello, Mo. Did you like the book I gave you?"

I sigh. "Actually, I haven't had much time to read recently."

"Oh?"

I pause for a second. I'm a private guy, and I don't like telling people about my weaknesses. But the whole day today has been strange, knowing I'm in school learning about music and social studies and science, while my father is sedated in a bed.

Like, I don't want to be here, but I also want to be here so I can forget. If that makes sense.

I open my mouth, and everything comes spilling out. About Abbu's illness. About his episodes. About his disappearance and now his being in the hospital. Everything.

And I don't even know why I tell him. It's not like I've known him long. If there's a teacher I'm close to, it's Pigao.

Trent, though. He's kinda like Imam Shamsi. Helpful. Kind. Warm eyes and sympathetic smile.

It's like he's saying, "You can tell me anything. I'll keep your secrets."

When I finish talking, Trent says, "I'm so sorry to hear this, Mo."

I shrug. I don't want his pity. "It'll be okay."

"Well, you can come hang out here at the library anytime," he says. "Some of the kids do that. Like your friend Frank."

Frank?

Oh, he means Frankie. I was confused by his use of the word *friend*, I guess.

I go back to where I left my things. Unfortunately my friend Frankie is already sitting there. "I heard what you said," he tells me. "To Mr. Trent."

I blink, trying to think back to what I'd said. It was basically a word vomit about my biggest problems in life. He heard all that?

I try not to look horrified, but I don't think it works.

Frankie gives me a small smile, and oh my god, there is zero snark in it. It's open and innocent and slightly painful, like he's hurting but doesn't want anyone to know.

It completely changes his look. From villain to average dude, in one second.

I'm still trying to figure out what's happened when he says, "Don't worry, I won't tell anyone."

"Er, okay." I'm not sure where he's going with this conversation.

He looks down at his hands. "My, um, mom. She has bipolar."

I sit down on the chair next to him. Actually, I fall, but let's not talk about that. "Oh," I say.

Ugh, what a stupid response. Come on, Mo.

Frankie smiles sadly again. "Yeah. I know it's a different illness than schizophrenia, but she goes through some of the same things as your dad. Not being around. Getting mad. Hearing things. Seeing things. Seeing people."

Whoa.

He stops talking, and we sit and stare at each other. Here's what I'm thinking:

One, this is the first time I've met a kid with a parent like mine. A kid who knows what I go through. Who goes through the same stuff.

In case it's not obvious, this is HUGE.

Two, I have something in common with Frankie, my archenemy. My nemesis. The person who's made my life miserable since the day I stepped into Alice Walker Middle School for the first time.

Three, I now understand Frankie's terrible attitude. Like, the reason behind it. We've both got the bad-boy persona down perfectly, don't we?

"I've got anger issues," Frankie adds with a shrug, like he knows what I'm thinking.

"Yeah?" I laugh a little. "I take out all my anger by boxing. Well, and painting."

"Cool," he says. "Better than taking it out on kids in school."

"True."

Okay, this is officially a weird conversation. I don't know

what to do. How to react. Is he my friend now? Should I forget our past? Should I forget how he's tormented Rayyan?

Um, no. Not happening.

Well, maybe it will happen. You know, eventually.

The bell rings, so I grab my backpack and stand up. "Nice talking to you," I say before rushing out of the library.

31

Naila Phupo is sitting at the kitchen table, looking into a shoebox.

"How's Abbu?" I ask.

She looks up. "Behtar hain." He's better. "Not sedated anymore."

"So he's awake?" I squeak. "Is he coming home?"

She shakes her head and goes back to looking inside the shoebox. "Not right away. They're going to monitor him for a while. Make sure the medications have time to help him."

"But . . ."

She looks back up at me. "But what, beta?"

I sigh and sit next to her. It's hard to explain, this feeling. I don't want Abbu in the hospital because it's scary, but I also don't want him out. That's when he gets bad, when he's got no supervision and nobody to make sure he takes his meds. That's when disaster strikes. "But he'll get worse again, once he's out."

She nods thoughtfully. "Maybe. But he can't stay in the hospital forever, can he? It costs a lot, for one."

Ugh. I'm so stupid. I hadn't even thought of that. With Mama's job, we've always had health insurance. But I'm not sure how that works now that she's on a fellowship. And she's not even in the country anymore.

Nope, I'm not thinking about her.

I nod to the shoebox. "What's in there?"

"Pictures." Naila Phupo takes one out of the box and shows it to me. It's a Polaroid picture of a little boy, about four or five. He's sitting on a tricycle, scowling at the camera.

"Who's this?"

She lets out a little laugh. "That's your abbu!"

Whoa. I've never seen his kid pictures before. "He was always angry, huh? Even as a kid?"

She laughs louder this time. It's still a small sound, but much happier. "Oh no, he was pretty cute and happy as a kid. I was three, I think, when this picture was taken. He was five. I'm not sure why he's scowling here; maybe the sun was in his eyes."

I'm not buying it.

I keep staring at the picture, trying to figure it out. Except for the scowl, he looks like a normal kid. I can't wrap my head around this image. I've thought of him as a monster for so long.

I can't let go of that.

Can I?

"Here's one with me." Naila Phupo pushes another picture at me. Two kids are sitting on a couch, a plate of something between them. French fries, maybe? One kid is Abbu, obviously. The other is a girl with clips in her hair and a cheeky smile. She's holding out a fry to the boy, and he's scowling at her.

"There's that scowl," I point out. "But you were cute!"

"Shukriya. Want to see more?"

I nod, trying not to seem too eager. Rayyan comes into the kitchen, looking for a snack. He grabs an orange and sits down on Phupo's other side. "What're you two doing?"

"Trying to change the narrative," she replies.

I stare at the picture in my hand. She's right. Just these two images of Abbu in a different lifetime have made me think of him as someone else. Not a monster, but my dad.

If we go through the whole shoebox, what will happen? Will it completely change how I think of him?

That's an alarming thought. My fears may be scary, but they're also comfortable.

Familiar.

I have a feeling this box of pictures is going to turn that familiar upside down. But then, Abbu lying in a hospital bed, sedated, has already done that. So why not go all the way? I pull the box toward me. "Let's see what else is in here."

Naila Phupo pulls it back. "Main dikhatee hoon. Sabr karo." I'll show you. Have patience.

We spend the next hour going through the shoebox. There are pictures of Abbu and Phupo throughout their childhood and early teens. Abbu changes from a chubby kid to a thin preteen, and then a tallish teenager. The nineties fashions are atrocious, all baggy jeans and backward baseball caps.

Oh, and the hair! Teen Abbu has longish hair styled in a wave at the front, in a boy-band look.

He's scowling in some pictures, but grinning in others. It's that smile I hardly ever see, the one where his eyes gleam and he looks . . . normal. Happy, even.

I wish he was this person again. It would be, I dunno, heaven or something.

Not just for me, but for him too. Because I'm a hundred percent sure he doesn't like how he is now.

"When did Abbu get schizophrenia?" I ask.

Naila Phupo chews her lip. "Hmm, I think it was the late 2000s. Maybe 2006 or 2007. He was in college and started getting symptoms. I was in high school, and really busy with life. I didn't really know what was going on, but I heard our parents whisper about it. Our mother would cry a lot, worrying about him."

"But they helped him, right?"

"They tried. There were doctors' visits and hospital stays, and lots of medicines being delivered all the time. Trying different things. Seeing what had the least side effects." Naila Phupo sighs. "But then bhai decided to move away. He transferred to a community college in New York City, and just . . . I don't know. Disappeared on us."

"Why would he do that?" Rayyan asks.

She shrugs. "I think he was feeling overwhelmed with all the attention. My parents started fighting about who was responsible for his illness. Abbu would blame Ammi for how she raised him. Ammi would accuse Abbu of never being around. Bhai already had no idea how to deal with this huge *thing*, but having everyone treat him like he was a problem just made things worse, you know?"

"Maybe the voices told him to move," I whisper, thinking about my research on the laptop the other day. There was an entire video about auditory hallucinations. They're the whispers that haunt my father all the time. Telling him what to do, how to feel. Filling his head with hurtful ideas.

Rayyan stares at me. I don't think he knows about the voices.

I go back to the pictures. There's one from Abbu's high school graduation, and Phupo tells me his favorite subject was math. "He wanted to be an investment banker," she says. "You know, before."

My eyes grow wide. Don't those kinds of bankers make serious money?

How hard must it be to watch Mama do incredible things with her career, while Abbu's stuck at home, scared of going out, not sure what's real or what's imaginary.

Suddenly his anger makes a lot more sense.

"And art," Naila Phupo adds. "He loved art, even though it didn't fit into his career path."

I try to imagine my rough-and-tough father painting. Did he prefer oils or watercolors or something else? Did he pour out his worries and anger and hate into his art, like I've been doing? Why did he stop?

I remember how he acted when he saw me with my paints and canvases after Thanksgiving. He looked like he hated them.

He looked like he was in pain.

"He didn't like it when I painted," I whisper.

Naila Phupo shakes her head. "That's not true. It just brought back bad memories. I promise."

"How do you know?"

She puts down the picture she was holding and turns to me. Takes my hands in hers. "We talked, you know. When he was in New York, yes, but more when you two moved here. It wasn't long conversations or anything, but we'd hang out, as you kids say. Drink some chai, watch some TV after dinner." She smiles. "He's proud of you. He loves you."

I pull my hands away. I want to believe her, and I know she wouldn't lie. She's not like that.

But I don't think she's right.

She's looking at me with big, understanding eyes.

"Parents who love their kids don't stop taking their meds,"

I blurt out. "He just doesn't care enough about me to get better."

She leans forward and wraps me in a sideways hug. "It's not that he doesn't care," she says. "It's that he doesn't even know how to take care of himself, let alone another person."

I clench my jaw. "How is that my fault?"

Listen, I know I'm being a brat. But at this point, I feel like I've earned the right.

Rayyan surprises me by chiming in. "Yeah, how is that Mo's fault? He's just a kid."

Phupo straightens up and nods sadly. "It's not. But you also have to remember that it isn't your abbu's fault either. He's drowning, Mo. He's been drowning for almost twenty years. He can't be expected to help others swim when he's barely holding on himself."

It's weird. Even though Phupo's words are kinda disheartening, they also make me feel good. Happy.

Because it means Abbu wasn't trying to be a monster. He wasn't *trying* to be a bad father or husband or brother.

Who knows? Maybe he even tried his best at being good at those things.

It was the illness that was holding him back, like Moriro's magurmuch. The beast that destroys you by swallowing you whole.

Maybe he actually loves me a lot. I just can't see it.

Maybe.

32

The week flies by in a sort of limbo.

I'm thinking a lot. Worrying a lot too. Abbu's still in the hospital, although Naila Phupo says he's improving. She also says the doctors don't want to distract him with lots of visitors.

It's okay. I don't know if I want to see Abbu right now.

Like I said, I've been thinking and researching. Also, feeling. There are lots and lots of feelings. When you've hated someone or something for a long time, finding out that they're not the baddie you made them out to be . . . it's sort of a letdown.

What do you do with all those feelings? All that anger?

I have no clue.

Today is the science fair. Rayyan's been super excited since he woke up in the morning, but I'm not. With everything going on in my life, I really don't want to think about some science project.

Correction. I'm not gonna let myself think about it.

Cause here's the truth: I may be dying of a broken heart.

Yes, that's a real thing. Pigao told us about it a few weeks ago. Broken heart syndrome, brought on by extreme stress and emotional situations.

Basically, my life.

"We're gonna win, I'm sure of it," Rayyan gloats, looking around the gym.

Seventh and eighth graders have set up their projects on folding tables. Sixth graders are in the cafeteria. It's Friday, the week before winter break, and school has ended early. The last two periods are for science-fair viewing, which means students, teachers, and even parents can visit.

To be fair, our heart model is one of the more sophisticated projects. Pigao came by earlier and said it was fantastic.

I half expected candy, but I guess he only gives that out in class.

"What do you think, Mo?" Rayyan says. "Do you think we'll win?"

"Um, I dunno." I'm not really paying attention. I'm trying to ignore my broken heart, knowing Mama won't be here to see my project. Or Abbu, or Zed, or Patel Uncle. My previous life in New York City is gone, and it's never been more obvious than right now.

Right here in this gym.

"What are you looking at?" Rayyan asks, squinting.

"Nothing."

This is what I'm really looking at: Frankie, sitting on the floor in the corner, playing on his phone. He's frowning, I think.

"I'll be right back," I tell Rayyan, and walk over to Frankie. When I get closer, I realize he's reading a text. "Let me guess," I say. "Your parents aren't coming."

He looks up quickly. "What? How did you know?"

I shrug. "I recognize the expression. Mine aren't either."

Look, I'm not sure why I mentioned my parents at all. I never do. Like, ever. But his bombshell in the library has made me see him in a different light. And it makes me want to poke the bear a little bit. See what happens.

Frankie frowns again. "My parents are divorced," he says. "And my dad lives in Denver."

"And your mom?"

He stiffens. "Why do you care?"

I sit down on the floor. "Well, see, *my* mom isn't coming, that's why I asked. We can start a rejected-by-our-moms club. Monthly meetings and everything."

He scoffs. "My mom didn't reject me. She's just . . . sick."

"I just realized the same thing about my dad," I tell him. "That he doesn't hate me. He's just sick."

"You didn't know this before?"

Yeah, this makes me sound so bad. "I . . . I knew he was

sick, but I guess I never really thought about what it meant."

Frankie doesn't say anything, just raises his eyebrows.

"You know, like how someone with a heart condition can't run around too much, but his kids get mad if he doesn't play soccer with them or whatever? Like that."

Frankie nods. "It's one thing knowing the facts. Emotions are completely different."

"Exactly."

We stop and stare at each other. I can't believe I'm talking to this dude without wanting to sucker punch him. I'm sure he's thinking the same thing, because he starts to smirk. "Seems like you're the one eating crow now, eh?" he says.

I roll my eyes. "I still haven't forgiven you for hurting my cousin."

The smirk dies. "Look, I can't help it sometimes. Getting angry. It's just . . . it happens. Sometimes I hate everyone around me. Even myself."

"Ever tried boxing?"

He squints. "Er . . . no?"

"Never mind, I'll show you someday. All you need is a tree, a pillow, and a rope."

He laughs lightly and goes back to his phone. "My mom's in the manic phase right now. She was supposed to come to the science fair, but instead she's in a casino in Louisiana, because she's sure she's going to win a million dollars."

"Wow," I say. "This makes me feel better about my mom."

"Why?" he asks. "Where is she?"

"In Greece, taking care of refugees."

"Dang."

"Exactly."

* * *

We sit on the floor until the dismissal bell rings. Pigao told us to stay in the gym for an hour after dismissal, for parents who come late.

Ya know, for those lucky kids whose parents are actually interested.

Rayyan comes over to where I'm sitting with Frankie. "Er, what's going on?"

Frankie looks up at him. "I'm not gonna ask for your lunch again."

"O-okay." Rayyan blinks. "Like, ever? Or just today? Because I already ate it today."

I snort.

Frankie gives me a dirty look and then looks at Rayyan again. "Look, I'm trying to apologize. For everything."

"Can you elaborate?" I say, half joking.

See, just because I'm seeing Frankie in a new light doesn't mean I don't wanna hold him accountable for his past deeds.

"That's fair." Frankie gulps. "I'm sorry for all the years I've bullied you. Hurt you, pushed you, said mean things."

"Eaten his lunch . . . ," I remind him.

"Yeah, eaten your lunch."

All this time, Rayyan's eyes are bulging, and he opens and closes his mouth like he doesn't know what to say.

I sigh. "Now you forgive him, bro. He's got anger problems. He's gonna work on them."

"Really?" they both say together. It's actually funny.

"Yes," I say firmly, because I am so tired of people not trying to do better.

Rayyan folds his arms on his chest. "But . . . that fight we had? It may have gone in my NJHS file. That's a big deal."

"Don't worry," Frankie says. "I'll talk to Mr. Trent. He's really nice. Gives me poetry books to read."

Well, that's one mystery explained, Mister Let Me Count the Ways. I clap my hands. "Okay, then it's settled. We're all turning over new leaves. Frankie, you're gonna work on your anger. And Rayyan here—not Ryan—is gonna stop watching horrible press conferences of his dad's death and only focus on his life. And I . . ."

I stop, because I don't know how to go on.

"You what?" Frankie asks suspiciously. "What will you do?"

I take a deep breath. "I'm gonna try to repair my broken heart."

"How?" Frankie asks. Not smugly, or in a disbelieving tone, but like he actually wants to know.

"I'm gonna try to love a monster," I reply.

Rayyan smiles and holds out his right fist. "Deal."

I place my hand over his, and then Frankie puts his over mine. We're like a triple-decker fist sandwich, but not the kind that hurts.

The kind that heals.

In the end, some unexpected people show up to the science fair.

First is Frankie's neighbor slash babysitter, Mrs. Patel, in a blue-and-white sari and a bindi on her forehead. I don't tell her I also knew a Patel once. Basically, it's a very common Indian name, but I'm happy Frankie has someone like that in his life. She looks kind.

Frankie hugs her very hard, so.

Second, Naila Phupo. I mean, we all knew she was going to show up, but it's still nice to see her. She oohs and aahs over our heart model, like she hasn't seen it ten times already. "I'm sure you will win!" she says cheerfully.

Third, Carmen Rodriguez.

Well, she's not completely unexpected, since she's in the same grade as us and is also showcasing a project. But it's still a little surprising to see her right there, at my and Rayyan's table, snapping gum with white teeth, looking like a shark.

"Hi," I say. I've kinda stopped crushing on her ever since she called me teacher's pet.

She looks at me like my face has poop on it. "Listen, Mo, I don't want you to get the wrong impression," she says.

"About what?"

She's annoyed that she has to spell it out. "Well, Mrs. Nguyen says there's no group project in music, so I don't need a partner."

"I know, I was there," I tell her.

"So, we can go back to not talking to each other."

I laugh. Seriously, this girl. "I'm not the one who talked to you in the first place," I tell her. "You came and talked to me. Every time."

She looks shocked, like she had no idea. Then she snaps her gum again and walks away.

Yeah, my crush is over. Thanks, but no thanks.

Fourth, Nathan Mamoo, with—get this—his entire family. I guarantee I look like a fish out of water, because my eyes are wide open and so is my mouth. "You . . . you didn't have to come," I whisper.

"Yes, I did," he says, giving me a tight hug. "I missed out on your childhood. All the birthdays and the science fairs and the Christmases. I'm not missing anymore."

I want to be a meanie and point out that I don't celebrate Christmas, but I stay quiet. This nerdy uncle is growing on me. "Thank you for coming," I say.

He smiles and introduces me to his wife, Tina, and their kid—my cousin Olivia. She's adorable. Like, really cute.

Reminds me of the younger kids in the Sunday school art class.

I grin at her. "Hi, cousin."

She grins back shyly. "Hi, cousin."

* * *

An hour later, the guests are gone and we're packing up our project to leave. Our heart model wins third place.

Frankie and Aiden's potato battery wins second place.

I'm only a little bit annoyed.

A couple of girls from the other eighth-grade section win first prize for, get this, a balloon-powered car. How did I not think of that? It's seriously cool.

There's a shiny medal for each of us, and a certificate signed by the principal. I think it's cheesy, but Rayyan is bursting with joy, so I smile too. And it's only ten percent fake.

I want to be happy, I really do. It's been a good day, overall.

But for the first time in a long time, I'm allowing myself to miss Mama. She'd be so proud of my project.

And you know what?

I'm also missing Abbu. If he wasn't in the hospital, he'd be here for sure. Loud, embarrassing, whispering mean things and hating on everybody's projects.

But he'd be here.

And that would be enough.

33

Christmas break is here. I'm bored out of my mind, and it's only Saturday.

This is the sequence of events so far:

1. Rayyan and I make breakfast and almost burn the house down.
2. No email from Mama. Of course.
3. Naila Phupo goes out to the backyard in the morning. She finds me boxing and freaks out. Then she rips away the pillow (it was in bad shape anyway) and makes me promise not to hurt myself anymore.
4. We don't go to see Abbu even though it's the weekend. Maybe tomorrow.
5. Naila Phupo gets lots of phone calls and she acts all weird.

Rayyan says she must be on her period. I say ew, gross, and make him promise never to talk about such things again. Also, that assuming women have their period because they're acting differently is a form of misogyny.

6. Rayyan feels bad and spends the rest of the day hanging out with his mom, telling her he loves her.

* * *

On Sunday morning, get this: Naila Phupo doesn't make breakfast. Not even toast and omelets.

She hands Rayyan and me protein bars and then tells me to get ready. "We're going to see your abbu today," she explains in a rush.

I drop my protein bar on the table, because there's no way I can eat now. I trudge upstairs to get dressed. Naila Phupo does the same. "This bar is yucky!" Rayyan yells from the kitchen.

"Eat an apple!" Phupo yells back.

Okay, this is weird. Since when does Phupo let him eat whatever he wants?

Half an hour later, we leave Rayyan at home and head to the hospital. That's another weird thing Phupo has done, leaving him alone. She's always so overprotective of him.

"He'll be fine," she assures me as she backs out of the drive-way. "He's got your phone, and he won't open the door, even if someone knocks or rings the bell."

I wonder if she's trying to convince herself, or me. "He could've come with us," I say. "I wouldn't mind."

She shakes her head. "No. We didn't need him today."

I frown. "What?"

"Nothing." She messes with the radio until some nineties music comes on. "Oh, listen. Madonna!"

I roll my eyes and look out the window. Rayyan was right—she's acting strange. But I don't wanna say anything, so I try to get in the groove like Madonna suggests.

Spoiler alert: I can't. I'm going to see Abbu, and he won't be sedated, which is good news, of course, but also bad news, because he may be angry or upset or mean or . . .

I practice pranayama until we get to the hospital.

We park, get out, and go inside. Naila Phupo literally drags me, like she thinks I'm going to run away. I mean, it's not impossible. I do think about it for a second or two.

"Be on your best behavior, okay, beta?"

"Yeah, sure," I mumble. I need to get my bad-boy attitude back. I can't go into this being all vulnerable and stuff, with my heart on my sleeve.

I swallow a few times.

Back to pranayama. In and out. In and out. Deep breathing.

* * *

The rest of the visit is one surprise after another.

First, we don't go to Abbu's room. Naila Phupo takes me to a big place that's set up like a living room. Couches. Televisions. Bookshelves.

It's nice. Quiet.

Patients sit around. They don't seem like they have mental problems, but you never know. I think of Frankie's mom. Has she ever been to a place like this?

I'd looked up bipolar disorder the night before. Those who have it also get episodes, like Abbu. Only they're called manic and depressive. Manic is when you're hyper and extreme: happy, jumpy, excited, blah blah. Depressive is when you're low, like sad, weepy, or tired.

I felt sorry for Frankie when I read all that. At least Abbu is predictable.

Sort of.

Not knowing how your mom is gonna be the next day must be horrible.

"Look, there's bhai." Naila Phupo points out Abbu. He's standing near a couch, the TV remote in his hand. He looks up and sees us, and his face changes.

That's the second surprise. Abbu smiles. His eyes crinkle in the corners. He hasn't smiled like that in a long time.

He comes toward me, arms out.

I'm really not sure what to do at this point. I mean, hug him, of course, since that's expected. But what do I feel?

Quick, somebody tell me what to feel. How to think.

I'm very, very sure he's still the same. Staying a few days in a hospital doesn't change you. Schizophrenia is still inside his brain, corrupting him.

But his smile is different.

So I hug him back with all my feelings. All my heart.

Not the anatomical heart, but the emotional one. The thing poets talk about.

How do I love thee? Let me count the ways.

"My son," he whispers in my ear. "It's good to see you."

"You too."

* * *

The third surprise is more like good news. Like, surprise, we've found the cure for cancer! Only not so drastic.

A doctor comes to meet us, me and Abbu and Phupo. He looks desi. Maybe even Pakistani. "I'm Dr. Yasir," he says, shaking my hand like I'm a grown-up.

"Hey," I reply. He hasn't introduced himself to Abbu or Naila Phupo, which means he's already met them.

Cool, so this meeting is for me? I'm not sure what's going on, so I swallow and try to focus on the memory of Abbu's smile earlier.

Yasir takes us to his office. It's big and bright, with paintings on the wall. I've never seen a doctor's office like this before. It's more like the study in a house. Lots of family pictures on the shelves.

"Please, sit. Let's have a talk," he begins. "We know things have been hard for you and your family, Mr. Mirza."

Abbu grunts, like he thinks this guy is a bit cheesy. "Just hit me, doctor. Am I gonna live?"

"Ha, that's funny." Yasir smiles. "Anyway, you've been doing well this week, which is a change from your previous hospitalizations. We're very pleased with the results. I think we have a better shot at managing your symptoms now than we did before."

Abbu grunts again. He hates talking about his symptoms. Absolutely detests it.

I cough. I'm not sure what I'm doing here. Shouldn't this be a private meeting between him and Abbu?

Naila Phupo's phone buzzes, and she snatches it up. "Er, sorry," she says nervously.

She reads the message, then turns to look at the door. It's closed. There's a window beside it, but it's covered with a blind.

She keeps staring at the door like she's waiting for it to burst open. Which makes me stare at it too, wondering what's going on.

And then, surprise number four, the door does indeed open.

Well, first there's a knock, and then Yasir says, "Come in," and then the door opens, but anyway.

The door opens slowly. Carefully.

That's when I get the biggest surprise of all.

Shock, really.

I stand up on shaky legs, but then I feel dizzy and sit back down. Maybe I'm imagining things.

Maybe this meeting got so boring, I fell asleep and started dreaming. It's happened before. Mostly in school, but still.

Maybe I also have schizophrenia and this is my first hallucination.

Normally that thought would stress me out. Paralyze me with fear.

But not today, oh no.

Because in front of me is Mama, smiling faintly, looking like she never left.

34

Mama is here.

Finally, finally, finally.

She came back.

She left those poor, thirsty, sick refugee children and came back. Who cares about the whys and hows and whens? All I care about is that she's back.

If wishes were horses, then beggars would ride.

Me, I'm the beggar. And my mother being here with me, in the same room, in the same city, in the same country, is the horse.

A horse that should be impossible, but it's not.

I'm gonna call it the unicorn of wishes.

* * *

Once upon a time, there was a stork and a she-stork. (Yup, a female stork is called a she-stork, look it up.)

The two birds had a great life. They lived in a cute little nest next to a lake and had lots of babies. Every morning, they flew out of their nest together to look for food.

One day, as they're searching, they see a field of millet, which is a stork's favorite food or something. The stork really, really wants to grab some millet.

The she-stork doesn't. She wants to get back home to their babies. Plus, where there's a field, there will be a farmer. This is basically a dangerous and foolish mission.

The stork doesn't listen, of course. He loves millet, and this is too good an opportunity to pass up. He tells his wife to sit in a tree and wait for him. Then he flies down and starts eating.

One grain. Two grains.

He's barely started when the farmer shows up. "How dare you eat my millet, you thief?" he grumbles. "I'll teach you a lesson!"

He throws a net and catches the stork. It takes all of two minutes, probably. Then he begins to haul the bird away.

The she-stork goes wild in the tree. She loudly clatters her bill (that's the sound storks make, look it up too) and flies around in panic. "I tried to stop you!" she cries. "Didn't I say don't eat the millet? Don't eat the millet?"

The stork knows he's about to die. The farmer isn't going to let him go. "I was a fool," he agrees from the net. "Go back to our nest and be a good mother to our babies."

The she-stork goes back to the nest, crying all the way. She feeds her babies and puts them to bed. Then she flies to the farmer's house to see if she can save her husband.

Only she's too late. When she reaches the cottage, she sees that the farmer has already killed the stork and chopped him up into pieces. I dunno, maybe they ate storks in those days.

The she-stork is devastated. "Fie! Fie!" she screams at the farmer. "You have committed a great wrong."

The farmer disagrees. "It was his own fault," he replies. "He shouldn't have eaten my millet."

Technically, this is true. The she-stork thinks for a minute. She's sad, obviously, but she wonders how she can still get the stork back. I mean, he was stupid, but he was still her husband. "When you've cooked the meat, give the bones to me," she says.

The farmer rolls his eyes, because what's a stork gonna do with bones? But he feels a little guilty, so he collects all the bones and puts them in a pile on the ground.

The she-stork flies down to the bones and starts singing. That's one thing you can't look up, because normal storks don't sing. Their voice is loud and honking and not exactly melodious.

But c'mon, this is a folktale.

Anyway, the she-stork sings, "I tried to tell you. 'Don't eat the millet! Don't eat the millet!'"

At her singing—surprise, surprise!—the bones on the ground

begin to move. They come together and are remade into the stork. Not the flesh-and-bones bird, but a skeleton, like Indiana Bones.

Is it magic? Who knows?

Nothing in the folktales is true, as you know.

The storks fly back to the nest together. One alive, and one a strange dead collection of bones.

But the she-stork doesn't care, because her husband is back with her again. Hooray!

The stork is very sorry, of course, and promises never to eat a farmer's crop again. Which, ya know, wouldn't be too difficult since he's actually dead, but it's the thought that counts.

35

"You're back?" I ask nervously.

"I'm back," Mama replies, also a little nervously.

Look, I get it. Life as Mrs. Mumtaz Mirza isn't a picnic, even if you never change your last name. Being Abbu's wife comes with a lot of stress. I'm sure they loved each other at some point in their lives, but I don't see even a speck of it now.

What I don't get is why (and how) she left those refugee kids she loves so much.

We're sitting in a corner of the living-room-style place in the hospital. Yasir thought it would be nice for me and Mama to talk alone for a bit.

Apparently all the adults knew she was back, which explains Naila Phupo's strange behavior. Wait till I tell Rayyan it wasn't female problems in general, but one female problem: my mom.

He'll laugh at my joke, I'm sure. He's been encouraging me to be funny ever since he found out about my joke phobia. "You never know how brave you are until you try," he's told me several times.

So I guess here I am, trying this bravery thing. "For how long?"

Mama exhales slowly. She's thinner than she was when she left, and her eyes are sunken. For the first time, I wonder what it's like living in a camp with the bare necessities. With people who have escaped wars and things.

Like, does she get scared? Worried?

"I'm back for good," she admits.

Um, what?

I stare at her like she'll give me some more info, but she doesn't. Just stares back like she's waiting for me to say something.

I blink rapidly. She's back? In what form? Like, a real stork or a dead stork brought back to life from bare bones? 'Cause, you know, I don't really want the dead version of Mama. That would be worse than the alive version, and she's never been nice to live with.

"What about the refugee kids?" I mumble.

"The water system has been set up, mostly," Mama explains. "I've been training some of the staff at the camp, and they'll be able to take on my duties."

"What about your fellowship?"

"There's still a lot of research to be done, but I can do it remotely."

Wow. I hadn't known remote work was an option. That means she didn't actually have to stay away from me—us—for two years to begin with.

I must have some kind of angry slash pained look on my face, because Mama sighs again. "I know I've let you down, Mo," she says wearily. "I *know* I should've done things differently over the years. Especially this year."

I'm actually shocked, because I didn't know she knew this. She always acts like she doesn't think of me and how her decisions affect me. She's always been, like, this aloof genius.

Brilliant in research skills, not so much people skills.

"Yeah, you kinda have let me down," I respond in the same tone. Normally, I'd never say this to an elder, but this is me being brave, I guess. "Abbu too."

Mama stiffens, and some of her arrogant face comes back. "Look, Mo. You're my son, and I know I should be doing better with you. That's my responsibility. Your father is a different matter. He's an adult. I can't do everything for him. He has to start taking responsibility for himself at some point."

My chest sparks with anger, just a little. Mostly I'm sad. Isn't this exactly how I felt too, until Naila Phupo explained it to me the other day? "How can Abbu help others swim when he's drowning himself?"

Mama looks stunned. She doesn't speak for a while. Then

she whispers, "When did you become so wise?"

"Since I started living with my aunt and cousin."

Another exhale. "It's been good for you, this move?"

Another spark of anger. "It's not like you care. You . . . you left us. We couldn't function without you, but you left us."

She grabs my hand. I shiver because it's been so long since she did that. Since she held me or hugged me or kissed me. Even before she went to Greece, it was hard to get a hug from her.

I squeeze her hand to let her know I'm glad she's back, even though I'm acting all mad-sad right now. I'm just processing.

I'll be fine. I'm always fine.

Mama says, "I didn't just leave you, Mo. I arranged it with your aunt ahead of time. We discussed it on the phone and made arrangements. I even researched the school and talked to the principal."

The picture of her working on something non-water related is strange. This time the spark is warmer, full of something like love. "You did?"

For the first time since she arrived, she smiles. "I wouldn't leave you without making sure you'd be okay." A deep inhale. "Tell me you know that."

Well, I didn't know that, but I'm not going to admit it now.

So I nod, and lean forward, and she leans forward too, and somehow it turns into one of those hugs that just go on and on and on.

I think she cries.

I definitely cry. I'm not even ashamed or worried about my reputation.

"I'm sorry," she whispers. "I'll try to do better."

"Me too."

* * *

The more we talk, the clearer things become.

For instance, Mama and Naila Phupo have been in touch all this time. Not a whole lot, but some. Mama's known about my grades and the Sunday school art class, even my heart model. "That aunt of yours emails me every few days," Mama says with an eye roll.

"She's great," I reply, grinning. "But did you know the heart model won third place?"

Mama's eyebrows go up. "Really? That must have happened while I was traveling. I'm sure there will be an email with dozens of pictures waiting for me."

My grin fades. "Pictures?" Let's be honest, Mama would never look at pictures of me doing everyday things. She likes images that mean something, like blueprints and flowcharts.

"Mo, my dear, those pictures are my everything. At night when I'd lie on my cot and try to forget all the things I saw that day—the blood and fever and the people who got sick drinking dirty water—at night I'd look at your pictures and thank God that you were safe and healthy and sleeping on a clean bed, not hungry or scared. . . ."

She stops.

I swallow, because I've never seen her so open. Even her

hands are held out, palms up, willing me to believe her.

"We should talk about our feelings more often," I say.

She slumps back and laughs a little. "Yeah, we really should. You've become smart."

"I'm in eighth grade now," I reply. "Practically an adult."

"Oh yes, practically. Tell me about eighth grade. Made any friends?"

I shrug. "More like frenemies."

* * *

Abbu and Naila Phupo are waiting for us in Yasir's office.

They're both silent and looking a little anxious.

Yasir, though, is smiling. He's like Bopoluchi after she killed all the robbers, or Azur Jamshed after he drove away Shri Badat. Like, "My job here is done, give me a medal and move on."

"Come in, please, Mrs. Mirza," he says, standing up.

Mama frowns. "It's Dr. Eckert."

Abbu snorts.

Mama turns the frown toward him.

Okay, so everything isn't perfect. Just because Mama's back doesn't mean she and Abbu have a fairy-tale life now.

No worries. I'm not an innocent little boy. I know things don't always work out between people. Maybe Mama will turn over a new leaf and start taking care of Abbu.

Maybe Abbu will turn over a new leaf and start taking care of himself.

If wishes were horses, et cetera et cetera.

More likely, things will go on as before, but we'll hopefully stay in Houston now. I'll have to explain to Mama the Pledge of Allegiance to the Texan flag situation. She'll probably write a protest letter to the governor or something.

Ha.

Mama and I sit down. Yasir passes out some papers. "Now that everyone's here, let's discuss the treatment options for Mr. Mirza. As you know, schizophrenia doesn't have a cure, but there are ways to manage the condition so that patients can live a full, healthy, and happy life."

"I'm not a patient," Abbu grumbles.

I wait for Mama to say something, but she bites her lip and stays quiet. I'm so proud of her.

"Okay," Yasir says quickly. "What would you prefer? Participant? Attendee? We could refer to you as a case number?"

"How about just Mumtaz?" Naila Phupo interrupts.

"Perfect!" Yasir looks at the paper in his hand. "Now, let's talk medications. We can give you a shot every three months that will reduce most of your psychosis symptoms."

He means the really bad symptoms, like delusions of aliens watching him, and hallucinating. Hearing voices that say horrible things.

My heart pumps furiously. If Abbu doesn't have those, he could be a different person.

It's too good to be true.

Normally, I wouldn't believe it, but Yasir's saying it, and he's a cool dude. And very smart, according to all the diplomas on his wall. It's gotta be true.

Yasir goes over a bunch of research that's been done to show how good the shots are. How new medication is helping treat people with schizophrenia—and other mental illnesses—so much better. "Things have really come a long way since you first developed the disease, Mr. . . . uh, Mumtaz," he says.

"What if Mumtaz refuses to get the shots?" Mama asks, with another dirty look in Abbu's direction.

"That's where we come in," Yasir replies. "We can work with you long-term. Provide you with a case worker who checks in regularly. You'd go to family therapy. You'd have a support system, and resources, and lots of options."

There's a silence as we all think about this.

Lots of options. That could be good, I guess.

It could also be bad. Just depends on which options you choose.

"It's all up to you, Mumtaz," Yasir adds.

Abbu looks at me. That special smile is gone, but his eyes are kind. Soft. "What do you think, Mohammad?" he asks. "Can I do it this time?"

Me? I'm supposed to decide? "Er, I don't . . ."

Naila Phupo reaches over and squeezes my hand. "What if we all help, Mo? What if we all work together and help your abbu?"

"Everyone?" I look at Mama. "Are you going to be part of this too?"

Mama nods. "I'll give it a try. I'm here now, and my remote

work is pretty light at the moment. We can rent an apartment near your aunt, and . . . and I'll try, I promise."

She promises. I never expected this.

She says she'll try. She's never said that before.

It's enough. Mama and Abbu both trying will be enough.

It has to be.

"At least our hearts are still beating, right?" I say in a low voice.

My parents look at me, confused. But Naila Phupo gives my hand another squeeze. "You'll have me too, beta. Don't forget."

I relax. More than Mama and Abbu, I trust this woman. She'll be there for me, making sure I'm okay. I know this.

"Yes," I say firmly. "I think Abbu can do it, if we all work together."

Look, you may think I'm being naive. But here's what I've learned from all the folktales I've read over the years. Where there's hope, there's life. A positive attitude, hoping for the best, where there's a will, there's a way . . . all that stuff is real. It makes us reach inside ourselves, past the skin and bones, past the anatomy, to the soul.

EPILOGUE

This isn't one of those stories that end in happily ever after.

At the most, it's a story that ends in "They tried their best."

It's the end of April, and here's what has happened so far:

Abbu is doing so much better. I mean, he's still loud and intense, but the worst of his symptoms are almost gone. He doesn't hear voices anymore, ever since he took that first injection in the hospital after Christmas.

He's on his second dose now, and Yasir says he'll get even better soon. As long as he keeps up with the shots, he should be okay.

All I know is, Abbu's been smiling more and shouting less.

Oh, and he's going to therapy to manage his anger, which is ah-mazing! After a session last month, he came into my room and told me he was sorry for calling me useless and stupid.

I forgave him. Of course I did. He's trying, and that's all I need.

I cried after he left my room. Like, full-on, tears-down-my-face crying. It was stupid. Don't ask me why. I don't think I'll ever get all friendly with him, you know? No tender father-son moments in our future, I don't think. Ew.

But.

I've officially stopped thinking of him as a monster, so I guess that's the biggest, best moment of my life.

I finally understand how Badri Jamala felt, when she got freedom from White Giant. Even though I'm only free from my thoughts, while she got free from, ya know, an actual giant, it's more or less the same thing.

It feels light and airy and giddy and . . . free.

I feel free.

My broken heart syndrome seems to be fixed. I mean, I still get some of that chest thumping and fluttering in my belly once in a while, when I worry that this is all too good to be true.

But overall, I'm a new person.

Yasir reminds us constantly that we should have low expectations, that we shouldn't assume everything will always be great. Abbu will have relapses, and sometimes schizophrenia will get the best of him.

I know that.

I'm still enjoying the victory for now.

Mama is doing okay in what she calls "civilian life." She

stayed home for exactly eighteen days. The duration of my winter break. She cooked a Christmas dinner (Naila Phupo helped, even though she kept talking about Christmas being a haram holiday) and took me shopping, and hung out with me. But by the time school opened back up, she'd gotten a job lined up at a consulting firm in Houston.

So I guess that means we're staying.

I'm not sure how I feel about becoming a Texan, especially since it's starting to get hot even in April. Rayyan says the summer will be fire, but we can go swimming in the apartment pool.

What apartment?

Oh, yeah, we moved into an apartment in late January. It's half a mile from Naila Phupo's house, which means I can stay at Alice Walker. Also, I can walk over to Phupo's as long as the weather's good. I spend most of my time there anyway, eating her food, hanging out with Rayyan in his room.

He says he misses me, but I think he's happy to have his room back. My bed is still there, though, because I stay over on weekends. Mama thinks all this family stuff is too much, but I don't.

I love all this family stuff.

Even Nathan Mamoo, Tina Mami, and Olivia. We're getting to know each other slowly. Olivia calls me Momo, which is adorable.

Mama was shocked to know I'd been in touch with her brother. Turns out Abbu was the one who didn't want us to meet. He'd felt that Nathan Mamoo was judging him or something.

Yeah, Mamoo can do that sometimes. When I told him I was into art, he crinkled up his nose and offered to get me an internship at his IT company.

Tina Mami patted his arm and told him I was too young for internships.

Rayyan says he'd be down for an internship anytime, so maybe that connection will come in handy in, like, six to eight years. Right now, we're happy teaching art to a bunch of hooligans.

Imam Shamsi told them to make get-well-soon cards for Abbu, and now the apartment is full of messy artwork. I've hung it on the fridge and from the mock fireplace. (Don't ask me why Texas has fireplaces, it's silly.) Abbu pretends to hate the cards, but I know they make him happy.

Make him feel special.

My own oil paintings, though? I keep those in the back of my closet. I don't paint much, just when I'm feeling upset.

It happens. Not as much as before, but it does happen.

Oh, and Frankie. Lots has happened with Frankie too. We aren't exactly friends, but at least we don't call each other names or start fights in the hallways. I've told him about family therapy, and he's been trying to convince his mom to go ever since.

She hasn't agreed yet, but I'm hopeful.

Nobody deserves broken heart syndrome, not even stupid Frankie.

Our family therapy doesn't always happen either. Abbu makes a lot of excuses about it, and Mama always has some work event. And when we do go, there's a lot of arguing between the two of them. They blame each other and talk about how good the old days were and how things are different now.

I sometimes talk about my feelings, which, you know, ugh.

The therapist says this is all part of the healing process, even my parents arguing.

I'm not sure, but I'm not an expert. All I can say is, my nightmares are less frequent. So I'll take this therapy as a win.

A victory over a monster.

It's all a victory, even though it's messy and there are no clear winners. We're all battle-scarred and stressed and exhausted. But there's also hope. I wanna be like Muchukunda when I grow up. All warrior cool, and blessed with eternal bliss.

Hey, I don't know what that means, but it sounds awesome.

* * *

It's the end of April, and we're all in the school gym, waiting for Rayyan to be inducted into the NJHS. He's all smiles. He's gained seventeen pounds, so he looks great.

After the induction ceremony is over, we're gonna go get some ice cream or something. There's this amazing gelato place around the corner that Rayyan used to go to with his abbu a long time ago.

I may even invite Frankie. He's in NJHS too, much to nobody's surprise.

"Maybe we'll all be best friends in high school," I joke. Although, it's more fact, since we hang out in Trent's library sometimes.

Okay, we hang out a lot. Not talking, just reading books at the same table, or whatever. Sometimes sharing a bag of chips.

"I hear they study Shakespeare's plays in English Literature," Rayyan says glumly. "Imagine how insufferable he'll be then."

"Perfect," I reply with a little smile. "Wouldn't want life to get too boring. I still have to keep up the bad-boy image."

Rayyan shakes his head and smiles, because of course he knows I'm a big marshmallow behind that image.

And let me tell you, his smile is as bright as the Texas sun.

A NOTE FROM THE AUTHOR

Dear reader,

My father was severely mentally ill, possibly with schizophrenia. This was a long time ago, in Pakistan, where not much awareness or understanding of mental illness existed. He never got proper care, or medication, or even a surefire diagnosis. My childhood was just as horrible as I've depicted Mo's in this story. The nightmares he has in the book were my personal nightmares. Many of the incidents I describe in this story happened to me as well. Many others are fictional. I didn't have anyone like Naila Phupo to support me, but I wanted Mo to have her. It was my way of rewriting my past and imagining a better future.

My father passed away several years ago, and I never had a good relationship with him. I wanted to write this book as an apology for my lack of understanding of his illness. I know

now that he wasn't in control of his actions and that, as Naila Phupo says, he was drowning and couldn't be expected to take care of others. I also wanted to offer you, my readers, a sense of hope. If you know someone with mental illness, knowledge and understanding are key. There is a way forward, but often it means others around the patient have to step up and do their part. It's not fair, but it's the only way.

Remember, the strongest heart is one that's still beating, that's full of hope and bravery.

—Saadia Faruqi